Sconed To Death

Sconed to Death

LYNN CAHOON

KENSINGTON BOOKS
KENSINGTON PUBLISHING CORP.
www.kensingtonbooks.com

KENSINGTON BOOKS are published by

Kensington Publishing Corp.
119 West 40th Street
New York, NY 10018

All Kensington titles, imprints, and distributed lines are available at special quantity discounts for bulk purchases for sales promotion, premiums, fund-raising, educational, or institutional use.

Special book excerpts or customized printings can also be created to fit specific needs. For details, write or phone the office of the Kensington Sales Manager: Attn.: Sales Department. Kensington Publishing Corp., 119 West 40th Street, New York, NY 10018. Phone: 1-800-221-2647.

First Printing: June 2019
ISBN-13: 978-1-4967-1683-5
ISBN-10: 1-4967-1683-3

ISBN-13: 978-1-4967-1684-2 (eBook)
ISBN-10: 1-4967-1684-1 (eBook)

10 9 8 7 6 5 4 3 2 1

Printed in the United States of America

Remembering Bobby McGee—
thanks for talking the Cowboy and I
into taking the Las Vegas leap.
You're a forever part of our story.

Acknowledgments

Writing a book takes time and concentration, things that are sometimes in short supply in a writer's life. But the good thing about writing is working on a book keeps me focused on things I can control while the world explodes all around me. Sometimes I'm lost in a story, either on my computer or in my head, when my husband needs to talk or wants to know what's for dinner. I did the same thing as a reader before I started writing. I'd be deep into a story and my son would judge how good the book was by the number of "Moms" he had to say before I looked up from my reading. So if you, dear reader, get lost in the stories I tell, you're not alone.

Chapter One

I have measured out my life with coffee spoons.
—T. S. Eliot

There is nothing like the taste of coffee, first thing in the morning. Maybe it's the warmth flowing through your body. (Or maybe it's the jolt of caffeine.) The mixture did miracles for a wake-up call.

Cat Latimer sat at the country farm table that could seat up to ten, twelve if her guests squeezed close, and inhaled her first cup. Fall had come softly to the small Colorado town of Aspen Hills. Cat loved the mild weather as well as the fallen leaves covering the yards and the sidewalks. Covington College had opened the last week of August for fall semester, so the town streets and shops were filled with college students.

The kitchen in the big house was warm and cozy, even though it was as large as some commercial kitchens. She'd started to think of the area as Shauna's domain, but they spent more time together here than anywhere else in the entire house. Especially during retreat weeks.

Cat watched as Shauna Marie Clodagh took a batch of brownies out of the oven. She had adapted well to Colorado life and had taken on the role of house mom when the writers were in session. That gave Cat the time to be the writer in residence, a role she didn't understand most days. But if Cat was being honest with herself, she loved running the Warm Springs Writers' Retreat almost as much as she loved writing novels. Well, almost.

The back door opened and Seth Howard wandered into the kitchen. Stripping off his jacket, he hung it up on the coatrack and went to the sink to wash. The guy looked like he worked with his hands (as he should), his broad shoulders and blond hair making her think of Thor. "Smells wonderful in here. I hope I can snag a brownie or two for the drive to Denver."

"If you feed Snow and the feline herd for me this morning, I think I can arrange that." Shauna got plates out of the cupboard and served a cheesy bacon skillet dish she'd been experimenting with all week. They'd gained a horse in the last few months along with a cat who just happened to be pregnant. Now, the barn was booming with life after sitting silent for years.

"Done and done." Seth crossed over to the table after grabbing a cup of coffee and leaned down to kiss Cat. "Good morning. I didn't know if I'd see you before heading off to the airport."

"It's not that late." Cat glanced at her watch. "Just because the two of you like to start your day at five doesn't mean everyone has to. Most creative types like to give our brain time to wake up. But you're right, I'm usually up earlier than this."

"Whatever makes you feel better, slug bug." He sat next to her and opened the paper. "I have to say, I like it when all the guests show up on one flight. What do these guys write again?"

"Cozy mysteries. They all are a part of a critique group out of the Midwest. Cincinnati, maybe?"

"I believe they're from Chicago." Shauna set plates in front of everyone. "I'm so excited to do the cooking class with them. It will give me a good indication of whether or not my recipes are ready to be included in the cookbook. I can't believe I'm putting together a book! I thought that dream would never happen."

"We still have to get you an agent and hopefully a publisher, but if no one snatches this up, we'll do it ourselves." Cat thought about the huge amount she and Shauna would have to learn to figure out the ins and outs of self-publishing, but if her friend wanted to publish a cookbook, she wasn't going to say it was too hard. Besides, it would be a great addition to the retreat.

"After we do this trial run, I'll have the proposal ready next week." Shauna smiled at her. "Get that scared look off your face. We're going to get picked up by a publisher, I can feel it."

"Your mouth to God's ears." Sometimes getting published was more about luck and determination than talent. However, Shauna had all three. Cat knew she wouldn't give up until she had the finished project in her hands. And if it was important to Shauna, Cat decided it was important to her too.

"So, cozy mysteries? What are those?" Seth had

finished the paper and pushed it into the center of the table as he finished his breakfast.

"Low on gore, low on sex, high on fun." Cat laughed. "I thought about writing one before I started with Tori's book, but I got distracted. I think you'll like this group. I got an e-mail from one telling me how excited they all were to be coming."

"Well, like I said, having them all on one flight has made my life easy." Seth glanced over at Shauna, who was writing in her notebook, her breakfast forgotten. "You going to be ready to teach class tomorrow?"

"Teaching is kind of an overstatement. I'm going to cook and they'll help." Shauna held up her notebook. "I'm writing it all out today. That way when I'm cooking, I won't forget a step and ruin our final product. And, I'm sending them home with a folder that has all the recipes we'll do on Sunday."

"Sounds good." Cat focused on her breakfast. "If you're cooking this, they're going to be wowed."

"It's one of the recipes. I'm doing three savory and three sweet." She peered at her notes. "You think that's enough? I want them to feel like they got their money's worth since the extra day is costing them more."

"We'll be fine." Cat took the last bite of her breakfast, then, as she dropped her plate off in the sink, cut a brownie and sat it on a napkin. She filled up her coffee mug. "I'm heading upstairs to write. Let me know when you're back."

"That will work." Seth was on his phone now, probably checking the scores. Shauna was studying her lists. Cat shook her head.

"I could have said I was going to start a new

career pole dancing and you two would have had the same reaction." Cat paused at the door to the hallway.

"Not really." Seth didn't even look at her. "If you'd said that, I would have definitely had a reaction. I'm not sure I want my girlfriend in that line of work."

"Well, let's hope the retreat keeps doing well so we don't have to cross that bridge." She smiled at him. "Drive safe."

"You got it."

She headed to the staircase and climbed the two flights to the third floor where she had her office. The third floor also had four bedrooms, one for her, one for Shauna, and two more rooms they used during retreat weeks. One was for Seth as he'd started staying over during the retreat just in case. The other was a guest room for out of town speakers. So far, they'd only utilized it once, but it was nice to have it available. Instead of turning right toward the bedrooms, she turned left to her turret office.

She'd teased her ex-husband, Michael, that the only reason she'd wanted the house was this room. It was over his study on the first floor and a row of rooms they hadn't remodeled on the second. Why they'd even considered buying the too large Victorian in the early years of their marriage had been a testament to the hope they'd felt. A life that never materialized as she divorced him and moved to California, unable to stay in the area. When he'd died, he'd left her the house. An act of kindness she still appreciated.

Opening the door, she found the office bathed in golden light. The room was windowed on three sides, and the other had wall-to-ceiling bookshelves that she'd filled with her favorite novels as well as her teaching library. She hadn't been a professor long, but she'd loved the idea of teaching a lot more than the practical side of the profession. She'd loved books, which led her to two career paths—teaching about books and being a librarian. Since then, she'd found a third path that she'd never thought would come true. She was a full-time author. And with the income from the retreat, she didn't have to think about working a day job. Of course, the money Michael had left her also helped her stay out of the job-seeking lines.

She opened her Word document and reread a couple of pages where she'd left off yesterday. She made a few minor changes, glanced at her outline, then fell into the world of Tori and the magical boarding school she'd been sent to once her powers started to manifest. Like Covington College in Cat's real life, Tori's high school was starting up football and the fall concert season. She hoped Tori would enjoy listening to the new bands she was being exposed to as much as Cat did. She shook her head. Tori wasn't real, but sometimes, it felt like she was, and that wasn't a bad feeling, not at all.

A knock pulled her out of the story and, when she glanced at the clock, she realized she'd been writing for almost four hours. Seth should be returning in less than an hour. And she was starving. She stood and crossed over to the door. "Sorry, I lost track of time. Do you need help getting everything ready?"

"Actually, I've made lunch and thought you might be hungry." Shauna walked over to the wall of windows and looked out over the back pasture where Snow, her horse, grazed in the field. "I still can't believe she's mine."

Shauna's now deceased boyfriend had done all right by her. He'd actually done all right by everyone. Kevin had left three sons. One boy he'd fathered young, then abandoned. The other two were twins he'd fathered with a one-night stand. He'd taken care of their mother in the will, and even his friend who'd been like a brother, and there wasn't any fighting for more money. Cat guessed when the money was enough, there weren't any hard feelings. Shauna was comfortably well off and had dividends in Shield Holdings, now that Kevin's will had been probated. But the most precious thing Kevin had left her was grazing in that pasture.

Cat moved over to stand by Shauna. "She's a great addition to the place. Well, she and the brood."

"We really need to think about what we're going to do with those kittens. I've got Angelica scheduled for her surgery next month. The vet wanted to wait until she was done nursing. They'll be ready for new homes in a couple of weeks." Shauna turned toward Cat. "Did you want to keep one or two more?"

Cat hadn't been raised with pets. Her mom had been adamant that she didn't need another mouth to feed. "I'd always really wanted a dog, but I'm falling in love with that little white one."

"Princess? She's a cutie. We can keep them all if you want. I'll pay the vet bills." Shauna smiled as Snow kicked up her heels in the pasture, then took off on a run. "I don't have anything else to spend my money on."

"You could travel." Cat settled on the couch

leaning her head on her arm as she rested. "You don't have to stay in Colorado."

"Are you trying to get rid of me?" Shauna plopped into the other side of the couch. "I like my life here. When I don't, I'll let you know. But for right now, it's good. Maybe we should plan a trip for the two of us next month after the retreat. We could go back east and check out the historic sights. Or head back to California to catch some waves. Do you think Seth would watch the menagerie?"

"Let's talk about this next week when the retreat is over. I'd love a quick trip out of town. The timing's great. I'm between contracts right now so I don't have anything due." The book she was currently writing was the next in the series, but without a contract, she didn't know when or if it would be published.

"Are you worried?" As usual, Shauna got to the heart of the words Cat hadn't said.

She continued to watch the horse run circles in the pasture. Was she worried? Or was it the fact she didn't have control over what would happen next that was bugging her. "Alexa, you know my agent, says not to worry, that they'll come back for more books. It's just hard to be waiting on them to make a decision."

"Then it's settled. We'll take a trip and get you out of this funk. Besides, I need the distraction too. Getting out of town is the best thing we can do for both of us." Shauna patted her leg. "Come down stairs and let's eat. I want to run the retreat schedule by you. I've ordered pizza and salads for dinner tonight for all of us. And I set up movies in the living room, just in case they don't want to jump into writing after traveling all day."

"You're really good at this hostess thing." Cat followed Shauna out of her office after saving her work on the computer. Worries could wait until after the retreat. Right now, she had to morph into an author in residence and be a good hostess too. The only problem was Shauna was better at the role than she was.

They were sitting eating at the table when a series of hard raps came on the back door. Cat started to stand, but Shauna waved her down. "I'll get it."

When Shauna opened the door, a short, blond-haired woman pushed her way in. "You're not going to get away with this."

"I don't know what you're talking about." Shauna crossed her arms and glared at the woman.

"Oh, don't play that innocent act with me. It might have worked on Kevin, but I know what you're about. I know you're cooking my recipes and planning on putting them into a cookbook." The woman poked Shauna in the chest. "Just because you're pretty doesn't mean you can steal from people who are more talented than you in the kitchen."

"Give me a break, Dee Dee. I can bake circles around you." Shauna stepped forward and poked the woman in return. "I've been to that place you call a bakery and you don't have to worry about anyone stealing your recipes, because no one likes your food."

"That's not true." Dee Dee's voice went up a few octaves and she stepped closer to Shauna.

Cat decided she needed to move in between the women before someone threw the first punch. She needed Shauna here tomorrow for the cooking demonstration. It wouldn't be good if she wound up in jail on assault charges. She crossed the room and moved her body in between the two women. "Now, Dee Dee, calm down. You know Shauna wouldn't steal your recipes."

"That's not what I'm hearing." Dee Dee seethed. "It's all over town."

"Maybe you should check your sources before you come over to my kitchen and start causing trouble." Shauna tried to step forward, but Cat's hand on her stomach stopped her.

"Shauna, you should be more open to discussing this." When Shauna glared at Cat, she shrugged. "I think maybe you just identified the problem. Dee Dee, who told you about Shauna stealing your recipes?"

"Sure, you'd like it if I told you, then something bad could happen to the woman and I'd probably be to blame." Dee Dee stepped toward the door. "You just remember, you're on notice. If I find one recipe of mine in your rotation, I'm going to sue. Both of you."

Cat and Shauna watched as Dee Dee stormed out. Cat tried on a laugh for measure. "Well, that was interesting."

"The woman is crazy. She tried to sue the grocery store, saying they stole her bread recipe for the in-store bakery. But the store got it from their chain headquarters and proved that to her lawyer, so she had to back down." Shauna sank into her chair and glanced up at the cabinet where she kept the scotch whiskey. "The woman is a menace."

"Well, you haven't stolen any of her recipes, right?"

When Shauna didn't answer right away, Cat came to sit beside her. "Shauna? What's going on?"

"There's really only a few ways to make a scone. And maybe I had one there and then came home and tried to replicate it. Of course, mine's way better than what she serves in that shop of hers." Shauna tried a weak smile. "Isn't imitation the best form of flattery?"

Chapter Two

Seth got back with the guests right before the pizza delivery from Reno's arrived, so as Shauna and Cat checked them in and handed each guest a key, Seth helped take the baggage up to their rooms. Bren Baker was the first to step up to the registration desk. Bren was an attractive woman with short black hair. She had a rock on her finger that must have run the buyer back a few bills. Cat handed her a registration card.

"I know you write cozy mysteries, but do you want to tell me what type?" Cat watched as the woman pulled a pen out of a very expensive purse or a very good knockoff.

"I'm the small-town queen of the group. My series is set in Texas, outside Dallas." She frowned at the markings, then, looking around to see who was watching, pulled out a pair of glasses.

"Uh oh, Bren's pulling out the cheaters. She's getting serious." The woman behind her laughed as Cat handed her a form to complete as well. "Bren hates to mar her beauty with glasses."

"Boys don't make passes at girls who wear glasses," Bren shot back at her friend. "You should know that, Colleen. I've tried to coach you on how to score your next husband enough times."

"Bren, the only men who are here are Rick and our driver, Seth." Colleen turned to Seth, who was bringing in the last load of luggage. "Seth, that's your name, right?"

"Yes, it's Seth. And no, I'm not on the market. My dance card has been taken away by that lovely lady who's giving out the registration cards." He slapped the other man, Rick, on the arm. "Thanks for helping with the luggage, man."

"No problem. I'm sure you have to carry a bunch all by yourself. It's not usual to find a male author at one of these, right?" Rick took the card Cat handed him and pulled a pen out of his shirt pocket.

"Actually, we get a lot of men for the retreats. Getting away to write isn't only a female author's plan." She smiled and handed the next to last card to the woman who seemed to be holding up the wall. "You must be Anne Rosen. The e-mail you sent me was lovely."

The woman, a light blonde with an even lighter skin tone, nodded. "Thank you for having this. I am so excited to get to writing. I'm setting up a new series for a proposal and I want it to be so amazing, the publisher can't turn me down."

"Anne, you could send in your grocery list and they'd publish it." Colleen handed the completed card to Shauna.

"Thanks. Now I just need your credit card and

I'll get you a room key." Shauna held out her hand as Bren glared at her friend.

"I was first in line," Bren muttered.

Colleen shrugged and handed her card to Shauna. "You snooze, you lose. Besides, this way I get to chat with Seth as he helps me upstairs to my room. Maybe he has friends who'd like to date a slightly pudgy author who tends to lose everything she puts her hands on except for plot bunnies."

Shauna handed her back her card and a receipt to sign. Then she handed Seth a room key. "Seth grew up here. I bet he knows a lot of eligible bachelors."

"I'm not much of a matchmaker." He blushed and picked up the bags that had Colleen's name on them. "Let's get you settled so you can come down and eat. Reno's has the best pizza in town."

The two walked off toward the stairs and Bren handed Shauna her card. "Leave it to Colleen. She always has to be first. She was the first in the group to get a contract. The first to publish. She's a tad competitive."

"Yeah, but you got a better contract and a marriage proposal from that rich guy. Maybe slow and steady wins the race." Anne spoke softly and Cat could hear the soothing in the tone. This wasn't the first time they'd had this tiff and Anne was the one who patched it all together. Cat was sure of it.

She waited for Bren to sign her credit card receipt. Then she took the key from Shauna. "Let me help you to your room. Seriously, you are not going to want to miss Reno's pizza."

Shauna nodded and turned toward Anne as Cat and Bren moved toward the stairs.

"You have a lovely home. Has it been passed down in your family?" Bren rubbed the polished wood of the stair rail.

"No. I got it when my ex-husband passed a year ago." She smiled as she started up the stairs. "It's a long story, but I'm sure you'll hear most of it before you leave on Sunday. Are you originally from Cincinnati?"

"No, why would you ask that?" Bren's tone turned to ice.

Crap, Shauna must have been right. This group was from Chicago. "Sorry, I got mixed up there. You guys don't live in Cincinnati?"

"Of course not. There's no way I'd be from such a small town." Bren checked her watch as they walked to her room. "I write about the places. I don't want to live there. We're all from Chicago. Oak Park, specifically."

Cat opened the door and turned on the lights. She showed her the bathroom and set her luggage on the bed. "Let me or Shauna know if you need anything. We're at your service this week so you can get as many words in as you want."

Bren nodded, then checked her watch again. She reached for the key Cat held. "Sorry, I need to make a private call."

She'd been dismissed. Cat wondered how Bren was received in this writers' group she was part of. Hopefully she'd relax and be a little friendlier as the week went by. Cat decided to chalk it up to being tired from the traveling and she'd give Bren the benefit of the doubt.

Seth was coming up the stairs with Anne and her luggage. Rick was following behind the two. Cat moved over to the side as they passed. "Looks like you have the last two handled."

"I'm efficient like that." Seth grinned at her. "The pizza arrived a few minutes ago and I'm hungry."

"Then let's get this party going." Cat waited for Rick to pass before going down to the first level. There she found Shauna talking to a young girl who must be the Covington College student. Each session, Cat opened a slot for a student Covington chose in exchange for a lecture from one of their English professors and full use of the library during each session. So far, it had been a beneficial exchange. Especially since Covington also paid the room and board charge for the student.

"Cat, this is Molly Cannon. She's our Covington guest." Shauna smiled at the girl. "She's been telling me what a big fan she is of your work."

When Molly turned toward her, the shock and astonishment on her face was laughable, but Cat turned it into a welcoming smile. "Molly, we're so happy to have you. What do you write?"

"I'm writing a young adult, but I'm not as good as you are. I love Tori and her stories." The girl swallowed. "It's such an honor to meet you. I mean, I knew you owned this place, but I didn't think I'd actually get to meet you. I thought you were some sort of figurehead or something. You know, like James Patterson, only with the retreat? He has a lot of people writing for him, so I thought . . ."

Cat saw her take a deep breath, then shake her head.

"Sorry, I'm rambling." She took another breath. "I'm very happy to meet you."

"Same here. If you're a Tori fan, I'd be glad to sign your books if you have them with you. I do a workshop on Wednesday to talk about an author's life. You might be interested in what I have to say."

"Oh, definitely." Her head bobbed several times.

What was it with this group? One was a stone-cold witch—okay, she appeared to be one. And one was a rabid fan. It was going to be an interesting week. "I can show you to your room if you'd like."

The front door opened and the flower shop delivery guy came inside.

Shauna nodded to him and grabbed a key. "You take care of the flowers and I'll show Molly to her room."

The disappointment was obvious on Molly's face but she followed Shauna toward the stairs.

Cat heard Shauna's next words. "You know I'm Cat's best friend. I bet I can tell you some stories about her that you'd love to hear."

"Really?" The awe in Molly's voice was evident. And Cat realized Shauna had taken the heat off her. Molly would be hanging around Shauna for inside information on her favorite author.

"Two dozen roses." The delivery guy put the vase on the registration desk. "You must be starting up one of those retreat sessions."

"Yeah, it's a tradition." She handed him a ten-dollar bill. The roses came every month like clockwork before the opening day of the retreat. Linda Cook, wife of the late author Tom Cook, sent them. At first, Cat thought it was in tribute to her husband, who'd died at the first retreat, but now, she thought it was a blessing on the success of the retreat. Either way, Cat loved the gesture and the flowers.

She glanced around the registration desk, then put all the cards and receipts in the top drawer and shut it. Shauna would take care of the paperwork soon. Right now, it was time to eat pizza and get to know the guests. Her stomach was growling, but she thought it would be rude to be the first one eating.

She went into the dining room and saw the line of pizzas and salad on the table. Shauna had already set out plates, forks, and napkins. And a tub of sodas and waters sat in the corner of the room. She grabbed a Coke and took several sips, hoping the rest of the group would arrive soon, before she succumbed to the smell of cheese and tore into a slice.

She didn't have to wait long. Seth and Rick were the first ones down and Molly and Shauna followed. Cat pointed to the plates. "Get your food while it's hot."

By the time most of the guests had returned, Cat was sitting at the table with Molly on one side and Anne on the other. Bren still hadn't come down from her room.

Colleen sat her pizza down and looked around. "Where's Bren?"

"She had a call," Cat answered.

Anne and Colleen exchanged a look. "Figures," Anne muttered as she started on her salad.

"What do you mean?" Cat lowered her voice just in case Anne didn't want the entire table to hear her answer.

"Let's just say Bren is in a relationship with a short

leash. I'm actually surprised he let her come at all. He's very particular on what she does and when." Anne shook her head. "Not my circus and definitely not my monkey. I would have left him the first time he pulled this crap."

Cat wondered if that accounted for the distance she'd felt with Bren. Her mother used to always say that everyone was fighting their own battles. She decided she needed to be more charitable with first impressions.

The mood had darkened a bit after the question about Bren, so Cat glanced at Shauna. "Do you want to talk a bit about what's going to happen tomorrow? I think all of you are attending Shauna's cooking demonstration, right?"

Cat had aimed the question at Molly since she knew the other writers had signed up specifically for the cooking demo section.

Molly nodded vigorously. "I'm so excited about it. I mean, I don't write about food, but food is part of our lives, right? A big part, and if you're writing a full character, what they eat makes a big statement about who they are."

"So since I love pizza, if I was a character in Cat's books, that would tell the reader something about me?" Seth glanced at Cat. "I don't understand."

"Molly's right. Food can help build a picture of a character. Let's say instead of pizza, you cooked your own food, only from what you could raise or hunt. You had very little food from the store. That would be a different guy than the one who ate out every night at a local diner reading a book." Cat expanded on the idea.

"Do you interview your characters before you write about them?" Anne asked.

"Actually, no. I'm a bit of a pantser. I let the characters form while I'm writing. But some people find that helpful. What about you?"

Colleen laughed. "Anne spends more time getting ready to write than she does actually writing the book. You should see her charts. They're scary."

"Everyone has their own process." Cat smiled at Anne, but deep inside, she agreed with Colleen. She had never understood plotters. By the time they figured out the story, Cat would have been tired of it. She liked the mystery of her process. She never knew one day to the next how the story was going to twist and turn.

"My process definitely slows me down. I'm hoping this week to try out some different practices for this new story I'm starting. It might not work, but I'd like to be a faster writer. I'll try anything." Anne picked up her slice of cheese pizza and folded it lengthwise. "This tastes like Chicago pizza."

"That's because Reno started in Chicago. He moved out here ten years ago to get away from the cold winters. He may have misjudged Colorado winters." Seth took a slice of the everything pizza and then stood to take the empty box into the kitchen. "I think the real reason he came out here was his wife was from these parts and he followed her out west."

"That's romantic." Colleen beamed. "I like a touch of romance for my stories. True or not, everyone needs a happily ever after."

"You read too many fairy tales as a kid." Rick

shook his head. "Real life doesn't work like the movies. You have to fight for a relationship."

"Speaks the man who hasn't had a date in the last year." Anne's words might have sounded harsh, if the tone hadn't shown the care behind them.

He shrugged. "I'm waiting for the perfect woman. One who isn't challenged by my softer side."

"You just want someone who's rich so she can support you," Colleen teased.

Rick held up a hand. "I promise not to turn away any megarich women who want to sponsor my writing habit and use me as a boy toy. I am totally in line for that. I could quit my job at the car rental place and just write."

"How many of you have a non-writing job?" Cat always wondered how people fit in being creative when they had to go to the cube farm every day and be productive for a living wage. She knew many authors who combined teaching with writing. And a number of lawyers who wrote at night, hoping for that one big break.

"I work a full work week. Not that I want to, but my writing isn't paying the bills. Yet." Rick nodded at Anne. "Tell her where you work, Anne."

"I work as a server at one of the upscale restaurants downtown. And the tips are totally worth it since I live outside downtown. I'm putting as much as I can away in my IRA so hopefully, when I'm old, I won't have to wait tables." Anne pointed at Colleen. "She's got the best job ever."

"Oh, what do you do?" Cat turned toward Colleen, who looked like she wished she had disappeared out of the dining room before she was asked.

"I work for a bookseller. It's crap pay, but it's

all they can really afford. And if it's slow in the store, they don't mind if I write. It's the best of both worlds."

"We have our local independent bookstore owner who comes in on Friday to discuss the fate of the book market. She's been very well received from other guests." Cat looked up and saw Bren coming into the dining room. She sat at the edge of the table closest to the door and took a slice of the pizza that was in front of her. "Hey, Bren. Glad you could join us. We're talking about what other jobs you hold besides the writing."

"I only write." Bren glanced down at her plate. "I like the solitude."

"Bren has a sugar daddy," Rick teased. Then yelped as he leaned down to rub his leg where Colleen had kicked him. "What? We all know it's true. There's no shame in having a relationship with someone who gets you."

Unless that relationship isn't very positive, Cat thought. But she kept that thought to herself. She wasn't here to solve everyone's problems. Her job was to make sure that the group had a good time and hopefully, got some words down.

"He's not a sugar daddy. He just would rather me stay home and nearby than go have a job and not be available to him." Bren didn't look up. "Let's just leave it at that and talk about something else."

Cat glanced at the clock. Almost eight. Time to get them moving toward the living room and the movies. "Shauna set up a few movies for your choosing for a treat if you want after dinner."

"I'm going back to my room," Bren announced.

"I have several things I want to get done before I sign off for the day."

"I'm in." Rick stood and grabbed one of the brownies. "Can we take food out of the dining room?"

When Shauna looked at him, questioning, he shrugged. "My mom was strict. Food was eaten in the dining room or kitchen. Nowhere else."

"Do you keep that same rule?" Cat asked. She wondered about household traditions and which ones continued through the generations.

"Heck no. I'm a slob. You should see my apartment. My writing desk is filled with empty coffee cups and candy bar wrappers." He grinned. "I just want to be mindful of your rules."

"Well, don't be a total slob in the public rooms, but your room is your domain while you're here." Shauna started picking up the empty trays. "Just remember I'm your housekeeper too, so you have to be able to look me in the eye."

He grabbed another brownie. "I'm pretty sure I'm immune to guilt now, thanks to my mother, but I'll keep it passable."

"I'm ready to fall into a story. The trip has just worn me out." Colleen filled a cup with hot chocolate and followed Rick out. "Don't think just because you get to the DVR first that you get to pick the movie."

Anne held back until they were gone. "You must think Bren's rude, but she's dealing with some things. She used to be fun and amazing. I've known her since high school. We both wanted to be writers someday. I used to think Bren could rule the world."

"She doesn't have to be nice to me. I have thick

skin. But thank you for your concern." Cat nodded to the living room. "I have a feeling you're going to have to be the deciding vote on what movie you watch."

"Being the peacemaker, it's the bane of my existence." Anne smiled as she grabbed a glass of water and strolled out of the room.

Chapter Three

Sunday morning was supposed to be a quiet time of reflection and rest. Instead, Cat was up at five and working with a frazzled Shauna to set up her *mise en place* for the day. The group's breakfast was already set up out in the dining room as an egg casserole finished cooking in the oven. Shauna's class didn't start until ten, but she wanted to be prepared.

"I know this is silly, but I really want to be prepped and ready at least an hour ahead," Shauna announced for the third time since Cat had wandered in to get some coffee and had gotten stuck with chores.

"I agree. But calm down. They all seem like nice people. I don't think you're going to have any rabble-rousers in your class." Cat finished cutting the strawberries and held up the cup of sugar. "You want this in these?"

"Yeah. I want them to have time to settle." Shauna

glanced around the perfect kitchen. "It is going to be okay, isn't it?"

"Most definitely." Cat grabbed her coffee cup and took a long sip. Maybe they were done—if Shauna could just relax for a few minutes.

Seth popped his head in the kitchen. "Hey, Cat? Can I see you for a minute?"

She patted Shauna on the shoulder as she walked by. "Sit down, have a cup of coffee, and relax for a few minutes. Nothing bad is going to happen."

When she met Seth in the hallway, she reached up and gave him a quick kiss on the cheek. "Thanks for rescuing me from that. Shauna's a complete wreck."

"That's not why I asked you to come out here. We have a visitor." He put his arm around her and led her to the foyer. "Nate? This is my girlfriend, Cat Latimer. She runs the retreat."

"Cat, nice to meet you." Nate, a short, pudgy man, had a surprisingly firm handshake. "Nate Hearst."

She smiled and glanced at Seth. "Are you two friends? I don't believe I've seen you around town."

"Actually, Cat"—Seth threw a warning glance at Nate that clearly said, 'let me explain first'—"Nate's from the health department. He's had a complaint about our kitchen."

"From one of the guests?" Cat felt floored. She started going through last month's guest list. No one had mentioned anything about being unhappy. But she could have read the group wrong—it happened.

"No, I believe it's from one of the townspeople. It came in on our tip line. They don't write down phone numbers, but I'm pretty sure I know what business complained." Nate held out a sheet. "If I could just visit your kitchen, I'm sure we can clear this up quickly."

"Sure." Cat took a step toward Shauna's kitchen. Maybe she should warn her. Shauna would be incensed at the insult. Her kitchen was as professional and clean as it would be in a restaurant. "Maybe I should go talk to Shauna first."

"I can't let you do that." Nate reached for her arm and, all of a sudden, Seth stood between them. A look passed between the two men and Nate broke first. He held up his hands. "I still can't let you warn her of my inspection."

"Okay, but if she bites your head off after you realize it must have been a prank call, you're going to feel really foolish." Cat pointed to the dining room. "That's where we feed the guests. The drinks are all on ice to keep them cold. The baked goods are fresh each day and we go over the fruit on a daily basis to make sure nothing is getting too ripe. Hot dishes go on a hot plate right out of the oven. I tell you, we're on top of food safety."

Nate stepped into the room and picked up a blueberry muffin. He broke it open and took a big whiff. Then he bit into it and sighed. "My mom made the best muffins, but these are even better."

Cat wanted to point out that if he thought they had health violations, it was stupid to eat something from the kitchen, but she realized the guy was just doing his job. And she didn't have to make it harder on him. "I don't understand. Why are you here on a Sunday?"

He finished the muffin and wiped his mouth with a napkin. "I got the call on Friday but Seth's bragged so much about Shauna's cooking, I wanted to wait until I knew a retreat was in session."

"You're not going to shut us down, are you?" Now Cat was confused. The guy seemed nice enough.

"Not unless I find some pretty serious health issues in that kitchen you're trying to keep me out of." Nate nodded to the door. "Is that the way?"

Cat glanced at Seth, who made go-ahead motions with his hands. She had to trust someone. She opened the door and showed Nate inside.

Shauna sat at the table with her back to the door. "I don't have time for this. Just grab your coffee and get out. I'm never going to be ready for this thing. I never should have agreed to do it. What was I thinking?"

"Um, Shauna? Someone's here you need to talk to." Cat walked over and put a hand on her friend's shoulder. "Now, there's probably nothing wrong, but I want you to be calm, okay?"

"What are you talking about?" Shauna spun around in her chair and frowned at Nate. "What are you doing here?"

"Do you know each other?" Cat looked between Nate and Shauna. Maybe this was all a bad practical joke. Seth loved jokes.

"He's the guy I told you about from Bernie's. He's always trying to buy me a drink." She turned back to her notebook, dismissing him. "I told you, I'm not dating right now. I'm in mourning."

"Over a jerk, from what I heard," Nate muttered, but then held up a hand to stop the tirade. "I shouldn't have said that. Besides, I'm not here on personal business. Although I do think you should reconsider my offer. One drink wouldn't hurt anyone. You might find you like me. I'm a likeable guy."

"If you're not here to talk to me, why are you here? I've got a class in less than ninety minutes." Shauna walked over to the fridge to look inside for what Cat thought was the thirtieth time.

"I'm with the health department. Someone called in a complaint about unhealthy conditions in your kitchen."

Shauna slammed the fridge door. "Are you freaking kidding me?"

"Calm down. I didn't say I believed them, but I have to investigate all complaints." He glanced around the kitchen. "You've done a nice job updating this. Seth, I take it you did the remodel?"

"I did." Seth walked the guy around, showing him all the new appliances and upgraded electrical. "We got all the building permits. There's nothing out of code here."

Nate took out a thermometer and sat it in the fridge, then another one for the freezer. He started a timer on his watch, then made some notes on his clipboard. "I'll take a sample of your drinking water, but if you're on city water, you'll be fine. The town replaced all these lines a couple of years ago. Replaced all those iron pipes. They were solid but tended to flake off into the drinking water."

Cat had walked over and stood by a visibly shaking Shauna. "We'll get through this."

"This is Dee Dee's fault, I know it." Shauna lowered her voice so only Cat could hear. "That witch hates me."

Cat didn't argue with her. Someone in town had a gripe with the retreat. Instead of focusing on that, she decided to lighten the mood. "You didn't tell me Nate was so cute," she whispered.

The look Shauna gave her made Cat laugh and both men turned to look at them.

Cat shook her head. "Private joke."

Nate removed the temperature gauges and wrote down the results. "Like I thought, no issues here. Sorry for the inconvenience. But maybe I could have another one of those muffins for the road?"

Shauna didn't move, so Cat went and got a plastic bag. She put two muffins and two cookies into the bag. "Thanks for making this less painful."

"It's my job. I'll see you in six months." He started to walk with Seth out of the kitchen.

Cat caught up with them. "Wait, why will you see us in six months?"

"I have to do a follow-up visit. To make sure you don't backslide." He smiled and waved at Shauna. "And maybe you'll be out of your mourning time by then."

After they left, Shauna sank into her chair at the table. "The man is so sure of himself. It's infuriating."

Cat dumped out the coffee from her cup, which had gone cold while she'd dealt with Nate's visit. She refilled her cup with fresh. "I don't know. He seemed really nice. You should at least talk to him. He likes your cooking."

"Everyone likes my cooking. Doesn't mean I have to date the entire male population of Aspen Hills." She glanced at the wall clock. "I'm going upstairs to shower and change. When the timer goes off on the casserole, would you take it out to the dining room? The condiments are all already out on the sideboard."

"Sure. Are you okay?" Cat couldn't identify the emotion that her friend was feeling. It wasn't sadness.

"I'm fine." Shauna smiled. "I just need to compose myself before I have to be on for the writers' group."

"Okay, but you'll tell me if something's wrong, right?"

Shauna nodded. "Definitely."

Had Shauna ever directly lied to her? It was obvious that Shauna was dealing with something and Cat knew she wouldn't tell anyone until Shauna figured out how she felt. Shauna's knee-jerk response was to shut down. Which wasn't a bad idea when you didn't know what you wanted to say.

The class started promptly at ten and Shauna was so in her element. Cat wanted to videotape the session, but she figured that would have changed the dynamics, and right now, the flow between Shauna and the writers felt perfect. Cat stood at the edge of the kitchen, wanting to be available in case Shauna needed something, but honestly, she could have been sitting at the kitchen desk and writing. Shauna was the perfect teacher.

"When you want to cream your butter, make sure it's not right out of the fridge." Shauna held up a cube of butter. "You should be able to push a fingertip into the wrapping and keep the shape."

"Maybe that's something we could use to find the killer in our books?" Colleen reached out to push her own finger on the paper-wrapped butter. "The killer left a fingerprint in the butter."

Rick wrote something down in his book. "It's mine, I've claimed it."

"Doesn't work that way and you know it." Bren smiled at Shauna. "Don't mind us; we're just always trying to find new ways to kill people."

"And new ways to uncover the killer," Anne added. "Sometimes that's even harder. What can an amateur sleuth know that would have gotten by the police who are paid to investigate? And you can't put your main character in jeopardy all the time. She, or he, has to be intelligent enough not to walk into the dark basement after hearing about the serial killer's release."

"But we don't do serial killers," Rick added. He picked up his coffee. "It's all very structured."

"Then it's like a recipe." Shauna tried to turn the conversation back to the class. She turned on the mixer to cream the butter and sugar. "We have two more dishes to make after this, but I want to get these muffins in the oven so we can have them for afternoon snacks."

"Does it matter what type of berry you put into the mix?" Anne chewed on the end of her pen.

"You have to watch the water content, but no, you can put any kind of fruit in these." Shauna held up a pint of huckleberries. "These are a regional berry. And only fresh for a few weeks out of the year. But you can freeze them, just like blueberries. Blackberries have bigger seeds, so they can be a problem."

Seth peeked into the doorway and waved at Cat to come out and join him. She caught Shauna's gaze and pointed to the door. When her friend nodded, Cat knew the jitters had gone away. Just like she'd told her they would. She met Seth in the hallway. "Shauna's a natural at this."

"I knew she would be," he agreed. "Man, she was a bundle of nerves this morning when I came in for coffee." He motioned toward the study. "Do you mind if we go in there? I don't want Shauna to overhear."

"What's going on?" Cat opened the door to Michael's study, but then sat in one of the lounging chairs she'd set up for people to relax and read rather than behind the large desk.

Seth perched on the other chair, his hands folded together in his lap. "Nate told me that he thinks it's Dee Dee from the bakery who called him in. He says that Dee Dee and Kevin used to be an item before Shauna arrived on the scene and . . . well, you know what happened then."

"That's crazy. Even if Kevin was still alive, Dee Dee was out of the picture." Cat rubbed her face. "Shauna has enough to deal with right now. She doesn't need another one of Kevin's ex-girlfriends giving her grief."

Seth shrugged. "I get it. Nate gets it. But Dee Dee is apparently still hot about how she and Kevin broke up. Well, we were wondering if you wouldn't mind going and talking to her to get her to stop calling in complaints."

"You think me going to talk to her will have any effect?" Cat shook her head. "I've got guests to deal with this week. I don't have time to coddle some woman's feelings."

He reached for her hand. "I know you're good at this emotional, touchy-feely stuff. Nate's tired of dealing with her constant harping. If you could get her to back off, he would be really grateful."

"And if I don't get her to back off?" Cat wasn't liking where this conversation was going. Not one bit.

"Nate's afraid he'll have to actually cite us for some dumb regulation one of these days. He doesn't want to be in that position."

Cat closed her eyes. Seth was right. The fewer times the health inspector came to your door, the less chance of him finding something that could possibly shut the retreat down for stupid reasons.

"Fine, I'll go talk to her." She glanced at her watch. It was two. Shauna and the writers would be engaged until three thirty, so if she was going to get this task off her plate, she probably should go now.

"I know you can handle this. Just spread some of your charm." Seth pulled her to her feet. "Get it done and over with. Maybe you'll get lucky."

"I'd be luckier if I could be upstairs in my room with my feet up reading a book." She walked with him out to the foyer.

"That was last Sunday. Today, you're a career woman who needs to take care of a threat to your business." He walked out with her and stopped at his truck. "I'm meeting Nate for beers down at Bernie's. Call me and let me know how it goes."

He leaned down and kissed her.

"Sure, you go have fun and let the girl handle the problems." She squeezed his arm. "I'll call you as soon as I'm walking back."

"You can do it." Seth let out a war cry that made Cat laugh as she turned right to walk the few blocks to town and to the bakery.

Chapter Four

The walk to town was perfect. The trees were just starting to drop leaves and the crunch of dried leaves under her feet made her think about all things autumn. Chilly nights with a bonfire. Hot chocolate in the evening by the fire. More time to read. All these memories made her happy. By the time she arrived at the bakery's front door, Cat had almost forgotten her unease at confronting Dee Dee. There were small café tables set around the front so patrons could sit and drink coffee or eat their baked goods on-site. Only one table was occupied. A man sat drinking coffee and reading his paper. He turned his head away from her when she walked up, probably not wanting to engage in conversation. Some people got to enjoy their quiet Sunday afternoon however they wanted. Instead, she was here playing nice and trying to calm down Dee Dee.

Cat pushed open the bakery door and a bell rang over the doorway. The air smelled like yeast-filled treats mixed with the strong odor of coffee. Not a bad place to spend your day, all in all.

"Can I help you?" Dee Dee Meyer came out of the back, wiping her hands on a towel. The smile fell off her face and her tone turned cold. "Oh, it's you. Come to make trouble?"

Cat crossed over the black-and-white tile floor directly to the counter. "Actually, the opposite. I've come to throw a truce flag. What is it going to take for us to be friends? Or at least stop sniping at each other."

Apparently, that honesty hadn't been what Dee Dee had been expecting at all. She narrowed her eyes and considered Cat. Then she turned around and poured two cups of coffee. She set one cup in front of Cat. "You need something in this?"

Cat shook her head and sat on the stool. "Nope. Black is fine."

"My kind of girl. I can't believe how many people turn their coffee into hot chocolate. If you want hot chocolate, then get one. Don't fill your coffee with all that junk and think you're drinking java." Dee Dee sat on a stool across from Cat. "I'm surprised you came here. I would have thought you would be too busy, what with the group you have in this week. I hope they come in and at least sample my food before leaving for home."

"We have a flyer with all the restaurants and eating establishments that we give out in their welcome baskets. That way, they don't have to worry about where they're going to eat since we only provide breakfast." Cat sipped her coffee.

"Well, at least that's something." Dee Dee rolled her shoulders back. "Look, I've got a special order

I need to get finished before six. What are you really here about?"

"World peace and popcorn for everyone." Cat smiled, but Dee Dee didn't follow suit. "Fine, I want you to stop calling the health department about my retreat. I think you're being a bully and using other people to do your dirty work."

"How do you know it's me who's been calling them?" Dee Dee didn't meet Cat's gaze.

Cat tried another tactic. "Look, I don't want to fight. I want to settle this. We can be good for each other. My writers' groups love to visit new places to eat. And you could be someplace we strongly encourage people to go to."

"You'd do that? Even after all of this?" Dee Dee caught herself. "I mean, if I had done something like you described. I couldn't be held accountable for what Nate does."

"I think you know better than that." Cat took a five out of her front pocket to pay for her coffee. "Look, just give me a call when you want to really talk. Like you mentioned, I've got a house full of guests to take care of."

Dee Dee let Cat almost reach the door before she responded. "Thank you for coming by. I'll curb my less attractive personality traits and try to be more neighborly."

Cat turned around but Dee Dee had already disappeared back into the kitchen area. Cat called after her. "That's all I'm asking for."

Cat crossed over Main Street and started to make her way home. She couldn't help thinking about how the bakery had been empty. Was that because of the day of the week or because of the way people felt about Dee Dee? There was a direct correlation between relationships and the ability to keep a business alive. People bought things from people they liked. Either way, it wasn't up to Cat to heal the woman, just keep her out of the way.

The Written Word bookstore was next to the bakery, but Tammy Jones had already closed up for the day. The town seemed quiet and it almost felt spooky being so empty.

Tammy would be at the retreat on Friday, so they could talk then. Maybe she'd have some insight on her neighbor, Dee Dee. For now, all Cat could do was hope that her talk did some good. She hummed to herself as she strolled back to the house. She might just get a hot bath and some reading time into her day after all.

The class had disbanded by the time she returned and Shauna was in the kitchen washing the dishes. Cat took her jacket off and hung it on the coatrack. "Let me help you clean up and you can tell me how it went."

"Actually, I just want to relax and think. I can clean while I'm doing that. It calms me to have something to do with my hands while I'm thinking. Can we debrief tomorrow morning? I want to implement some changes for next time, but I want to let my thoughts settle before I jump."

"If you're sure." Cat grabbed a soda out of the fridge. "Are the guests getting ready for dinner?"

"Molly is showing them where The Diner is so they'll be able to find the place." Shauna grinned. "That group is so funny. All they want to talk about is their books. And life. And how life affects their books. You can tell they've been friends for a long time."

"I love having these types of groups. There's no drama." Cat nodded to the kitchen door. "I'll be in my room soaking and reading if you need me."

"Don't forget dinner will be on the table at six and your uncle will be joining us." Shauna rinsed off a dish and stuck it in the dishwasher.

"Works for me." Cat paused before leaving the kitchen. "You did good today. I'm proud of you."

She didn't wait for a response. Shauna had needed something to get her out of this funk. Between working on the cookbook, riding Snow, and now prepping for the class, her friend hadn't had time to grieve. Idle hands, her mom had always said when Cat felt blue. Then she'd assign her another chore, and by the time it was over, so was her funk. Cat hoped her mom's recipe for joy worked on Shauna as well.

For her, she was going to relax until tomorrow when the retreat started for real. Then she'd have to be friendly and charming. Sometimes Cat wondered if they should do retreats every other month, just so her introverted tendencies could have plenty of time to recuperate after a session. Unfortunately, with the utility costs and the remodel loan she'd taken out to open the retreat, they needed the monthly income.

Cat was in the tub, her head back and her eyes closed, when a knock came on her door. "If I just ignore them, they'll go away," she muttered, not opening her eyes.

"Cat? Are you in there?" Shauna's voice called

through the closed door. Then Cat heard the key turn in the lock.

"I should have thrown the dead bolt." She opened her eyes and checked the level of the bubbles.

"Cat? Are you in here?" Shauna called out again; this time, Cat knew she was in the bedroom.

"I'm taking a bath. Alone. And I don't need anything, so go away," Cat responded, closing her eyes again.

"Your uncle is here. And he needs to talk to you." Shauna's voice came from near the bathroom door.

"I'll see him at dinner." Then Cat realized the retreat was already in session. She sat up with a start, splashing water out of the tub. "Crap, did something happen to one of the guests? Please tell me they're all right."

"They're fine. It's not the guests." Shauna went silent for a minute. "Cat, Dee Dee Meyer found someone in her kitchen."

"How does that affect me? I'm clearly not in the bakery." Cat didn't understand what Shauna was saying and why it would be so important to drag her out of a hot bath.

"Cat, she found some dead guy. And Dee Dee told Pete you were in her shop earlier today."

Cat pulled herself out of the bath and wrapped an oversized towel around her. She went over and opened the door. "Yeah, but there wasn't anyone dead or alive in the shop except for Dee Dee when I left."

"Well, your uncle needs to check your timing so he can mark you off the suspect list." Shauna shook her head. "Why were you over there in the first place?"

"To try to convince her to stop being a jerk and calling Nate over perceived health code violations." She waved toward the door. "Go tell Uncle Pete I'll be right down, but I'm not happy about giving up my relaxation time to talk to him about something that has nothing to do with me."

"Bad things seem to happen to that girl," Shauna said as she made her way toward the door to the hallway. "She comes over here all hot about something stupid and she winds up finding someone dead in her own bakery. She doesn't have any kind of luck."

Cat leaned against the doorway. She'd known better than to get involved in Nate's secret plan to stop Dee Dee from making false reports. What was the saying? No good deed goes unpunished? She dried off and went to get ready to talk to her uncle.

Uncle Pete, or Chief Edmond, as the rest of the town residents called him, sat at her kitchen table, a laptop open in front of him and a phone to his ear. He filled out his police uniform a little too well. Cat noticed a few buttons straining. He had a mug of hot chocolate and a plate of cookies sitting nearby. Cat took one of the cookies as she sat, earning her a glare from her uncle.

"Look, Paul, just wait for the crime scene guys outside the bakery. No one gets inside until after they've done their work." He paused, listening to his deputy, Paul Quinn's, response. He rolled his eyes. "I'm sure that's important to Ms. Meyer, but she cannot go back into the bakery until I clear it. Just tell her to go home. I'll call her later."

Shauna handed Cat a cup of hot chocolate as

well, along with her own plate of cookies. "You two aren't going to want dinner after this."

"I'm going to have to take a rain check on dinner, Shauna." Uncle Pete sat his cell down after ending the call. "There's no way Paul Quinn is going to be able to keep the crime scene undisturbed. That's the third call I've gotten from the kid since I assigned him the task."

"Why did you give the responsibility to Quinn?" Cat knew Paul Quinn from school. To say he was a screw-up was being kind.

"Would you believe all my other deputies were busy or out of town?" Uncle Pete ran a hand through his thinning hair. "I went down to a skeleton staff as the Guns and Hoses charity event is this week in Denver. We have one kid who might just take it all."

"All what?" Cat was confused by her uncle's explanation.

Shauna laughed as she sat down at the table. "Cat, it's a boxing match. The police officers against the firefighters, right, Pete?"

"Exactly." Uncle Pete rolled his shoulders. "Although with this murder, I might have to call some of the guys back."

"Did Dee Dee recognize the dead guy?" Cat sipped her coffee. "Maybe he was a customer who wandered into the kitchen and had a heart attack."

"That's not quite what went down." Uncle Pete opened a new window. "Besides, I'm the investigator. I ask the questions and you answer them. I know it's an unusual process for you."

"Oh, bite me."

"Cat!" Shauna's reaction was priceless. She couldn't have been more shocked if Cat had turned purple and started doing the hula in the kitchen. "Show some respect."

Uncle Pete held up a hand. "Old family joke." He grinned at Cat. "She knows better than to push this line or she'll wind up in one of my cells until she can show better manners."

"You don't scare me." Cat leaned back in her chair. "Go ahead, let's get this over with. I might be able to get some reading in before I have to switch over to hostess mode."

"You want to tell me why you went to the bakery today?"

Cat went through the whole thing. How Seth and Nate had asked her to go over and make nice with Dee Dee. Then she repeated almost word for word the actual conversation, at least what she could remember. Finally, she shrugged. "Then I left. There was a guy out at one of the outdoor tables reading a paper. Or wait, maybe he was there when I went in? I'm not sure."

"Dee Dee's security feed doesn't show anyone sitting outside and reading the paper."

Cat folded a cookie in half. "I don't know what to tell you. The guy was there when I walked up. That's right, I remember now. But either I didn't look that way or he was already gone when I came back out."

He stared at her. "You're sure that there was a man sitting at the outdoor table?"

Cat nodded. "I'm certain."

Uncle Pete drummed his fingers on the table. "Then why didn't her security feed pick him up? Unless I have the wrong discs. I better get back on scene and see if I can find the right ones."

"Do you want me to package up some food for tonight?" Shauna started to stand, but Uncle Pete waved her down.

"Don't worry about it. I've got leftovers from lunch I can warm up at the station." He turned to Cat. "Anything else you want to tell me?"

"I can't think of anything. Except the next time Seth and Nate ask me for a favor, you can bet I'm going to say no." Cat sipped her coffee, then set the cup down, noticing the looks Shauna and Uncle Pete were sharing. "What?"

"There is no way you'd step away from helping anyone. It's not in your nature." Uncle Pete closed his laptop and stood. "I just wish your helpfulness wouldn't lead you into murder scenes."

"It wasn't a murder scene when I went there. Just a local bakery." Cat held up her hand. "But yeah, I get your point. For the next week, I'm going to be here, playing hostess and talking books. You'll have to solve this case without me."

"You think you're funny, don't you?" He kissed her on the head. "I just hope it's that simple and you don't get pulled into this. I worry about you when you're off playing Nancy Drew."

"One, I don't play Nancy Drew. I think of myself more like Miss Marple. I just like to solve puzzles. And two, sometimes things just happen. I don't go looking for danger." Cat followed him to the door. She put her hand on her uncle's arm. "You make sure you eat something."

"Leftovers aren't as nice as one of Shauna's dinners, but it's food." He smiled at her. "I've been taking care of myself for a lot of years."

Cat went back to the table and sank into the chair. "I wonder who was killed."

"You noticed he left that part out of the conversation too?" Shauna stood and walked over to the stove. "I know he doesn't want you getting involved in the investigation, but I felt like he was holding back something. Usually, he comes out and tells us what's going on."

"Well, maybe he thought it didn't really concern us." But as Cat returned to her room to try to read a little before dinner, the thought kept rolling through her mind. Why had her uncle been so secretive?

Chapter Five

The local paper sat on the table the next morning when Cat went down to the kitchen for a cup of coffee. She took a long drink and held up the page, reading the headline. When the words sank in, she choked on the coffee. "Seriously? This is who was killed in Dee Dee's bakery? Greyson Finn? The famous Denver chef?"

"Apparently." Shauna sat next to Cat, her own cup in her hands. She pointed to a line in the article. "Your uncle is going to be upset about that. . . ."

Cat read aloud. "'According to an undisclosed source in the Aspen Hills's police force, the investigation is stumped on why Mr. Finn was even in the small Colorado town.'" She glanced at Shauna. "Quinn's in big trouble."

"Since he was the only other officer on scene and we both know your uncle didn't call up the press to tell them a gossip story." Shauna pointed to the picture of the Denver restaurant that Finn had opened just last year. "Kevin took me there a lot. The menu was amazing. He had a magic touch with food."

"So why would some big-shot chef even be in Dee Dee's bakery?" Cat sipped on her coffee as she read the rest of the article. "It doesn't mention how they knew each other at all."

"See, that's the weird piece." Shauna looked up at the clock. "Seth will be here in about ten minutes. He's staying over starting tonight, but I guess he wanted to watch the football games yesterday so he stayed at his apartment."

"Better there than here." Cat liked having Seth in the house, but sometimes, his love of sports made it hard to be around the guy. He was always watching one game or another. And she'd tried to sit and read while he watched a game, but he was always pointing out things to her and asking if she saw some move. If they ever made this living situation permanent, she would have to set up a game room for him and explain that even though she loved the guy, she didn't love his sports.

"I like football. But yesterday was too hectic for me to even think about watching any type of television. All I wanted to do after dinner was sleep." Shauna started cutting up fruit on a chopping board. "Of course, when I tried, all I could think of was that poor man who was killed. I would have never guessed it was Greyson Finn."

The back door swung open and Seth came into the kitchen carrying a bushelful of apples. "Mr. Henry stopped me on the way here and said he'd promised you apples."

"What a sweet man." Shauna hurried over to direct Seth to a sideboard. "I know just what I'm going to do with these. Apple pie or apple crumble."

"Both." Seth headed toward the door.

"Where are you going?" Cat picked up an apple and took a big whiff and groaned. There was nothing like a freshly picked apple.

"Oh, you thought that was the extent of his gift? There are four more bushels in the truck. I think you're going to have to figure out some more ways to cook with apples or to put these up for the winter." Seth disappeared from the kitchen toward his truck parked at the side of the house.

"How long will they stay good?" Cat took an apple over to the sink and washed it. Then she used Shauna's cutting board to slice it up and remove the core.

"Not long enough for us to eat enough pie." Shauna paused thoughtfully at the pile of apples. "I'll put out a basket for the guests. But I'm going to have to make applesauce or freeze some pie filling to get these down to a manageable amount."

"What are we having for breakfast?" Seth dropped the last basket on the floor since the sideboard was full. He grinned. "Besides apples."

"I'm making ham and cheese omelets, and there's a pan of hash browns on the stove." Shauna moved to the fridge. "Give me five minutes and I'll have a plate ready for you."

"Works for me." He glanced at the clock. "I'm going to take my bag up to my room then. Same accommodations?"

"Yes." Cat blushed as he winked at her. "Stop that. We've got guests in the house."

"Who love teasing you about your boyfriend." Seth grabbed his bag that he'd left at the door. "I'm thinking next week we should go into Denver for the weekend. We can see a show or just hang out."

"Sounds great." Cat decided to hold back on discussing the plans she'd made with Shauna till after the retreat ended. Besides, she could do both. She just had to plan it out. She touched his arm as he walked by. "Thanks for being part of the retreat crew. I really appreciate your help."

"Darling, you're paying for my help. I donate my charming personality and wit with the guests." He pulled her into a hug. "I've got your back."

Cat leaned in to the hug, then remembered the bakery incident. "Hey, you and Nate got me in trouble last night with Uncle Pete."

"How did we do that?" Seth tilted his head down to watch her closer.

"You sent her to the bakery, and when a dead guy was found there, Pete had to look at Cat as a suspect." Shauna carefully folded the omelet in half. "You don't have time for the story and to get your stuff put away, so which one will it be?"

"Who was killed?" Seth held up a hand. "Wait, I'm not sure I want to know. Let me run this upstairs real quick and you can tell me about it over breakfast."

"If you're not down soon, Cat gets the first plate," Shauna warned as Seth sprinted to the hallway door.

Cat went to the fridge and took out the orange juice and poured three glasses. "I still don't understand why Greyson was hanging out in Aspen Hills. You would think he'd be too busy with running a restaurant for a day trip."

"Don't tell me you're going to start investigating." Shauna plated up the omelet and put hash browns next to it. Setting it aside, she started the next omelet. "Your uncle isn't going to like it."

"I didn't say I was investigating. I'm just wondering, that's all." But as she sat down with the first plate, she wondered if she was lying to herself as well as her friend. She itched to find out more about Greyson Finn on one hand. On the other, she wondered if she was getting addicted to the high of finding out secrets. This couldn't be good for her. Not really.

"Well, you have enough on your plate with this retreat. You don't have time to snoop into this guy's death." Shauna folded over the second omelet. "Even if it is dreamy Greyson. You know he was voted Denver's best bachelor in the last two years. He even got a trophy from the city council."

"Sounds like a wimpy trophy." Seth came back into the kitchen and pointed at Cat's plate. "Hey, that's my food."

"No, it isn't. You weren't here, so I got it. You snooze, you lose." Cat put her arms protectively around the plate. "Although if you want this half-eaten omelet, I'll take the new one that Shauna's just finishing."

"Oh, no you won't." Seth stood between Cat and the stove.

Shauna handed him a filled plate. "Now there, children. Mummy loves both of you equally."

Seth took the plate and sat next to Cat. He gently elbowed her. "You're lucky she had more food ready. I'm starving. Now, tell me what's going on with this dead guy."

They spent the next half hour filling Seth in

on what had happened at the bakery. When they finished, he shook his head. "Pete must be tired of all of this activity. I don't think we had a murder in Aspen Hills for years before . . ."

He stopped before he finished his statement.

Cat nodded. "You might as well say it. Before the retreat opened."

"Now, that's not true. Michael was killed before you even moved back to town." Seth took his plate to the sink. "And with that clarifier, I'm heading upstairs to check on the home security system. I've got a whole list of things I want to get done this week so you get your money's worth from your handyman boyfriend."

Shauna laughed as he disappeared out the doorway to the hall. "You have a way of getting under his skin, you know?"

"We've always been this way. Other people would tell us to stop fighting and Seth and I would look at them confused. We hadn't been fighting. We were discussing something. When we're fighting we're not talking at all." Cat ate the last of her hash browns. "Breakfast was really good. If no one's down yet, I'm running upstairs to play with some new ideas about some spin-off books. That is, if I get a new contract."

"Just pop into the dining room and say hi if anyone's awake. I don't know yet if we have morning larks or night owls, but I suspect there might be someone in there eating breakfast." Shauna wiped down the table with a clean cloth. "I'm going to chop some apples for a couple of pies for tonight."

"I'll come down and take the group to the library." Cat put a lid on her travel mug and grabbed a couple of cookies. She had some research to do anyway. And it would be better if no one knew she was looking into Greyson.

When she got to the stairs, Rick Talbert was coming down, dressed in running clothes. His red hair peeked out from a ski hat. He slipped on gloves as he went down the last couple of stairs. "Good morning. I'm going for a quick run before breakfast. If I don't get exercise done in the morning, it doesn't happen."

"It's a beautiful morning. Not too cold." She glanced backward at the front windows. "We have a treadmill downstairs if you want to use it."

"I like being outside for as long as possible. I'll run outside during the winter as long as it's not icy on the sidewalks. Which means, I don't get to run as much as I'd like. Chicago winters can be pretty brutal."

Cat started up the stairs. "Well, I won't keep you. I'm heading to my office to work for a bit, but I'll be taking the group over to the library just before ten."

"Looking forward to it." He made his way through the foyer and out the front door.

Wondering if any of the other guests were up, Cat paused at the second-level landing, but she didn't see anyone out of their room nor did she hear anything. Maybe Rick was her only lark this session, as Shauna had called the early risers. When she got to her office, she booted up her computer and started looking into the life of Greyson Finn. The work was interesting. And if caught, she could claim it was research.

An hour later, she had a couple of full pages and more questions than she had answers. Nothing she had found linked the local chef to Aspen Hills or Dee Dee. She shut the computer down and locked her office, just in case one of the guests confused her turret room for the attic, where they had additional writing areas set up for guests. Cat didn't like the idea of anyone else working in her office.

As she went downstairs, she reminded herself that she needed to stop this addiction. Uncle Pete was the family member in law enforcement, not her. She was an author who also had a retreat—one that was currently going, and she needed to focus on that.

She heard voices in the dining room so, instead of going into the kitchen for coffee, she went in to see who was up. "Good morning," she called out as she went to the sideboard to fill a coffee cup. She'd left her travel mug upstairs. "How is everyone this morning?"

"I'm so ready to get started writing. I'm beginning a new series this week. I've got it all planned out and I hope to have a large dent in my word count by the time I go home on Sunday." Colleen waved Cat over to an empty chair next to her. "I know some people like the spontaneity of writing whatever comes to mind when they sit down, but I want some guidelines. Especially when I'm opening a new world."

"Sounds like an ambitious goal." Cat sat next to Colleen and, since all the guests were in the room, took the time to go through the schedule. "We have a pretty relaxed setup except for the few seminars during the week. If you don't want to attend one, just let me know. That way we won't wait, thinking you're just running late."

"I love the idea of learning more about Hemingway. He's in the same time period that I like to set my books." Bren sipped on her orange juice. "I'm doing a series about Frank Lloyd Wright homes."

"That's unusual." Cat grabbed one of the muffins from the middle of the table. "How did you come up with that hook?"

"I live near the museum in Chicago. I've always been interested in architecture. But this way, I get to do research on a house and then make up the story as I go. So much better than having to stick with the truth."

"So Bren lies for a living," Rick, who was sitting next to her, said around a mouthful of eggs.

She playfully slapped him on the arm. "We all lie for a living. We write fiction."

Cat thought she saw a spark between the two, but just as soon as it was there, Bren had turned away and it was gone. Was there a romance going on there? Interesting.

Anne spoke, her voice soft but thoughtful. "I'm going to be working on a young adult book this week. Something totally different than what I usually write. I just want to spread my wings and play with something different."

"That's challenging." Cat was impressed. Some of the group had come with firm goals in mind. "We always encourage guests to set goals for the week before you arrive since it will help center you at the retreat. You won't believe how fast the week goes by."

"I'm running every morning." Rick stood and

refilled his plate. "Anyone can join me if they want. I'll be in the lobby at six."

"Six is way too early to get up if I don't have to go to work in the morning." Colleen shook her head. "You go right ahead and run. I'll be tucked into bed waking up slowly."

"I'm coming down early all week and writing in the living room by the fire," Molly announced. "It's beautiful in there."

A cell rang and all eyes went to Bren.

"Sorry, I've got to take this. We're meeting in the lobby at nine forty-five, right?" She stood and paused at the doorway for an answer. When Cat nodded, she answered the phone. "I was just about to call you. Breakfast was . . ."

Bren's voice trailed off as she walked away from the dining room.

Rick shook his head. "That guy has her on a really short leash."

"We shouldn't talk about Bren behind her back," Anne admonished. "What happens in a relationship is between the couple and not anyone else's business."

"You sound like you're stuck in the sixties." Colleen held up her hand to stop Anne's next words. "But I agree. We shouldn't talk about Bren and her relationship. It has nothing to do with us."

Rick looked like he wanted to argue, but he sighed and took the wrapper off a blueberry muffin. "Whatever."

"I guess I'll see you all in a little bit then. You're going to love the library. And it's nice enough you can walk there and work if you want to for a change of scenery. And there's the attic too, if you need more of a quiet area." Cat took her cup and walked to the doorway. "The dining room will have drinks and snacks all day to keep you energized. We stock it with some items before we retire at night in case you're a night owl, but you might run out of coffee."

"Everything's perfect," Anne said. "I just can't believe I have a week to do nothing but be a writer. This is heaven."

Cat felt the positive energy as she went back into the kitchen. Shauna was peeling apples. "That didn't take long."

"What? For me to get started on the apple invasion?" Shauna smiled. "There's something very calming about cooking. It gets my mind in a Zen mode where I don't have to really think. I can just be."

"No, I was thinking about our guests. Here's what I think I figured out." She refilled her coffee cup. "Rick's in love with Bren. Not sure if she realizes how strong the attraction between the two of them is. But Bren's in some sort of bad relationship with a guy who keeps pretty tight tabs on her. The rest of the group is concerned but won't address it because it's her personal business."

Shauna looked up at the clock. "First official day, and before the first seminar, and you've already got the dirt on your guests."

"It's not dirt." Cat grinned over the rim of the cup. "But knowing the group helps when I'm trying to support them in meeting their goals for the week. I think sending them the goal sheet when they signed up really helped center a few of them. They are ready to go."

"So as long as Rick doesn't turn into a raving

lunatic or Bren's significant other doesn't show up and disrupt the week, you've got a handle on things." Shauna sat one peeled apple down and picked up a second.

"Way to bring my good mood down." Cat held up her hand. "So sometimes I live in Pollyanna Land."

Chapter Six

Cat got them to the library five minutes before Miss Applebome's lecture was supposed to start. She handed out the library cards that the college had printed off for the guests and stopped at the spot where Molly sat. "You don't have to sit through this seminar. I know you know about the library."

"It's fine. I like spending time with the group. It helps me understand people better if we have a common experience." She leaned over. "Besides, we're all going to Reno's Pizza after this for lunch, so I didn't want to miss that. I love that pizza."

Cat nodded. That logic she understood. Reno's had the best Chicago-style pizza west of Chicago. The owner, Don Reno, was the third son born into a family pizza restaurant dynasty. He'd moved and brought his franchise to Aspen Hills, Colorado, years ago. The place was amazing. She often wondered why Don hadn't moved his business to Denver, where he could have made a lot more money, but she never mentioned the idea to the chef-owner.

She wasn't stupid. "So can you make sure they know their way back to the house after lunch?"

"Definitely." Molly flipped back her hair. "I like being in charge."

Rick shook his head. "Don't get used to it. If you want to be part of this group, there's only one leader, and that's Bren. She's got the Queen Bee persona down to a science."

Miss Applebome cleared her throat and Cat knew that was the woman's gentle reminder for Cat to leave the room. She moved toward the door. "See you all back at the house. And my cell number is on the library cards, just in case you need something."

As she closed the door, she heard Miss Applebome's welcome to Covington. The head librarian met with all the new students before they got library privileges and she'd insisted on this two-hour introduction session for the writers' retreat guests as well. The library was her domain and she controlled access and information.

Cat paused in the lobby area. She should go home and work on her edits. She should go home and help Shauna do something with the apples. She should do a lot of things rather than what she was planning on.

She sat at the computer that had the library's research lists. Cat keyed in Greyson Finn's name. Several cookbooks were first on the list, but there were also several more recent articles from different Denver magazines and newspapers. She wrote those down and went to hunt the stacks.

After she pulled the periodicals, she sat at one of

the tables and started reading. She took out the notebook she'd tucked into her tote before she left the house. She had just finished the pile of magazines when someone sat at the table next to her.

"Cat Latimer, I haven't seen you in the library for years. What are you researching?" Jessica Blair pulled up one of the magazines and stared at the cover. "Are you setting up a list of restaurants close by for your guests?"

Jessica had been her best friend when she was married to Michael. They'd both joined the English Department the same year and shared the English 101 class load. She'd lost touch with Jessica when she'd moved. Leaving friends behind had been one of the sacrifices of moving. Especially couple friends.

Cat closed her notebook and stacked the magazines. "Just looking up some things. How have you been? I don't think I've seen you since I moved back."

"Then we should do lunch or drinks one of these days." She glanced at her watch. "But not today. I've got a class in fifteen minutes. I just wanted to tell you how much I've enjoyed your books. One of my best students, Molly, is a superfan."

"She's in my retreat this week. I'm looking forward to talking with her more." Cat tucked her notebook into her tote. "I'll walk with you. We can catch up for a few minutes. Maybe we can do dinner next week?"

"Not dinner. My kids are screaming for help with their homework most nights. Lunch would work better. I'm in my office on Wednesday's. Can you get away then?"

Cat pulled out her phone and opened her calendar program. "What time?"

"Let's do eleven and head over to The Diner. That way we can miss the student rush." She paused at the doorway to the English building. "I'm so glad I ran into you. I was so sorry to hear about Michael."

"Thanks. I know we were divorced at the time, but it still came as a shock." Cat glanced at her watch. "Look, I'll let you go. Next Wednesday at eleven. I'll meet you at The Diner."

"Sounds great." Jessica started toward the building, a student joining her as they entered.

Cat sat for a moment on one of the stone benches outside the building. All she'd ever wanted was to be a professor here at Covington. And yet, she'd given up that role because she couldn't stand to be in the same town as her ex. How many other decisions had she made on an emotion when really, she should have been looking at her future. With or without Michael, teaching at Covington had been exactly what she'd wanted in a career. Until her agent had sold her book. Not everyone got two dream careers in their lifetime. As the sun beat on her face, she smiled. She was lucky.

She stood and headed home. She hadn't mentioned to Shauna that she was going to be a while. Mostly because she knew if she had, Shauna would suspect Cat was researching Finn. Which she had been. But there hadn't been anything in those articles that had even hinted at a connection to Dee Dee.

As she walked by the bakery, she saw Dee Dee standing at the counter, waiting on a customer. She lifted a hand to wave when the woman turned her way, but Dee Dee quickly dropped eye contact. Cat kept walking. "So much for being friendly."

When she got home, the kitchen smelled of apple pie. Shauna wasn't there so Cat checked the whiteboard and read her message aloud. "'Gone to the store for supplies. Lunch is in the oven. Chicken enchiladas. There's Spanish rice on the stove, but you're probably going to have to warm it up. Back soon.'"

Seth stepped into the kitchen from the hallway. "Hey, I was wondering where everyone was. I just went up to your office to see if you were writing."

"No, I got held up at the library. Did you know Jessica Blair? She started teaching at Covington the same year I did." Cat wiped off the whiteboard and went to the oven to get out the casserole dish.

"She and her husband have a brownstone near the college. I did some work for them in the basement. They finished it into a game room for the kids." Seth grabbed two plates. "Were you friends?"

"Yeah. We used to double date a lot." She smiled. "Of course, that meant cheap pizza and a bottle of wine at the house before game night. I'm pretty good at Scrabble, just saying."

"I think that's the first time I've seen you smile about a memory that involved Michael, ever." He touched her shoulder. "It couldn't have been all bad, right?"

"It wasn't. At least not at first." She dished up the rice and enchiladas. "Do you want me to stick this in the microwave?"

"Sure." He grabbed two sodas out of the fridge. "So you ran into Jessica. What did she have to say?"

"Not much. She was on her way to a class. We made plans to get together next week to catch up." Cat dished up food for herself while she waited for the microwave to finish. "I've missed talking to her."

The microwave beeped and Seth took his plate out and put hers in. Then he took the plate and sat at the table, opening his soda. "I'm surprised she's working today."

"How come?" Cat stood and waited for her food.

He set down his fork. "I would have thought you knew. Especially since you've met her husband." He held his hands palms up. "Her brother-in-law was the guy who was killed last night."

"Her husband's last name is Blair, not Finn." Cat took her food out of the microwave and went to join him.

"Not true. His name is Finn. Her name must be Blair." He took a bite of the rice. "This is so good."

"That doesn't make any sense. I know. . . ." Cat paused, thinking about how Jessica had introduced them. Tyler. Always just Tyler. She'd assumed his name had been Blair. She cut into her enchilada and cheese oozed out onto the plate.

Seth took another bite before he answered. "Look, I remember because I said something about how different the name was when he gave me the check. He said Finn was a good Irish name."

By the time they'd finished eating, Shauna was back with groceries. Seth helped her carry in the bags from the car. Shauna started to unpack and glanced at the casserole dish. "Do you mind making me a plate while I finish this? I'm starving. I would have been home earlier, but I got caught up with all the gossip at the store."

"You get your gossip at the grocery store?" Cat took a plate out of the cupboard and dished up the food. She placed it in the microwave.

"I've told you that before." Shauna put two gallons of milk in the fridge. "Today was crazy busy since they all wanted to know about the murder."

"You don't know anything about the murder," Cat reminded her.

"Just put that in the pantry. After two days, I think I underestimated the amount of soda products this group is going to consume. They're not much on coffee though." Shauna directed Seth with two cases of soda. She turned back to Cat. "I never said I did. But everyone thinks since your uncle is a frequent visitor to the house, I must know something. It works for all of us."

"What do you say?"

"I tell them I don't know anything. They don't believe me, of course, and tell me what they know. I nod a lot, which they take as me confirming what they knew was what I knew. It works great all around." Shauna took her plate out of the microwave when it dinged. "So do you want to hear the gossip?"

Cat grabbed a bottle of water and sat. "Of course."

"Are the guests here or out?" Shauna looked at the door. "I'd hate to get them all excited about solving a murder. You know your uncle hates it when the amateurs step into his investigation."

Seth delivered the last case of water to the pantry, then sat. "That includes the three of us sitting here.

He was just complaining about the last time you got involved."

"When?"

"On our fishing trip last weekend. Face it, Cat, he worries about you. And Shirley's feeding that fear. She sent him an article about a woman who was killed because she was getting too close to finding a killer. You need to leave investigating to the professionals."

Shirley Mann was Uncle Pete's Alaskan girlfriend. They'd been having a long-distance relationship since Shirley had attended one of Cat's retreats. Cat wasn't quite sure yet how she felt about her uncle's new love life.

"Does that mean you don't want to hear what I found out?" Shauna looked at him, pausing.

"Of course I want to hear. Gossip is good for the mind." Seth took a sip of the soda he'd left on the table when Shauna had arrived.

"And they say women are chatty." Cat rubbed his back, turning her attention to Shauna. "What do the good folk of Aspen Hills say about the murder?"

"I guess Finn came into the store the morning he was killed. He told the butcher he was cooking a special meal for family. He came in often, but Conrad, he's the butcher, didn't think anyone recognized him. He's kind of a secret foodie so he'd been to Finn's restaurants a lot and studied up on the guy." Shauna took a bite of her lunch.

Cat and Seth shared a look.

"What?" Shauna quickly swallowed her food. "You already knew this?"

"We knew he had family. Remember I told you about my friend Jessica Blair? Greyson Finn is her brother-in-law." Cat paused for a minute, listening to a noise in the front of the house. "Sounds like the children are home. I'm going to go check in with them and see if they need anything."

"Tell them not to order dessert with dinner as I'm pulling out the pie and vanilla ice cream with a caramel drizzle. I hope they like it because we're going to have a lot of it." Shauna opened her tablet and started scrolling. "I'm looking for an apple muffin recipe now."

Seth headed the other way. "I'm checking in on Snow and her dwarfs. I'll see you at dinner. My mom used to make an applesauce for pork chops that was pretty good."

"I'll look into that. Thanks, Seth." Shauna focused on her tablet as Cat left the kitchen. They were all in sync again. It had taken some time after Shauna's boyfriend was murdered, but finally, the three of them seemed comfortable again. Cat thought about Jessica. In all the time they'd been friends, she'd never mentioned her husband had a different last name. She'd always been Jessica Blair. Cat should go visit her, take her food. That's what friends did when there was a loss, right? Supported each other? But was Cat even supposed to know that Jessica's family had had a loss?

The etiquette rules were confusing, at least in this situation. Cat shook off the questions and decided to go over after Jessica's last class. Maybe she'd been trying to hold it together to get through her day and that's why Finn's death hadn't come up.

"Hey, we're back!" Molly almost crooned the announcement. "Everyone's going to grab their laptops and write in the living room. Do you want to join us?"

Cat glanced at her watch. She had a couple of hours before Jessica would be home. "Sure. Let me grab my laptop and I'll meet you in there."

"Cool. I'm so glad Ms. Blair talked me into applying for this retreat. I'm enjoying getting away from the reality of school for a few days, even though I know it's going to suck trying to get caught back up when I go back to school next Monday. I tried to work ahead, but you know how those things go."

Cat touched the girl's arm before she could disappear up the stairs. "Jessica Blair suggested the retreat?"

"Yeah, she said I'd learn a lot from you." Molly tilted her head, studying Cat's face. Somehow she heard the underlying question of "why?" in Cat's words. "She said you two were friends—isn't that true?"

"No, we're friends. I'm just surprised she suggested the retreat. I'll have to thank her for that."

"Oh, yeah. She's a big fan. She even teaches a bit out of your first book. You know, the part she helped you write?"

Chapter Seven

"Maybe she said edit, and Molly thought it was more than that?" Shauna sat a soda in front of a steaming Cat. "Drink this and calm down. You know people like to expand their part of the story."

"But I never expected *Jessica* to do this. I mean, I don't think I even talked to her about the book, since it wasn't literary. Michael told me that the other professors would use me writing a genre book against me if I ever wanted to go for tenure. In fact, we'd discussed a pen name so no one would know it was me once it released." Cat scrubbed her face with her hands. She'd told Molly she'd be a little late for the write-in, but instead of going to the office to get her laptop, she'd ducked into Shauna's kitchen and unloaded. "And I was going to have lunch with her. Why? So she could steal more of my life to make herself look good in front of her students? I'm about to explode."

"You're more hurt than angry, I can see that. You need to talk to her, but this probably isn't the best time, not with a death in the family. So keep your lunch date next week and hear her side of the story. Maybe she had a good reason."

"And maybe pigs fly." Cat chugged half the soda down. It was cooling her down a bit. "Anyway, I've got a retreat to hostess. I can't be worried about what some nonfriend said or did."

"That's the spirit! Write her off your list immediately." Shauna stood and went over to the counter. "I'll put one of these pies into a box and you can take it over before dinner. That way we'll be down one pie."

"At least you'll be happy." Cat finished off the soda. "I'm going to go write a confrontation scene for Tori. That way, maybe I won't have to rip Jessica's face off when I see her."

"I always admire your way of dealing with stress." Shauna handed her a plate of cookies. "Put these out in the dining room, will you?"

Cat got more than one scene done before the group began to disband to get ready for dinner.

"We're going to Reno's again," Colleen announced. "I'm going to have to work out every day to get rid of all these carb-fueled pounds."

"You could run with me in the morning." Rick shut his laptop and stood.

"Yeah, no thanks. But I might take a walk around the neighborhood after dinner if anyone wants to join me." Colleen stretched her back. "I love having time to write, but it really makes me stiff."

"I do yoga in my room every morning," Bren announced. "It keeps me flexible."

At that Rick blushed and the other women, besides Molly, giggled. "Too much information," Anne said, putting her hand on Bren's back. "Let's go get ready. Meet down here at five?"

"Perfect." Colleen smiled at Molly. "Are you coming too, dear?"

"If I'm welcome." The young woman looked from person to person.

Colleen nodded her head. "Of course, you're welcome, dear. You're part of the group now."

Cat watched them go up the stairway, chatting about word count and plot holes. The group was bonding. Well, most of them already had fused, but they were including Molly in the mix and that made Cat happy. She went into the kitchen where a pie sat boxed on the table.

"The guests are on their way to dinner. Molly's going with them. She's bonding well with the group," Cat announced as she stared at the boxed pie.

"I think you should still go. It's the right thing to do." Shauna was working on something on her tablet. She didn't look up as Cat paused by the table. "I wrote out a sympathy card and signed your name to it as well."

"You should go." Cat ran a finger down the side of the box.

Shauna shook her head. "No. One, you're the face of Warm Springs Writers' Retreat. And two, you and Jessica were friends. No matter what happens after this heart-to-heart you'll be having."

"I'm not as mad anymore, but I don't understand why she would do it." Cat grabbed a bottle of water from the fridge and sank into a chair.

"You know I can't answer that for you. But Jessica can. Give her the benefit of the doubt until you hear the whole story. Then you can make a decision on what you want to do." Shauna stood and crossed over to the fridge where she took out a package of pork chops. "I'm trying the apple suggestion that Seth gave me. I hope the recipe I found matches his mom's."

"If not, he'll be sure to tell you." She sipped on the water. "You going riding this week with the retreat in session?"

"Probably not, but quit stalling. If you really want to talk scheduling, we'll gather after dinner." Shauna made shooing motions with her hands. "You'll be fine. Go talk to your friends."

Cat checked how she looked in the kitchen mirror, then picked up the pie. "I'll be back shortly."

"If you're not, I'll call Pete and see if you've been arrested." Shauna grinned. "Dinner's at six."

As she walked toward town, Cat took a deep breath to really enjoy the fall foliage. In her opinion the town looked its best in the autumn. The trees were a golden brown, the sidewalk matching the color due to the falling leaves. And mums bloomed in everyone's flower garden. Shauna handled the flower beds for the house. Cat hated any kind of gardening. She didn't like to get her hands dirty.

Cat approached the brownstone and old memories flooded her mind of dinners she and Michael had attended at the house. Long nights talking about the college administration and how unfair it was to new professors. Michael had always tried to be the voice of reason, bringing in the other side, until both women wanted to kick him. Then they'd play some sort of silly game and the bad feelings would disappear. Along with several bottles of wine.

She climbed the stairs and rang the doorbell. A harried man opened it and his face turned from pain to a look of welcome. "Oh, my, aren't you a sight for sore eyes." He pulled her into a hug. "I'm so glad to see you. Jessica will be upset she missed you. She took the kids over to her mother's. We have a thing tonight."

"Actually, I talked to her this morning. I heard about your brother." Cat stepped back from the hug. "I brought you this. I'm so sorry for your loss, Tyler."

"I didn't know if you knew. Jessica was always so determined to make it on her own, she didn't want anyone to know and prejudge her." Tyler leaned against the door frame. "I'd invite you in, but I told my mom I'd meet her at the funeral home at six. The body, I mean, Greyson, isn't released from the coroner yet, but she wants to make some decisions now. I think it's helping her cope. Keeping busy, you know."

"That's okay. I'm in the middle of a retreat, so I should get back to the house. I'm really sorry, Tyler."

"Thanks, Cat. I'm sorry about Michael. We didn't know what to do when he passed." Tyler ran a hand through his hair. "I'm a mess. I've got to go. Can we talk later?"

"Of course." Cat pressed the box into his hands. "Take care of yourself."

And then the door closed on her and Tyler was gone.

She didn't feel as warm and fuzzy on the way home. In fact, she barely saw the beauty of Aspen Hills this time. All she saw was Tyler's devastated face. The man had loved his brother. And his explanation of why they'd kept it a secret rang true. But somehow, there was something more that Tyler hadn't said. Something about Jessica.

Back at the house, she entered through the front door. The writers were still out. When she went to the kitchen, Shauna was busy cooking. She glanced up when Cat paused in the doorway. "Everything go all right?"

"Yeah. Tyler's devastated. I can't blame him." Cat went to the fridge and stared inside, finally choosing a soda. "I never had siblings, but I could see how hard it was on him."

"I have a brother. I couldn't imagine how I'd feel if he was gone."

Shauna's announcement shocked Cat. "You've never talked about him."

"He's ten years older. A banker or some financial guy, I can't ever keep track of where he is or what he's doing. He worked in Europe for a while, but now I think he's back in NYC. Wall Street type." Shauna turned the heat down on the pot of green beans. "I don't see him much or really at all, but I would be devastated if something happened to him. Probably because I'd think of all the things we should have done."

"You have some fun money now, you should go visit." Cat took a sip of her soda. "We said we weren't doing any retreats in December. Christmas in the city would be lovely."

Shauna went over to her desk and pulled out the

tablet she used in the kitchen. "I'll think about it. Right now, I'm going to send him an e-mail and tell him I love him. If that doesn't give him a heart attack, we'll be fine."

Cat took the cue and left Shauna in the kitchen. Instead of heading upstairs to her office, she decided to walk out to the barn. Visiting the kittens was always a mood elevator. And she really needed that. Maybe instead of a pie, she should have taken Tyler and Jessica a kitten.

When she reached the barn, the kittens were out in the middle of the yard, the mommy cat, Angelica, up on a straw bale, watching them with one eye open and a foot dangling over the side of the bale that one kitten was using as swatting practice. Cat sat next to her, stroking her black-and-white sun-warmed fur.

"Take in the sun while you can. Pretty soon we're going to have to think about moving you guys inside the house. The winters can get pretty cold up here." She scooped up one of the kittens, with soft gray fur covering his body and a speck of black on his nose. "Hey, buddy, how are you today?"

"I didn't expect to see you out here with the retreat going on. Let me guess, the writers are all at dinner?" Seth sat on another bale. His blue jeans were covered in dirt and he wore his overshirt opened, showing the what-had-been-white tank underneath. Even after a long day working with the landscaping, the guy looked hot. Or maybe it was because he had been working. When she didn't respond, he tapped her on the leg. "Earth to Cat? Are you okay?"

"I'm fine. Just thinking about siblings and secrets. Did you know Shauna had a brother?" Cat stroked the kitten, who started to purr, curled up in her lap. "I thought I knew everything about her."

"She mentioned him to me once, I think. Some business guy?" He laughed at Cat's shocked expression. "What? Can't I know something about her that you don't?"

"It's just weird that it never came up." She rubbed the kitten's soft ear.

Seth leaned over and swiped up an orange kitten to his lap. "I was complaining about Todd." When Cat's eyes narrowed at the name, he laughed. "You have to remember my cousin. The kid came to stay with us every summer until I went away to the army."

"I remember Todd. We couldn't ditch him." Cat smiled at the memories. "And he hated it when we went to the swimming hole. He said only rednecks swam outside manmade pools."

"He was scared of the wildlife." Seth shook his head. "Now, he's a teacher in Illinois with three kids. He called the other day and wanted to know where he should take them for a 'safe' Colorado holiday. I guess they're coming out west for a ski vacation in December."

"Did you mention Little Ski Hill? It's less than thirty minutes away. That resort would be awesome for kids, especially if they haven't skied before."

"I'm not sure I want them that close to town. I was thinking of suggesting Vail or Breckenridge. That way he can overspend for the week and be with people he considers his equals." Seth got the kitten swatting at his hand. "Sometimes family can be a headache."

Cat watched the now sleeping kitten on her lap.

"I went over to Tyler and Jessica's with a pie. He's really broken up."

"How's your friend?" Now the kitten Seth held was attacking any slight movement he made.

"She wasn't home. But she had to have known about Finn when we talked earlier this morning, didn't she?" Cat lightly stroked the kitten's soft fur. If she didn't watch out, they wouldn't be getting rid of any of the litter as she would be too attached to all of them.

"Probably. Maybe seeing you helped her keep it together while she taught her class. It can't be easy to get a substitute without some lead time." Seth set the kitten down and picked up the full black one. The orange kitten wasn't having any of it and climbed Seth's jeans to get back up on his lap. Then he started slapping around the other kitten. Seth picked up the orange kitten and held him in the air in front of his face. "Okay, Ali, you're the king of the hill."

"He's a fighter. He doesn't want anyone to get the best of him. Shauna said she found him in with Snow a few days ago. The guy's fearless." Cat felt the buzz of a text message from her phone. She pulled it out of her jacket pocket. "Dinner's ready. And we have a guest."

"Let me guess, your uncle?" Seth sat both kittens down and stood, brushing the straw off his jeans.

"Give the man a stuffed animal." The memory of their recent trip to the state fair burned her cheeks. The weekend had been good. Neither she nor Seth had talked about the business or Aspen Hills, or really, anything that could have started a fight. They'd been happy. She loved making good memories with him. "Come on, let's go eat. Uncle Pete hasn't been over since he got back from Alaska a few weeks ago. I'm getting a little nervous about the frequency of his visits with Shirley."

"He's a grown man. You can't ground him to his room." Seth held his hands out to pull her to her feet.

Cat sat the sleeping kitten on the ground where Ali the Great promptly attacked his sleeping sister and got a swat to the side of his face for waking her up. "That's a good girl; make sure you always stand up for yourself."

Seth chuckled. "You never had that problem. You were always sticking up for the others."

Cat put her arm around him as they walked back to the house. "Sometimes we all need a little help."

When they got to the house, a Charger with "Aspen Hills Police Department" painted on the side was sitting on the street in front of the house. "It's a good thing people around here know Pete's your uncle or they would have concerns about how often the police are here."

"I'm sure Mrs. Rice keeps everyone informed of his visits even if he's just coming for dinner, like tonight." Mrs. Rice was Cat's neighbor and the head of the unofficial community gossip chain. She was also vying to take over for Shauna as the cook for the retreat in case Cat needed a replacement. Cat prayed that day would never come. Especially since Mrs. Rice had called dibs on any job opening.

Seth opened the back door for her, and as she walked into the kitchen she saw Shauna and Uncle Pete already at the table. "Hey, sorry we're late. The kittens didn't want us to leave."

"I haven't fallen for a line that lame out of you since the two of you dated in high school." Uncle Pete sipped on his coffee. "You need to develop a new set of excuses."

"You caught us." Seth crossed the room and shook Uncle Pete's hand. "We missed you at the men's group last week. Don wants to pull together a friendly poker game. You on board?"

"You're asking a police officer to an illegal gambling party?" Cat went over to the sink and washed her hands. "I guess I'm not dating the smartest tool in the shed."

Seth pressed his hands to his chest and stepped backward. "You're killing me. Besides, didn't you know that technically, gambling is legal in Aspen Hills?"

"You're kidding, right?" Cat sat at the table and watched as Seth went to the sink. "That can't be true."

Uncle Pete nodded. "Actually, there's an exception in the Colorado Constitution that allows social gambling. So I would not actually be arresting anyone at the poker game. At least, not if they let me win."

"You're always trying to play that old card, but you know it doesn't work like that. It's a game of chance and skill. Who you are in your normal life has no bearing on chance." Seth sat at the table. "So can I tell Don you're in for next Wednesday?"

Uncle Pete leaned back in his chair and pulled out his phone. "My calendar says I'm free, so unless this investigation heats up, I'll be there. Too bad we lost one of our best members this week."

Cat narrowed her eyes. "Wait, are you saying that Greyson Finn was part of your poker group?"

"When he could make it. He came probably every other month." Seth shook his head. "Cat, I know that look. There is no way our friendly monthly game had anything to do with his death."

Uncle Pete held up a hand. "Hold on, Seth. Cat might have a point."

"The poker game isn't even that serious—" Seth started, but Cat shook her head.

"All I'm saying is maybe it wasn't just a friendly game to him. Why would he come all the way from Denver just for a card game?" Cat looked between Seth and Uncle Pete. Neither one of them had an answer; she could see it on their faces.

"Maybe your friendly game wasn't his only outlet for gambling." Shauna sat a pan of lasagna on the table next to the large salad and bowl of green beans. "Make sure you save room for pie."

Chapter Eight

"Great," Uncle Pete murmured as Shauna dished up lasagna on his plate. He took some green beans and passed the bowl. "I already have the governor calling me directly asking when I'm going to get off my butt and solve the murder of his favorite chef. Now I have to investigate the fair-haired boy's gambling habits? Shirley's offer is looking better and better."

Cat studied her uncle as Seth pushed a bowl of salad in her hands. "I'm not sure which of those bombshells to attack first."

"So, how is Shirley?" Shauna handed Cat a plate of lasagna. "Getting ready for the winter? It must get really cold up there in Alaska."

"Shirley's fine." Uncle Pete shoveled salad onto his fork. "And I didn't mean to spill the beans quite like that. You know we've been doing this long distance thing for a few months. Well, she and I talked about making it a little closer."

"Like moving to Alaska?" Cat couldn't believe what she was hearing. Uncle Pete was her only relative left in Aspen Hills since her parents had decided to make the snowbird thing permanent. "Are you crazy?"

"Now, Cat, 'crazy' is kind of a loaded word." Seth handed her the ranch dressing.

She took the bottle and, distracted, poured way too much dressing onto her salad. "I think it's crazy to give up a position like police chief and move out west like some pioneer in a covered wagon. Do they even have roads up there?"

Uncle Pete grinned. "Yes, they have roads. They even have a grocery store where we can get food so I won't have to be hunting and fishing to survive."

Cat grunted and decided that maybe eating would be more prudent than talking. She took a big bite of the pasta. This was one of her favorite dishes that Shauna made, and yet, today, it tasted like sawdust. She kept her head down and willed away the tears.

"Look, I haven't made a decision. And you're right. I have a career here that I typically enjoy. It's just when I have everyone including the dog catcher second-guessing my investigations, it makes me a little wistful to chuck everything and live a simpler life. One where the mayor, Covington's president, and the governor don't have my number on speed dial." He softened his voice. "I really didn't mean to spring that on you this way. I've ruined dinner."

"You haven't ruined dinner. You've just proven we're family as you feel comfortable sharing your thoughts with all of us." Shauna patted his hand. "Now, let's eat before this gets cold."

Cat swallowed hard, trying to make sure her

voice was steady. "I'm sorry I reacted badly. I would miss you horribly if you left me—I mean us."

"Well, nothing's set in stone. It's just a pipe dream right now." He smiled at her. "You wouldn't get rid of me that easily. You know there are planes that fly between Colorado and Alaska too, right?"

Cat let her lips curve into a smile, but it felt like the knife was still in her heart. A buzzing rang in her ears through the rest of dinner. As soon as she finished eating, she stood and put her plate in the sink. "Sorry, I need to check on something."

As she disappeared through the kitchen door she heard her uncle call out her name, but she pretended she hadn't heard it. She needed to get away from people before she burst into tears. It wasn't fair. It wasn't her life, and she had no right putting any guilt on Uncle Pete. But all that reasoning she'd tried to use during dinner hadn't eased the pain she'd felt at the thought of losing her uncle to the wilds of Alaska.

On autopilot, she almost ran straight into Bren, who was on her way upstairs. "Oh, I'm sorry." Cat looked around the empty foyer. "Are you all back from dinner already?"

Bren glanced down at the phone in her hand. "No, they're still at the restaurant. I had to leave early. Something came up. An emergency at home."

Cat grabbed her arm before Bren could dash upstairs. "Is everything all right?"

"I just told you I have a family emergency. I think that's all I need to say." Bren's eyes went dark with anger.

Cat let go of Bren's arm, feeling the heat of the glare. "Sorry, I didn't mean to pry."

"No, I'm sorry. I'm a little flustered. I need to go and make a call. Sorry I can't stay and chat." Bren started up the stairs and didn't look back.

"If you're sure you're all right . . ." Cat called after her.

"Sorry. Got to go." Bren sprinted up the stairs.

Cat had been going up to her office to hide but decided to make a left and head into Michael's study. It didn't matter how long he'd been dead, it would always be her ex-husband's study. One of the drawbacks of living in a house where you'd spent time together. Except now, it didn't make her feel sad for the lost years. Now, she felt grateful for the time they had spent together. She'd loved her life then. She loved her life now.

Maybe there was a lesson there she could apply to Uncle Pete and his sudden need to uproot his life. If she was honest with herself, it probably wasn't his uprooting that bothered her. It was his untethering to her. Which was a completely childish and selfish way to think.

She sank into the large leather desk chair and opened the laptop that she left in the study. Scanning her e-mails, she deleted most of them. She didn't need to know about a sale at the Bed and Bath store. And she didn't want to order a book or movie. Right now, she just wanted to do something totally mindless and let her subconscious work this out.

When Shauna came into the room, Cat was on level fifty of the game she'd found. She looked up from the laptop as Shauna closed the door. "Save the lecture. I know I was out of line tonight. I just can't bear the thought of him moving so far away."

"Pete's worried about you. He had to leave because he had a call, but he made me promise to go find you." Shauna sank into the lounging chair across from the desk. "I have to admit, I'm a little concerned too. I've never seen you that upset."

"Uncle Pete has been my rock for, well, ever." Cat closed the laptop. "He's always been the North Star I knew I could find my way home by. If he's not here, then what happens if I get lost?"

"You're a strong, brave woman. You can light a flashlight."

Cat shook her head. "I'm speaking metaphorically."

"And you think I'm not?" Shauna picked up a book that was sitting on the end table and glanced at the title. "You have to know that your uncle isn't what anchors you to Aspen Hills."

"Then what is? My folks are living in Florida. Uncle Pete was the last relative I had living here."

Shauna's eyes twinkled. "Are you sure about that? I think the three of us make a great team. And once a month, we get reinforcements from the writers' retreat. More people to get to know and care about. I'm surprised you can even lift your arms, we're so tethered to this community."

"I hadn't thought of it that way. I've always thought of Aspen Hills as home, but mostly because my family lived here. I guess home is more than just where you were born." She watched her friend put down the book and stand to leave. "Where are you going?"

"My work here is done." Shauna grinned as she

paused at the door. "I've got a retreat to deal with and so do you, once you're done with your pity party. The guests are back from dinner and in the living room."

"Except Bren."

Shauna frowned. "How did you . . ."

"She came in during my tantrum and basically flew up the stairs after telling me to stay out of her business. In a mostly nice way." Cat put the laptop away in the desk and stood to follow Shauna out to the hallway. "Something's going on with her. I've been sitting here trying not to think about her, but I have to say, I'm worried."

"We can't fix everything in someone's life in a week."

Cat nodded. "I know. But it's hard to see someone who it appears is being bullied and not say something. Her friends are worried too. Maybe it would be easier coming from an outsider."

"Walk that line carefully," Shauna warned. "If she doesn't want her fantasy shattered, she may not take kindly to you holding up a mirror."

"That's why I'm thinking about it and not up there in full-blown intervention mode." Cat shook her head. "It was supposed to be easy. People come for a week. They write. We feed them breakfast and give them a room. And it's done. No one said I'd become this involved with each and every person."

"You can't help it. You like people." Shauna gave Cat a hug. "The flowers Linda sent this month are beautiful. There are good parts to the retreat too."

"I love what we're doing. It's just . . ." Cat paused, not knowing exactly how to phrase what she felt.

"You didn't realize you'd like the people so much," Shauna provided.

Cat lingered before entering the foyer. "I was the same way with my students. I brought several home for dinner before Michael informed me that all of the students got room and board as part of their tuition. I thought if they were there on scholarship, they might need the meal."

"You've got a kind heart." Shauna nodded to the living room. "Now go play with your writer friends. I'm going to spend some time working on the cookbook now that the house is settled."

"Thanks." She turned back and faced Shauna. "I'll call Uncle Pete in the morning and see if we can meet for coffee so I can apologize."

Shauna smiled, a hand on the kitchen door. "He'll appreciate that."

Cat stopped at the sign-in desk in the foyer where the bouquet of roses from Linda sat. She leaned over and breathed in the sweet smell. Running the writing retreat was like teaching. Maybe she hadn't left the job she loved. Maybe she had just changed the setting? She went to the dining room to grab water and a cookie, then headed into the living room.

"I still think drowning your victim takes too long. And they might escape and go to the police." Colleen set her soda down on the coffee table. "Besides, it's overdone."

"If the killer stayed there to make sure the victim went under, then the deed is done," Rick countered.

"Unless the victim is a long distance swimmer and is able to hold his or her breath longer than the average person. Then the killer gets caught before there's even a death." Anne sipped her coffee, then looked up at Cat's shocked face. "Sorry, we didn't hear you come in. We're playing a round of Kill That Victim."

"Oh . . ." Cat sat on the edge of the couch, not sure how to respond.

"We do this all the time at restaurants after critique group. One day an off-duty police officer stopped by our table and asked what we were talking about." Colleen grinned as she relayed the memory. "He seemed relieved when we told him we were plotting our books."

Anne giggled. "Then he asked us to keep it down."

"No one asks my plotting group what we're doing. Of course, our conversations probably sound more like gossip instead of plotting since I write YA." Molly reached for a brownie off the plate in front of her. She looked at Cat, her eyes filled with expectant hope. "Do you have a plotting group?"

"No, I don't work that way." Cat could see the disappointment in her face. She'd known the next words out of Molly's mouth would have been either an invitation to join her group or a request to join Cat's. She turned toward Anne. "So how do you decide who wins?"

Anne shrugged. "Most nights we don't because they all think they're right about everything. It's kind of annoying, really."

Rick sat back in the couch, his face registering shock. "But I *am* right about everything. Haven't you learned that yet?"

The group dissolved into laughter. When it subsided, Colleen turned toward Cat. "So, we've heard rumors about the guy who was killed in the bakery. You're related to the police chief, right?"

"He's my uncle." Cat didn't like where this conversation was going. She'd had writers' groups that had decided to solve a murder before, and it never ended well. "But we don't really talk about his work."

Disappointment filled Anne's face. "Oh, we were hoping you could clear up the method of death for us. The rumors we heard at the library today, well, they just don't sound feasible."

"You know real life doesn't have to make sense," Rick added. "I've modeled a plot point on some real murders for a story and I got nailed by my editor. Unrealistic, he said. Seriously, it was real life. How can that be unrealistic?"

Cat couldn't help herself. She opened her water and took a sip, playing it casual before she asked, "So what are the rumors?"

"Two people said he was shot. One said the baker hit him on the head and stuffed him in the oven. And one said he had a heart attack and it wasn't even murder." Molly summarized the day's conversation.

"It's crazy how much people talk here. And to complete strangers." Colleen shook her head and then took the last cookie. "How did they know one of us didn't kill him?"

The room got quiet as they all looked at each other. Then one by one, they started laughing.

Anne shook her head. "I think the bigger question is which one of them did the deed and is hiding in plain sight. You know that's what happens in our books. It's always the one you didn't suspect until the reveal and then everything falls into place."

"If you've done your job right," Colleen added. "Sometimes everyone except the main character knows the killer way before the reveal. That's just sloppy plotting."

"Which none of us has ever done," Rick added dryly.

"According to a few of my reviewers, they always know the killer long before the end." Colleen glanced around the room. "It makes you wonder why they keep reading and reviewing you if they hated the book so much to give it three stars."

"Three stars isn't bad." Anne patted her friend's arm. "I love the one stars with just a few words. Like 'crap.' Or 'not for me.'"

"They don't really do that, do they?" Molly's eyes widened. "Professional reviewers aren't mean. The other students in my class are harsh, but I thought once I was published . . ."

"Oh, to be young and naive," Rick teased. "The best one-star reviews are the ones where they say, 'I didn't order this.' Or 'my e-reader wouldn't open it.'"

Anne smiled at Molly, who had reached for another cookie. "Don't listen to us. We're jaded. Most reviewers give thoughtful comments. I try not to read the reviews. They aren't for us; they are for the other readers. And if someone is having a bad day and leaves a snarky review, well, I can't control that. All I can control is writing the best book I can write."

Rick picked up his coffee cup. "I'll drink to that."

Cat studied the four people gathered around the

coffee table. Writers had a common bond. Most of them wanted to help each other through the mine-field of being an author. And she didn't know if she'd gotten lucky with her retreat guests that they were mostly of that type. Then again, maybe she drew a certain type to the retreat. People who were serious about their craft and their business.

"Did anyone have any questions about the week's schedule?" Cat decided to get the topic off reviews before they scared Molly from ever publishing any-thing. "Shauna's willing to do a one-on-one with anyone if you want to play around with a recipe."

Colleen nodded. "That would be awesome. I have a muffin I've mentioned in my current book but I've never made it or anything like it. Do you think she could help me develop a recipe?"

"She'd love that." Cat thought about the retreat schedule. "Tomorrow there's a session at ten with Covington's Hemingway expert that lasts about an hour. Wednesday, I do a fireside chat on the busi-ness of writing. And Friday the local bookseller is coming in for a session on working with authors. Last session, we did afternoon word sprints before dinner each day. We can do that too."

Molly raised her hand. "I can run those. I run a word-chasing group on campus every Friday night."

"You college kids sure know how to party," Rick teased. "When I was in school, Friday night was cheap beer night at the local bar."

"It is here too, but some of us take our writing seriously," Molly shot back.

"Children, stop fighting." Anne shook her head and smiled at Cat. "You can't take them anywhere."

"Thanks for the offer to handle that part, Molly.

Just let me know when you're having them and I'll come in and write too. I'm between contracts but I have a different idea I'd like to play with." Cat stood and stretched. "I'm heading to bed. You're welcome to stay up as long as you like. We restocked the dining room with treats and drinks, so don't be shy. I'm less of a night owl and more of a lark."

They said their good nights, but no one else followed Cat out of the room. She wanted to grab a notebook and start making notes about Greyson Finn's murder. Not that she was going to investigate. This was just something she wanted to get down before she forgot what the rumors had been.

And pigs fly. The angel on her shoulder pointed out the obvious. She was investigating, even if it was just on paper and in her head.

Chapter Nine

"Official day one in the books," Shauna announced as Cat came into the kitchen Tuesday morning. "Of course, for me, it feels like day three since I had the cooking demonstration on Sunday."

Cat yawned as she poured coffee, then sat at the table where Shauna was on her tablet. "They're a fun group."

"Did you stay up too late?" Shauna took in her appearance. "You look tired."

"I went to bed early, leaving the group in the living room still planning murders and desserts." Cat sipped her coffee and almost groaned as the warm, life-sustaining liquid filled her senses. "I just couldn't sleep. I'm still mad at Jessica for claiming to have helped me write the first Tori book, but on the other hand, she just lost her brother-in-law."

"I get it. You don't know if you want to rip her head off or give her a hug." Shauna pushed a plate of apple fritters toward her. "Have one of these. Maybe the sugar will perk you up a bit."

"I was hoping a hot shower would do the trick,

but I may have to sneak away this afternoon and take a nap." Cat rolled her shoulders, then took a fritter, setting it on a napkin in front of her. "They did hear a lot of rumors about how Greyson Finn died when they were at the library. They were trying to poke at me to see what I knew."

Shauna didn't look up as she swiped at her screen. "So what do you know? Have you started a notebook yet?"

Her friend knew her too well. Cat squirmed and took a bite of the pastry to delay her answer. Shrugging, she decided to admit it. "I've been looking into Finn's life and the guy didn't have enemies. At least none on the surface. His employees loved him. He has two restaurants in Denver and there were rumors that he was looking for a third site."

"But no smoking gun." Shauna turned the laptop around. "From what I know about your sleuthing method, you need to get close to the victim's life. I think it's a great excuse for a dinner out. You can get reservations at his restaurant for dinner this week. Do you and Seth want to take a quick trip into Denver to see what you can find out?"

Cat shook her head. "I've decided I'm staying out of this one. Uncle Pete's already wondering why I was over at the bakery the day of the killing. I think I'm going to focus on the retreat and maybe play with a new book idea I've been considering."

"That sounds almost believable." Shauna held up a hand when Cat started to object. "Look, I'm all for you staying out of the fray. Lord knows you've put yourself in harm's way enough times over things that you should have stayed away from."

"Then why the hesitation?" Cat finished the last

of the fritter and watched as Shauna chewed her bottom lip.

"I guess it's because you care about people. You jump in to help because you can't stop yourself." Shauna closed the laptop and got up to get the coffeepot. She refilled Cat's cup as well as her own, then sat back down. "If Pete hadn't been the one investigating Kevin's death and you hadn't helped out, well, I might not be sitting here looking for more apple recipes."

"Shauna, that's silly." Though Cat had wondered the same thing. "Anyway, that all worked out."

Shauna sipped her coffee. "I just wanted to say thanks. I appreciate everything you did for me then."

The back door opened and Seth strolled into the kitchen. "Snow and the dwarfs are fed and watered, so don't let them talk you into a second breakfast when you go out to visit later."

He stopped and stared at Cat and Shauna, feeling the energy in the room. "Did I just walk in on something? Should I go back outside for a while?"

A shared look of humor passed between the two women before Cat spoke. "You're fine. Shauna made apple fritters."

He went to the cupboard and grabbed a cup for coffee. Once he'd filled it, he joined them at the table. "I know I'll probably be sick of apple anything before long, but these are my favorite pastry. The ones at the bakery are okay, but there's this little coffee shop in Denver that has the best ones ever."

"Well, I hope mine are at least better than the ones at the bakery." Shauna eyed him carefully.

"And when have you been visiting the bakery anyway? Do you not like my baking?"

Seth's eyes widened and he shook his head. "I don't go there often. Just when I'm working on that side of town. Besides, the only time I get to enjoy your baking is during retreat weeks. A man can't live without donuts in his life for three weeks out of the month."

"I'm just kidding you." Shauna glanced at her watch. "Thanks for taking care of Snow. I'll go visit after lunch. I've got a batch of apple butter to make this morning. Is there anything you need from me for the guests? I'll freshen the linens and clean rooms after I get the apple butter in jars."

"I got called out on a porch repair job this morning. You don't need me here for anything with the retreat, do you?" He glanced at Cat as he finished one fritter and grabbed another.

"Nope. Professor Turner is coming this morning and then the guests are on their own until we gather in the living room this evening after dinner." Cat thought about her own schedule. "I guess I'll go up to my office this afternoon and do some marketing and scheduling."

"You're not writing?" Seth asked.

She shook her head. "In between contracts. I don't want to get too far into the next Tori book if they aren't picking up three more. I'm playing with different series ideas. The group's in for writing sprints so I'm going to join them and see what shows up on the page."

"And you're not investigating Finn's death?"

"What is it with you two?" Cat glanced back and forth between Seth and Shauna. "Do you think I have a need to get involved in every unsolved crime in the three-county area?"

"I would have said Colorado, but yeah." Seth glanced at Shauna. "Do you agree?"

"Actually, I don't think she'd go north past Denver. So maybe most of Colorado," Shauna clarified.

"I'm so glad you two are my friends. I'd hate to see how you would talk about me if we were enemies." Cat stood and threw away her napkin and refilled her coffee cup. "I'm going upstairs to work. I'll see you at lunch?"

"You don't want breakfast?" Shauna asked.

What she wanted was a nap. Cat shook her head. "I'm good. I'm going to push through and see if I can get a second wind this morning."

As she climbed the stairs to her office, questions about who killed Greyson Finn taunted her. How did he die? She could call her uncle, but he'd tell her to stay out of things. She couldn't very well reach out to Jessica and ask her for the gossip since it was one of her family who had died. Besides, she needed to have a different talk with Jessica. Friends didn't claim ownership of someone else's work. She hoped that Molly had just misunderstood Jessica's intent, but her intuition told her differently.

When her alarm went off at nine thirty, she had finished her accounting for her writer business. Thank God Shauna took care of this part for the retreat. Cat hated doing the monthly accounting work as it was. The retreat was a whole different level of stress. She saved her work and closed down her computer. Professor Turner tended to arrive early and had a habit of rearranging her living room if he wasn't supervised in his lecture setup.

She stretched and headed downstairs. She was most definitely taking a nap this afternoon. Maybe she'd skip lunch and just sleep after the guests left.

Cat glanced in the dining room and saw that Shauna had already set up the morning treats. She snagged an apple and smiled at the little handmade sign by the bowl. "EAT ME." Grabbing a bottle of water, she headed into the living room to make sure it was ready for Turner's lecture.

When he arrived at 9:45, he hesitated at the door. Cat had set up his lectern and a slide projector but hadn't moved the chairs into a replica of a classroom. She could see his gaze roll over the seating and a large sigh shook his body. "I see you already have me set up, Catherine."

"I do. I didn't want you to have to worry about moving furniture." Cat hoped her meaning was clear. "So how have you been? How's the project with the Hemingway papers going?"

"It's so exciting. I'm surprised you haven't heard the news. There's a book coming out about Hemingway and his spy activities. I'm sure I've seen the author on campus at the library working. Maybe you know him?" Professor Turner looked hopeful. "Don't you all have meetings together?"

She wondered how many authors he thought there were in the world. Maybe he imagined they all went to the Disneyland resort once a year and sat in the bar, talking about books? "Sorry, I don't know any nonfiction writers. I'm sure Miss Applebome would know if he came in without a card. She knows everything that goes on at that library."

"You're right about that. I should talk to her." He glanced up as Rick sauntered into the room, brownie half in his mouth and a coffee cup in his other hand along with a notebook shoved between his arm and his chest.

"What," he mumbled through the treat. Glancing around the empty room, his eyes widened. "Am I not supposed to be in here yet?"

"Of course, you are." Professor Turner gave him a welcoming smile. "I was just looking at your refreshments. Catherine, would you mind getting me a bottle of water before I start? My mouth gets so dry when I'm teaching."

Cat left to get the water and Professor Turner followed Rick to his seat, peppering him with questions on his knowledge of Hemingway. The guy liked to know his audience. Stepping out of the room, she ran straight into Jessica Blair. Anger flared inside her and her heart raced, but she was able to squeak out a welcome. "Jessica, I didn't expect to see you today. I'm so sorry for your loss."

She considered Jessica with flat eyes. For someone who just lost a family member, the woman looked normal. The classic professor. Jeans, a starched white shirt, and a blazer. Cat had worn the same uniform when she started teaching, but she'd switched the white shirt to wearing vintage vanity T-shirts with cartoon characters or favorite quotes by the time she gave notice.

"I knew you'd figured that out already when Tyler mentioned you'd stopped by. I know I never told you about Greyson being family."

"Actually, I didn't know until this week. And why would someone who said she was my friend hide something like her real name?" Not to mention the fact of Jessica claiming to have written at least part of Cat's first book. But she'd hold that discussion for another time. Besides, Jessica never answered any question about her actions directly. "Why are you here, Jessica?"

"I need you to tell your uncle that I couldn't have killed Greyson. That I was with you when he was killed. You could say we were in the library." Jessica nodded. "That we met there after my class to catch up."

"But we weren't in the library." Cat couldn't believe what she was hearing. "Are you telling me you were involved in Greyson Finn's death? If that's true, you need to go talk to my uncle now. Maybe there are extenuating circumstances or something. I know you couldn't have meant to kill anyone."

Jessica sighed like Cat was the slow student in one of her classes. "Look, I didn't kill anyone. I just need to make sure your uncle doesn't come around asking questions. Can you do me one favor?"

"Lie to my uncle?" Cat shook her head. "I'm not as quick with the lies as you seem to be."

"What's that supposed to mean?" Jessica's face turned beet red. "I never . . ."

A sound came from behind her. "Cat, did you find me some water?"

Cat and Jessica turned to see Professor Turner watching them.

"No, I was just about to get it. I'll be right in." Cat turned to Jessica. "As soon as I finish here."

"We are finished. Nice to see you, Professor Turner." Jessica's eyes narrowed. "And thanks for nothing, Cat. I thought I could count on you but you're as flaky as Michael said you were."

Stunned, Cat watched as Jessica stormed out of the house, slamming the front door as she left.

"My, she is in a mood today. Of course, I heard she had issues with the other professors many times. She just seems to think the world should provide her every need." Professor Turner checked his watch. "Oh, dear, it's almost ten. Can you hurry and get my water? I hate to be interrupted once I've started a lecture."

Jessica wasn't the only one who thought the world revolved around her. But why would she want Cat to lie for her? This didn't make sense at all. Cat realized Professor Turner was still standing there, waiting for his water. "Sorry, I'll grab a bottle right now."

"Thank you, Catherine." He turned to go into the living room, but then paused and turned back. "That Blair woman is trouble. I've heard rumors that she tried to pass off another professor's work as her own. Of course, she didn't get caught or the school would have dismissed her on the spot."

Cat watched as he entered the living room and then she hurried to get his water. Had there been rumors of Jessica's lack of care with claiming ownership of other's works? She hadn't told anyone at the college, even Jessica, about the book. Only when she had decided to become a full-time writer and open the retreat had she come clean to her former peers.

She deposited the water on the lectern and then headed upstairs to her office. She needed to find out all she could about her former friend before Uncle Pete came over to verify Jessica's bogus story. Cat shivered as she ran up the stairs, one question looping through her head. Had Jessica actually killed her brother-in-law?

Googling Jessica Blair only came up with the typical stuff Cat expected to find. Her profile on Covington's website. Glowing reviews from former students. And a list of classes she was teaching this semester and next. That was what made her pause.

Jessica was teaching exactly the same classes she had been when Cat left five years ago. Yet Cat knew that the college had hired several professors since she'd left. So why wasn't Jessica moving up the ladder? Cat wrote down the question and wondered if one of the other professors in the English Department might know. She'd start with Professor Turner since he was just downstairs, but a glance at her watch told her she'd been up here web surfing for over an hour. Turner was long gone. She'd have to find someone else to spill the dirt.

She went back to the department faculty list and her gaze stopped at Lori Reedy. The woman had been the dean's secretary for more years than Cat could remember. Deans may come and go, but the administrative staff stayed put.

She shut down her computer and grabbed her tote, shoving her notebook and a few pens inside. She had questions for Lori, and if she timed her arrival just right, she'd catch her coming back from her lunch hour. On a whim, she grabbed the latest Tori book and tossed it in the bag as well. Dropping off a signed book was a great excuse to get the woman talking.

Or at least Cat hoped so.

Shauna was in the kitchen finishing setting the

table for lunch. "Hey, I was just about to come get you."

"I can't stop to eat right now. I'll be back in about thirty. Go ahead without me. I'll heat up something when I return." Cat had her hand on the back doorknob when Shauna spoke.

"Catherine Latimer, where are you going?"

She turned, her hand on her shoulder tote, and met Shauna's gaze. "Why are you asking?"

"Because I don't want you to get into trouble. I overheard that spat you had with your friend. Although, maybe you should think about moving her to an ex-friend category. That woman is awful. But you shouldn't be going out to confront her. You'll probably knock her on her butt." Shauna held on to a plate like it was a steering wheel on a runaway car.

"I'm not going to confront Jessica." Cat walked back and pried Shauna's fingers away from the plate and set it on the table. "Seriously, I'm not that stupid. Although I do want to call her out on her lies, I'm more interested in why she needed an alibi."

"Do you think she killed him? Just because she wants an alibi doesn't mean she's a killer. Does it?" Shauna sank into a chair and pushed her hair out of her eyes. "Figuring out the lies has me all twisted. I'd rather be cooking. So if you're not heading to Jessica's to give her a piece of your mind, where are you going?"

Cat glanced at the door. "I'm going to find out why Jessica's career has dead-ended at the college. Uncle Pete says you have to find out as much as you can about the victim to find the killer."

"But Jessica's not the victim," Shauna pointed out.

Cat headed to the door. "No, but she's family. And she's trying to cover up something that she doesn't want found out. I don't think she killed the guy. She's a vegetarian for one thing."

Shauna rolled her eyes. "Vegetarians can kill people too!"

Chapter Ten

Lori Reedy had a desk in the waiting room outside the dean of the English Department's door. The telephone system sitting on the right side of the mahogany desk was as big as a small laptop and all eight lines were lit when I walked toward her. She didn't even look up. "Hold on a minute."

Then she went through each line and took a message for the dean, who was apparently out of town at a conference this week. The man hadn't told his dentist, his trainer, or apparently his poker buddies. Cat briefly wondered if the dean was in the same poker group as Seth and Uncle Pete. And the late Greyson Finn. When Lori was finally finished, she tapped the pile of notes on her desk to straighten them and, putting a paper clip on them, threw them into an in-box on the side of her desk.

"So what can I help you with, Ms. Latimer?" She folded her hands in front of her on the desk, looking a lot like Cat's fifth-grade teacher had each time she'd asked for a hall pass.

"I'm so glad you remember me." Cat smiled and pulled the book out of her tote. "I wanted to drop off one of my books since you've always been so helpful. I appreciated the flowers you sent for the department to Michael's funeral."

"His death was a considerable shock to the entire staff. And of course, since the two of you had been married . . . Well, I'm glad you found some condolence in the flowers."

Cat knew the department had sent flowers; the bouquet had been huge. But she'd guessed that Lori had been the one to order them. And she'd struck pay dirt. "I did, ever so much. My time employed here at Covington will always be some of my fondest memories."

Lori glanced at the book Cat held in her hands. "Not the type of thing they teach around here."

"Which is probably why I haven't been asked back to teach since I've moved home. Not that I have enough time to teach a class anyway." Cat backpedaled just a bit to try to keep Lori off guard. "Can I sign this to you?"

She shook her head. "Sorry, no."

Cat felt her eyes widened. "I don't understand."

"I've already read it and have my copy at home. I have the entire set actually. I really enjoy your storytelling." Now a smile curved on her face. "I sent a set to my sister in Des Moines. She likes witch stories too."

"That's nice to hear. I'll send you a copy of the new book when it comes out." She tucked the unneeded book in her tote. She started to step away, but then paused, seeming to consider something. "I started the same time as Jessica Blair. I see she's still teaching the 101 classes. If I had stayed, would I have been stuck with the freshmen classes too?"

"Oh, no, dear. You were being fast-tracked." She shook her finger. "And it had nothing to do with your husband's influence. You were a firecracker and all the students and other faculty loved you."

"But Jessica?"

The air held heavy for a minute, then Lori glanced around to make sure the room was still empty. "You can't say where you heard this, but Jessica isn't really a stellar teacher. The only reasons she's still here is Greyson Finn's relationship with the dean. Of course, now that Mr. Finn is gone, maybe he'll do the right thing and fire her sooner than later."

After saying her good-byes and thanking Lori again for buying the series, Cat walked home slower than she had to the college. She hadn't expected to hear something like that about Jessica. When they'd taught together, she'd been excited about teaching the new students. About making a difference in someone's life by reaching them with just the right book. Now to find out that she was only at the school because of Finn's connections? Man, that had to sting.

Cat sat on a bench just outside the campus. Her mind was playing with an idea. Had Jessica known that she owed her job to her brother-in-law? And if so, was that the reason she was so desperate for an alibi? But that didn't make sense.

If she wanted to keep the job, she wouldn't kill her golden goose.

Her stomach rumbled and Cat shook off the nagging doubts. She announced to the empty sidewalk, "One more reason I'm not supposed to be investigating. I have no idea what I'm doing."

A passing jogger gave her the side eye. He'd had his earphones in but apparently, he'd heard some of Cat's whine. She smiled, trying to look sane, and gave him a short wave. He automatically waved back and picked up his speed.

I'm not crazy just because I'm sitting here talking to myself. This time, Cat kept the thought inside as she stood and headed back home. When she let herself in the back door, Shauna and Seth were just finishing a lunch of grilled cheese sandwiches and tomato soup. The warm and comforting smell of the food made her almost weep with joy. What was wrong with her that she was so emotional?

She grabbed a plate and a bowl and filled them while the others watched. Finally, Seth broke the silence. "Did you find what you were looking for?"

"Maybe," Cat mumbled through a mouth filled with warm, gooey cheese. She swallowed before continuing, not wanting to choke on the food. "Jessica was on a short leash at the school. She wasn't even close to tenure track and they weren't giving her additional assignments. According to the dean's secretary, they only kept her on because of Greyson Finn and his influence."

Shauna pushed her empty bowl away. "The man seemed to have a lot of power for a chef."

"I think he was more than that. Maybe you could

consider him a community leader. I saw a lot of pictures of him at those high society charity events where people go to be seen in Denver." Cat sipped her soup, thoughtful about the effect one man could have on a region.

"He was going to build a restaurant here in town." Seth grabbed another sandwich. "The request for bids hit my e-mail last week."

"Seriously? Why didn't you mention this before?" Cat shook her head.

Seth held the sandwich halfway to his mouth. Then he set it down on the plate. "There are a couple of reasons. One, I didn't see the e-mail until this morning. I don't check it a lot when my schedule's full. No use knowing about work I can't take on."

That made sense, but Seth had said a couple of reasons. She decided to push. "And two?"

He sighed. "And two, I told Pete I'd try to keep you from investigating Finn's murder, so I didn't feed the beast. But I see you've already taken up the gauntlet."

"No, I'm not investigating the murder." Cat held up a hand before Shauna and Seth could speak. "What I want to know is why Jessica is so focused on me giving her some lame alibi for the time when her brother-in-law was killed."

"And?" Shauna prodded.

Cat didn't look up from her soup. "And, I want to know why she claimed to have written my book. I guess I'm still a little upset about that."

"If she had a good reason, in her mind," Seth

added quickly when he saw the red that creeped up Cat's neck, "would you forgive her?"

"I'm not sure. I don't think you can come back from a betrayal like that and be all, let's go get mani-pedis." Cat sighed and leaned back in her chair. She was no longer hungry and that was a bad sign. She was always hungry. "I'm really steamed at her."

"You have every right to be mad." Shauna picked up her plate and took it to the sink. "Sometimes people aren't who you think they are."

Cat wondered if Shauna was thinking about someone besides Jessica. Shauna had found out a lot about her almost-fiancé after his death. Things that she wouldn't have liked if she'd found out when he was alive. But she'd been blinded by love.

Cat didn't think that was all so bad. She took her half-eaten lunch to the sink. "I'm going upstairs to work. I'll be in my office if anyone needs me."

"I thought you didn't have a project going right now," Seth said.

Cat grabbed a bottle of water from the fridge. "There's lots to do besides just the writing. Now I need to do all the things I let slide."

"An author's work is never done." Shauna rubbed Cat's arm. "You're fine about this Jessica thing, right?"

"Of course." Cat put on a smile she didn't feel. Betrayal seemed to be her theme the last few years. First a husband, then a friend. Maybe she had "stupid" tattooed in invisible ink on her forehead. "Besides, I have you two. Why would I need Jessica?"

Cat heard Shauna's muttered comment when she left the kitchen:

"Which means she's not at all fine. I hope that witch Jessica gets what she deserves."

Cat didn't turn around to hear Seth's response, but Shauna's apparent outrage at Jessica's behavior made her feel justified in her own anger. She ran into Rick coming down the stairs and put on her hostess smile. "I didn't realize you all were back from lunch."

"Most of the group isn't." He glanced up the stairs. "Bren needed to come back and make a call so I walked back with her."

Cat didn't say anything, but she guessed she didn't hide the questioning look on her face.

"I know, she's an adult. But sometimes I think she's alone too much. And it wasn't that big of a deal. I was done eating anyway." Rick held up his laptop. "And now I'm going to set up in the living room and get some words down. I wrote this morning, but some things that Hemingway dude said, it's been tickling at my brain."

"I'm glad you got something out of Professor Turner's lecture. I know not everyone's as big a Hemingway fan as he is." Cat didn't say that Turner was a fanatic and most of the guests had found him dull. "But there's something to be said to studying the masters of the craft to see what you can learn."

"Exactly. I'm always reading biographies of the great writers. It gives me hope that someday, I might have a book written about me." Rick stepped toward the living room. "Do you want to join me?"

Cat thought his offer was more out of politeness

than wanting company, so she shook her head. "I'm heading upstairs to my office on the third floor. If you need me, Shauna knows where I'm hiding."

"The house is great. It has a writerly vibe to it." He strolled toward the doorway on the other side of the foyer. "See you this evening."

Cat watched him disappear. The house did have a good vibe. It had been comforting when she and Michael lived here, but now, it seemed welcoming. She wondered if houses could have souls or personalities, which took her to Tori's world and an idea for a new book. She raced up the stairs, hoping to get the bones of the idea down before the spark dissipated.

It was after five when she finally saved her document and closed up her computer. She'd written a chapter and made a quick outline/blurb for her agent to use if the publisher came back for more Tori books. The idea was strong. She knew it. Now it was just waiting time for the publisher to run the numbers and see if she'd made them enough money.

She met Shauna on the stairs. "I was just heading up to see if you wanted to come down for dinner or not. That must have been a lot of paperwork."

"I was writing. The story is strong. I might just write the book now and if they don't give me a contract, I'll self-publish it. Or hold on to it until I get my rights back and self-publish the series. It all depends. But at least I'm not at their mercy anymore. I know I have options." Cat followed her downstairs.

"I thought they liked Tori and the books." Shauna glanced at her, confusion on her face.

Cat shrugged. "They do, but one of the problems with being a storyteller is if there is a void, we'll fill it with a story. I'm just keeping my options open."

"Whatever makes you feel better." Shauna paused at the bottom of the stairs. "I'm just glad you're writing and not running around trying to solve this murder."

"The day's still young." Cat strolled into the kitchen. "What are we having for dinner?"

The kitchen smelled like her childhood home on Sunday afternoons. She turned and grinned at Shauna. "Fried chicken?"

"Yep. And mashed potatoes, a corn casserole, corn bread, and of course, apple pie à la mode for dessert. I had to up my weekday game because Pete was trying to say he was too busy to eat."

Cat grabbed the plates and started setting the table. "My uncle can't resist your chicken. I'm pretty sure that's the only reason he won't chuck the job and move to Alaska to be a hermit with Shirley."

"I don't know. I hear Shirley has her own talents."

Cat threw a towel at her. "Ewww. Stop talking about Uncle Pete and Shirley doing it. It gives me the hives."

"Who's doing it?" Uncle Pete asked as he and Seth walked into the kitchen at the same time.

"I knew they talked about sex when no one was around—I've just never caught them." Seth took Pete's hat and hung it on the coatrack. "Must be your sly investigation techniques."

"I don't know what you're talking about." Cat stepped over and gave her uncle a kiss on the cheek. "I'm really glad you could tear yourself away for dinner."

"Almost got caught at the station. There's so many calls coming in from the tip line, Katie's about ready to pull her hair out. We have a couple of interns from the college answering phones." He walked over and kissed Shauna on the cheek. "Thank you for making dinner. It smells wonderful in here."

The group finished setting the table and quickly took their seats for the evening meal. Uncle Pete sighed as he took a chicken breast from the plate and passed it on to Cat. "You cook like an angel."

"That's what you tell me all the time." Shauna grinned at the compliment. "But I appreciate people who like my food. It makes me feel needed."

"So where did you get the interns?" Seth piled mashed potatoes on his plate, then made a well for the gravy. "I didn't know Covington had a criminal justice program."

"They don't. These are pre-law students. I'm pretty sure each one is hoping to get a credible tip so he or she will be tapped to work the case by the prosecutor." Uncle Pete took the bowl of potatoes and mirrored Seth's movements.

"Now, where would they get an idea like that?" Cat broke open a piece of corn bread, the steam filling her mouth with the taste. She spread butter on both sides.

"I might have said it was a possibility." Uncle Pete shrugged. "Hey, it worked. They're happy and Katie doesn't have to answer all those calls herself."

"Are you any closer to finding out what happened?"

Cat set her fork down and looked at him. "Can you tell us how he died? The rumor mill is going wild."

Uncle Pete stared at her for a long second. Then he set his fork down. Using his napkin, he wiped his lips. Then he nodded. "I'm going to have to talk to you again anyway. Someone is saying you're her alibi."

"Let me guess—Jessica."

Uncle Pete didn't look surprised but instead he looked thoughtful. "Don't tell me you actually are her alibi."

"No. Not even. She stormed in here today and demanded I lie to you. So what's up with that? I don't think she has the guts to kill a fly, let alone her brother-in-law." Cat tore off a piece of chicken and pointed it at her uncle. "This isn't the woman I was friends with before Michael and I divorced. She's like a bad clone."

"Well, your friend has some explaining to do. She and the victim had been talking on the phone daily. His phone is filled with calls from her." Her uncle paused, looking at Cat. "Do you think she might have been having an affair with him?"

Cat almost spit out the chicken. "Jessica? No way. She was so in love with Tyler it was uncomfortable to be around them sometimes. Or at least . . . that's the way it was five years ago. Heck, how do I know? This Jessica isn't the same person I knew then."

Uncle Pete returned to his meal, looking thoughtful about what Cat had told him.

When they'd finished the main course, they all had a cup of coffee and a slice of pie with vanilla ice cream on top. Then Cat ventured the question again. "So how did Greyson die?"

Her uncle didn't look up from his dessert. "Someone hit his head very hard from behind and left him to die on the floor of the bakery. Someone with a lot of anger."

If that didn't describe the Jessica who'd come to visit today, Cat thought, *nothing did.*

Chapter Eleven

Seth's phone rang as they were sitting, drinking coffee. He glanced at the display, then stood. "Sorry, I have to take this."

Cat heard him answer as he walked outside. "Hey, Nate."

"I don't care what Nate wants me to tell Dee Dee now; he's out of luck." She got up and got the coffeepot to refill her cup. "Anyone else want some?"

Her uncle held up his hand. "Me. I've got some paperwork to finish up tonight."

The door to the kitchen opened and Seth walked over to Uncle Pete. "Sorry, you're going to have to take that to go. Nate was almost run down outside Bernie's a few minutes ago."

"Oh, no. Is he all right?" Shauna stood and grabbed a couple of to-go cups from the cupboard. "Cat, fill these. Seth, I take it you're going with Pete?"

"If you don't mind. Nate asked me to come and he's kind of shook up." Seth took the cup Shauna handed him. "Thanks."

"You'll need to bring your own car. If Nate needs to go to the hospital, you might just save him an ambulance bill." Uncle Pete took the coffee from Shauna. "Of course, if he's really hurt, you'll have to follow him."

"Do you need anything from me?" Cat followed her uncle to the door. "Maybe I should . . ."

"Maybe you should stay here and take care of your guests." Uncle Pete put on his hat and jacket. "Just because you're my niece doesn't mean you have to be part of everything that goes on in Aspen Hills."

"You don't think this is about the murder?" Cat pushed the question out before he could leave.

"The question is—why do you?" With that, he left with Seth following close behind.

Shauna picked up the empty plates and moved them to the sink. "Your uncle just wants you to be safe. He doesn't mean to keep you out of the loop on things."

"I know. I'm a serial investigator. Sometimes I think it's the writer in me. I see something and add it to something else, then all of a sudden, I have a solution to the problem. I don't mean to be a pest." Cat sat with her coffee, watching out the window until she couldn't see the tail lights on Seth's truck anymore. "But don't you think it's weird that Nate is almost run down right after Greyson was killed?"

"I have to agree with your uncle. I'm not seeing the connection." Shauna glanced at Cat's dessert plate. "You want more?"

"No, I'm going to go see what's going on with the retreat guests." Cat took her coffee cup and left the kitchen. She found the writers all gathered in the living room. Coffee and desserts sat on the coffee table nearby. Anne looked up as Cat paused at the door and waved her inside. "Hey, we were wondering where you'd taken off to."

"We just finished dinner with my uncle." Cat had expected to find the group chatting somewhere. "Do you mind if I join you?"

"Please." Bren moved over on the couch and patted the seat. "Come sit by me. I've been told I'm a horrible guest and need to be more social."

"You need to keep your phone in your room," Colleen muttered.

Instead of getting angry, Bren laughed. "You're right. And that's exactly where it is right now. In my room. I deserve to have a little time just on my own."

Cat didn't want to preach to the woman, especially since she was seeming to be growing a backbone, but she hoped Bren's newfound strength would continue, preventing her from returning to that scared woman she'd been on the stairs on Monday. "I'm glad to see you taking part in the group activities. That's part of the joy of the retreat. Writing hard during the day and then coming together to talk about the writing and the business at night. Although I have had guests who did the bulk of their writing after the group broke for the night. I'm just not a night owl."

"Me neither," Anne supplied. "If I'm writing tired, I get to a point where I'm writing words and sentences, but they have nothing to do with the story. It's like my brain takes over and downloads thoughts to my fingers."

Rick laughed. "I had to throw away a whole page

one day because I'd done that. I thought I was getting so much done, but it was all crap."

"So what were you talking about before I interrupted? Ways to kill people again?" Cat curled up on the couch and watched the group.

"Actually, no. We were brainstorming a title for Rick. He's a little blocked," Colleen said.

"You make it sound like I have digestive issues." He turned toward Cat. "I always have problems with titles. I want them to be cute and punny and that's just not my wheelhouse."

"This should be fun. Should I get out the whiteboard so we can brainstorm?" Cat jumped up and headed to the closet where she stored the presentation tools for the retreat. "Or maybe just flip-chart paper and some smelly pens?"

"I vote for the paper, but we'll clear off the coffee table and lay it here." Anne waited for Cat to bring the large pad of paper to the couch. "If that's okay."

"We'll just double sheet it and the ink shouldn't bleed through." Cat tore off two sheets and handed the box of food-scented pens to Colleen. She spread the paper on the now clear coffee table and Colleen dumped the pens on top.

Molly sat cross-legged on the floor and took the blue pen and opened the cap, holding it under her nose. "Blueberry!"

"I like the cinnamon one the best," Anne announced, grabbing the brown pen before anyone else could.

They huddled around the table. Cat looked to Rick. "So what do you have so far?"

He grinned. "Book Two of the Southern Chefs

Mystery series. The books are all about a group of chefs in Atlanta who solve mysteries together. We'd just started playing with the title when you walked in."

Cat wrote "Southern Chefs" in the middle of the page. "Let's see, food phrases that work as murder hints."

"What about 'Pecan Pie Poisoning'?" Colleen wrote it down in blue. "What are some other southern foods?"

"'Catfish Carnage'?" Anne wrote down.

Rick shook his head. "Too spot-on."

"Shh. No critique during brainstorming. This is our 'write drunk' time, to paraphrase a Hemingway quote." Anne threw Rick a red marker.

"Pretty sure Hemingway didn't say that, but whatever. So what about 'A Dead Man and the Sea'?" He wrote it down in neat block letters.

"You are really bad at this," Bren teased, picking up the black marker.

He poked her with a finger. "Hey, no critiques during brainstorming."

"And you wonder why we're just starting the process. It takes a while for everyone to start playing by the rules," Anne commented to Cat.

Cat was playing with the things she knew about the south. Low country. Shrimp and crab boil. Heat. "Slow Southern Slaying." She wrote that one down. "Fried Chicken." "Bless your heart . . ." Maybe something with that. She was lost in thought as she played around with the words, trying to make the title seem southern and about food, as well as being about murder. She murmured as she wrote, "Bless Your Dead Heart?"

"Arsenic and Old Lace." Bren wrote as she spoke the words.

"Isn't that already a title?" Colleen glanced over to where Bren sat.

"Tell us a little bit about the series. Maybe that will help," Anne prodded.

As Rick explained his premise, Cat thought about the words that kept popping into her brain. Like "Sweet Tea." Or movies about the south. "A Few Dead Men?"

"What about 'Sinners and Sweet Tea'? Or 'Chicken Pot Die'?" Molly got into the fun. "If it's a vampire cozy mystery, it could be called 'Chicken Fried Stake.'"

Rick pointed to the paper. "Write those down. They're really good."

Molly beamed at the praise and quickly wrote the ideas down on the paper with an orange pen that smelled like a Florida grove. "This is really fun."

They brainstormed for a few more minutes, then Bren stood and stretched. "I need sugar if I'm going to stay up much longer. Should we pop in a movie while we let the brainstorming ideas settle? Rick can pick one tomorrow morning and then whoever's idea it was, he has to list you in the acknowledgments."

"I'm putting all of you in the acknowledgments. This was really helpful." He followed her out of the living room. "Maybe tomorrow night we can brain-storm titles for the rest of the series?"

Anne shook her head. "I think he's only half kid-ding about that. Rick really hates thinking of titles."

"It takes a village." Cat nodded to the big screen

television and the bookcase filled with movies. "You're welcome to watch anything. Seth and I like to spend Saturday nights here with the latest releases, so I think you'll find the selection good."

She started to leave, but Colleen pulled her aside. "I just wanted to see if you were all right. I was in the living room when that woman came in and started yelling at you."

"I'm fine. She's just under a lot of stress." Cat hadn't realized any of the guests had been close by to hear the argument. Now she was really glad she hadn't gone off on Jessica. "Thanks for checking in with me though. That was sweet."

"Well, according to the lady I talked to in the library who was shelving books, I guess your friend can be a royal witch." Colleen looked around to see if anyone was paying attention to them. When she decided that everyone was occupied and not listening, she leaned closer to Cat. "She also said that Jessica was having an affair with the dead guy. Can you imagine that? I hear he's related to her and everything."

"It might just be a rumor. They spread like wildfire when something like this happens." Cat didn't want Colleen to get invested in solving the murder. One person in the house taking chances was enough.

Colleen didn't look convinced. "This woman was pretty sure about her facts. She said she used to see them meet at the bakery after it closed for business once or twice a week."

"Jessica and Greyson? They were meeting at the bakery?" It didn't make sense. Why not invite him over to their house? Unless they were hiding an affair. Cat wondered if Uncle Pete knew about this. "Who did you talk to? Do you remember?"

"Her name was Heidi. She said she's been at the library for years, almost as long as Mrs. Applebome." Colleen paused and Cat saw the moment the realization hit her. "You don't think it's just rumor, do you?"

"Not really my place to judge." Cat nodded toward the television. "You better get over there if you want a vote in what movie you're watching."

Colleen shrugged as she watched her friends. "It doesn't matter. I'll probably be asleep within the first fifteen minutes. Watching movies makes me tired."

Cat knew how she felt. Sometimes when she and Seth were cuddled on the couch, she'd wake up, the movie over and a blanket covering her. Seth would be sitting in one of the other chairs reading while she slept. The first time it had happened, she'd thought it had been Michael sitting there and she must have been dreaming. Thank goodness she hadn't called out his name.

She didn't miss her ex-husband and she definitely didn't love him anymore. But living in the house they'd bought during their short marriage brought back memories at the oddest times. Especially when she was tired. She realized Colleen was watching her. "Sorry, I spaced there for a minute. Anything I can do for you?"

"Just stay safe. I hear from Shauna that you have a habit of snooping around. I'm not sure this is the time to do that." Colleen blushed as Cat stared at her. "Sorry, I'm a bit psychic and sometimes I don't control what I'm saying as well as I should."

Rick passed by with a plate of chocolate chip cookies. "Oh . . . did you have to out your special power? Now she's going to think we're all freaks."

Colleen smiled and took one of the cookies. "Rick, the only one who's a freak around here is you."

As she walked away toward the group discussing movies, Rick watched her go. Then he grinned at Cat. "She really loves me."

"Do not," Colleen called back without even turning around.

Smiling, Cat left the group to settle in for the evening and decided to check on Shauna. When she went to the kitchen, it was empty. But the back door was open. Cat walked through to the backyard and the path that led to the pasture beyond. Cat would take bets on the fact that Shauna was probably out talking to Snow.

When she reached the barn, three kittens came running up to meet her. The fourth and fifth were on Shauna's lap, curled up and seemingly asleep. Shauna wiped her cheeks with the back of her hand when Cat walked through the door. "You caught me trying to unwind a bit. And, I realized having a horse is another good thing. They like apples. I can get rid of at least one more a day."

"I didn't mean to interrupt." Cat picked up one of the kittens and brought it to her cheek. "I was just checking in. I'm heading to bed. The writers are tucked into the living room with a movie, even Bren. She swears she's putting away her phone for the rest of the week."

Shauna sighed. "Sometimes women are in bad relationships. Maybe it's her, maybe it's him, but clearly, it's not working. You have to have your own life, you know?"

"I guess I've always felt that way. Even in high school, Seth and I were close, but we both had things that we did apart. My girlfriends and I would go to the theater. Seth and the boys would go to the woods." Cat sat on a straw bale. "He asked me once if I thought we were too different."

"You do have different tastes, but doesn't that make the relationship even stronger?" Shauna absently rubbed one of the kittens' heads as she spoke. "Kevin had his work. I think his hobby was making more money. But it gave me time to be at the retreat. Doing the things I wanted to do. I think he might have wanted the more arm candy type of wife, but that's not me."

Cat looked around the refurbished barn. The feel of the old wood mixed with new life gave the area a magical quality. "Seth's a good man. We have fun together. I'm afraid I've brought him knee deep into my world as he's now the official handyman slash driver for the retreat."

"It works." Shauna met her gaze. "The three of us are friends and that makes the work easy. We all have our roles."

"It does work, doesn't it?" Cat yawned and set the kitten down near its mother, Angelica, who promptly grabbed the baby and started to give it a bath. "I'm heading in. Do you need anything from me?"

"No, I'm fine right here. I'll be in later." Shauna's smile was sad. "I'm giving myself time with my memories. I get exactly thirty minutes a day, then I have to get out of my pity party and back to the real world. So far, the process is working."

"Then I'll leave you to it. But if you need me . . ."

Shauna shook her head. "Go to bed. I'm fine. And I appreciate your concern."

Cat walked back to the house. The stars were just coming out and the night sky was clear of clouds. The temperature would drop quickly now that the sun had gone down. Colorado nights were chilly even in the summer. In the fall, it was jacket and bonfire time. The house glowed as she approached it from the back. Warm and inviting, it called to her. The house was becoming her home again. But this time, instead of sharing it with Michael, she had opened the doors to the retreat guests as well as Shauna and Seth.

And the house seemed to like the energy the additional people brought. Cat pushed past the rambling thoughts and made her way to the kitchen. She grabbed a bottle of water from the fridge and headed toward the stairs. Pausing at the bottom step, she heard laughter coming from the living room where the guests still were involved in the movie.

Yes, she thought as she made her way to her room, *the change is good*.

The next morning, Cat met Shauna in the kitchen. The smell of caramelized apples made her stomach growl. "What are you making now?"

"Caramel apple waffles." Shauna stirred the pan, making the smell even more intense. "I thought I'd set out the waffle maker and batter and the guests could make their own breakfast this morning. I really like this group. They're always coming in and asking questions about the food and how it's prepared. I'm thinking a few of my dishes will be in some of their books come next fall."

"Which is all the more reason we need to get that cookbook of yours in front of my agent so she can start shopping it to publishers." Cat poured her coffee and sat at the table. "Come sit and tell me how your week's going. Everything okay?"

"You're asking about finding me in the barn yesterday?" Shauna filled her own cup and sat. When Cat nodded, she sighed. "It's just hard sometimes. I know Kevin wasn't the best boyfriend, but in his own way, he was a good guy. Having Snow around helps."

"Are the kittens too much?"

Shauna laughed. "Are you kidding? They are great. They typically pull me right out of my pity party. Are we really thinking of keeping all of them?"

Cat's eyes widened. "I hadn't thought we would."

"Then I'll make up a flyer. Do you have a favorite you want to keep?"

Cat thought about the five. She adored all of them. Maybe they *should* keep them all. Cat held up her hands. "I can't decide. And what if we give one away and they have a bad family? Can we vet the new parents?"

"We could just fix them all and keep them. We would have a full house, but they are happy in the barn and we could make sure there's a heat lamp going when it gets really cold."

Cat sipped her coffee, thinking. Then she gave up. "I can't make a decision."

Shauna shook her head. "We don't have to decide today. Just be thinking about what you want to do. It's your house."

"Yeah, but it's your home as long as you want to live here. You have a say too."

At that Shauna stood and walked over to the stove to stir the apples.

Cat felt the change in mood. "Did I say something wrong? Crap, you're not leaving and traveling the world like I suggested, are you? You know I can't replace you."

Shauna chuckled, then turned around. Tears flowed down her cheeks. "I'm just so blessed that you came into my bar that day and we became friends."

Crap, Cat hadn't meant to bring on the tears. She guessed that Shauna's thoughtful mood as she made her way back from the barn last night had carried over to the morning discussion. "I'm glad too. If I had a sister, I'd want her to be just like you."

"That's sweet." Jessica stood in the doorway watching the two of them. "I guess that explains why you haven't reached out to me since you've been back. Even though we were best friends before."

"Jessica, what are you doing here?" Cat wasn't going to play the "who do you like the best" game. She'd refused to play it during her school years and she wasn't getting dragged into it now.

"I came over to talk to you." She stared hard at Shauna, then she seemed to collapse. The anger on her face turned to grief. "You have to convince your uncle that I didn't kill Greyson."

"Tell me one thing first." Cat stared at her former friend until she knew she had her attention. "Were you having an affair with Greyson?"

Chapter Twelve

Jessica's eyes went wide. "Why would you ask me that?"

"Because that's what people are saying. And there's a lot of things about you that I didn't know." Cat wanted to call her out on the book thing, but she held back. This was more important. "Well?"

"No, I wasn't having an affair with Greyson. I love my husband. I love Tyler." Jessica looked worn out and defeated.

Cat stared at her. "Look, I don't know what you think you've heard, but my uncle doesn't really listen to me when he's investigating a case."

"That's not what everyone says. They say you should have gone into law enforcement instead of teaching or writing." Jessica pointed to the coffee-pot. "Do you mind? I've been up since four this morning and I'm starting to drag."

"Of course." Shauna hurried to grab Jessica a cup and then pointed to a chair at the table. "Why don't you sit down? I'm Shauna, by the way."

Jessica looked at Cat for confirmation, and when

she nodded, Jessica sank into one of the chairs. "I really am sorry for just showing up like this. I know I was a total witch the other day and all I can say is I wasn't thinking straight."

"Drink some coffee and tell us what's going on. I didn't even know that Greyson Finn was Tyler's brother." Cat wanted to grab her notebook, but after making such a big deal out of the fact she wasn't investigating, she thought maybe it wasn't the best thing to do.

"That's my fault. Greyson got me the job with Covington. I'd applied everywhere to teach, but no one seemed to want me. So when Greyson offered to talk to the dean in my behalf, I grabbed the lifeline. I just didn't want everyone to know the only reason I was teaching at Covington was my brother-in-law's influence." She sipped her coffee. "I should have told you, especially after we started hanging out after work. Tyler urged me to trust you. But Michael was so good at his work. And you, you would have been accepted at any college you applied at. I felt like I didn't belong."

Cat didn't know how to respond. She could see the hurt in Jessica's eyes. Before she could say anything, Anne walked into the kitchen.

"Oh, sorry, I didn't realize you had company." Anne held out a coffee carafe. "Any way I could get this filled? There's a group of us writing in the living room. Last night's movie session made us all hungry to get some scenes down before breakfast and your seminar."

Shauna stood and took the carafe to the coffee-pot. "I can handle this."

Jessica stood. "I've got to be going too. Tyler and

the boys should be up by now and we have to go over to his mom's. She's having a gathering for family before the funeral."

Cat walked her out of the kitchen and to the front door. "Look, I'll do what I can, but really, you need to talk to my uncle. If I'm hearing these rumors, you can bet he has too."

Jessica zipped her light jacket and pulled up the hood to cover her head. It wasn't raining so Cat imagined that Jessica thought it made her less noticeable. "I'll go talk to him tonight after I get the boys settled for the night. I didn't kill Greyson."

Cat nodded. She believed Jessica. Of course, her belief and three dollars would get her a cup of coffee before the jury convicted her. "Look. Just talk to Uncle Pete. I'll see what I can do."

Jessica was already halfway down the block before Cat realized she hadn't asked her the most important thing. If she wasn't sleeping with Greyson, why had she been seen meeting him at the bakery? Maybe Dee Dee would know that answer. She glanced at the clock. She had a seminar at ten. The bakery would be slammed until about two when the breakfast and lunch crowds were gone. If she went now, Dee Dee wouldn't even talk to her unless she bought something. And that would just be to tell her the cost of the donut. Cat made a decision. She'd go back after lunch. Then the bakery owner would have no reason to ignore her.

She went back into the kitchen to eat breakfast before she went upstairs to go over her notes for the seminar. Cat's thoughts kept returning to Greyson Finn's last hours. Had he been the man she'd seen sitting outside the bakery on Sunday? She wished she'd paid more attention, but at that time, her mind was on one thing. To get Dee Dee to stop calling the health department. Which made her think of Nate, and then Cat realized she hadn't heard Seth come in last night.

As if her thoughts had called him, Nate Hearst knocked on the kitchen door. Cat met Shauna's gaze and shrugged. She hoped Dee Dee hadn't called in another complaint. Cat went over and opened the door. "Hey, are you all right? Seth didn't come back before I turned in. Come on in. Tell us what happened."

"Nothing to tell. No broken bones but I have a few bruises on my butt because I tripped backward over the curb trying to get out of the way of that crazy driver. Your uncle is pulling surveillance tapes to see if he can identify the car plate." Nate took the cup of coffee that Shauna handed him and sank into a chair. "I really need to work out more. If I'd been thinking, I could have just turned and moved out of the guy's way. Probably just some drunk driver who didn't react in time."

"Seriously? Well, I'm glad you're okay. We were worried, weren't we, Shauna?" That got Cat a dirty look from her friend, but a hopeful one from Nate.

"Sorry to have worried either of you." He turned toward Shauna with a smile. "I appreciate the concern."

"So what has you out so early this morning?" Shauna turned away quickly. Cat assumed it was to avoid making eye contact with Nate.

"Unfortunately, my job. This is a spot check. It's part of my process. I'm hoping to close out this investigation today." He took a deep breath. "I take it you're in the breakfast prep stage?"

"Can you eat or is that against the rules?" Shauna flipped out a waffle from the maker and put it on a plate. She ladled two big scoops of the caramelized apples on the still hot waffle and then topped it with whipped cream.

Cat could hear the guy's stomach rumble. He looked around. "I have to let the temperature gauges set for a few minutes. I guess I have time. If I'm not interrupting your day."

"I'm in the feeding people part of the day." Shauna set the plate at an empty spot at the table. "Get your gauges set up and I'll refill your coffee."

Cat was glad this was just a follow-up. And, as she watched Nate hurry around the kitchen to get to the waffle, she thought the report would go in their favor. As long as he liked his breakfast. "You can clean up in the washroom off the pantry."

He quickly set up what he needed, then set his bag on the bench by the back door. He walked toward the direction where Cat had pointed. "This is so kind of you both."

"It's not me, it's all Shauna," Cat responded as he returned from washing his hands.

He sat and cut a piece off the waffle with his fork. Taking a bite, his eyes closed in pleasure. With his mouth full, he said, "I've never had a waffle this good."

"You should pour a little maple syrup over the top." Seth slapped his friend on the back as he came in from outside. "It's heaven."

"Are you here for seconds?" Shauna glanced up from pouring more waffle batter into the machine.

"Cat hasn't eaten so she's first, but then I can make you another."

"I could eat." He poured himself a cup of coffee and sat across from Nate. He pushed the maple syrup across the table. "I'm telling you, you have to at least try it."

Nate grabbed the container and poured some over his half-eaten waffle. He took a bite and groaned. "You weren't wrong."

"I tell you, Shauna's cooking is the best. You should try her clam chowder. It hits the spot on cold winter days." He sipped his coffee and nodded toward Shauna, who was getting Cat's waffle ready.

"You have to say that or I won't feed you," Shauna teased as she sat Cat's plate in front of her. "Let the man make his own mind up about what he thinks."

"I think you're a food goddess." Nate didn't even look up from his plate. "I might just have to pop in for breakfast again. On official business of course."

Cat looked up into Shauna's blushing face and raised her eyebrows in an unspoken question.

She shook her head, then announced, "Sorry, I've got to run upstairs to check on something. Cat, would you cook if anyone wants another waffle?"

"Sure, but what are you doing?"

"Thanks." Shauna ignored the question and hurried out of the room.

Cat and Seth exchanged a look, but Nate looked too focused on his waffle to notice Shauna's absence.

"I hate to ask, but I'd love a second one if you don't mind." Nate glanced over at Cat, who had just started eating.

"Don't worry about it. I can make a waffle." Seth

put a hand on Cat's shoulder to keep her in the chair. "So what's going on in your world today, Nate?"

"Not much. We were supposed to start working on a restaurant proposal, but with the death, I guess that's out of the works."

Cat's attention left her waffle and she studied Nate. "So Greyson Finn *was* opening a restaurant here in Aspen Hills."

Nate leaned back in his chair, studying her. "I never said who died."

"How many people have died here in the last week?" Seth asked as he poured batter into the waffle iron. "It's not that much of a stretch."

"Yeah, you're right." Nate scratched the back of his neck, considering his response. "I guess it doesn't hurt. Yeah, Greyson came in last week and was talking to my secretary about what he'd need to do to start the planning stage of opening a new restaurant. I guess he was going to do American western classics."

"Like a steak house?" Seth turned over the waffle.

"That would have been amazing." Nate nodded. "I didn't talk to the guy, but I have gone into Denver just to eat at his restaurant. A little overpriced for my city worker budget, but the food was great."

Seth sat the waffle with the apple mixture down in front of Nate and took his old plate to put into the sink.

Nate took a big breath in and sighed. "Not as good as this though. She really should think about cooking professionally. She's that good."

"She does cook professionally, for the retreat." Cat considered the next bite, then set it down on the plate. "Did Greyson say where he was going to put the new restaurant? Over near the highway?"

"That would have made sense in an access way. But no, he was planning on renovating an existing building downtown." Nate sprayed whipped cream over the top of the hot apples, then added maple syrup. Seth had converted another one.

Cat held her breath. She knew the answer to the question before she even asked it. "What building downtown?"

Nate had just taken a bite of the waffle and Cat had to wait for him to answer. He wiped his mouth with the napkin on his lap before he focused on her. "It's on Main Street. The one that currently holds the bakery? I guess he must have known the bakery was closing. No wonder Dee Dee's in such a bad mood."

Cat couldn't believe what she was hearing. Greyson was going to put Dee Dee out of business? If that wasn't motive, she didn't know what was. She needed to call Uncle Pete. Seth must have read her mind because he glanced her way.

"Nate, are you telling me that Greyson owned the building where Dee Dee has a bakery?" Seth spoke slowly, his implication clear.

"I guess. I mean, I didn't look at the plans. I told you, he was just in there talking about opening a new spot. My sister, she got all excited when she heard the news. Like normal people were going to be able to eat there anyway. That guy catered to the rich and shameless in my opinion." Nate finished his second waffle and looked longingly at the now unplugged waffle maker. He put his fork on his plate and leaned back. "That was the best breakfast I've had in forever."

"Did Dee Dee know about the new plans?" Cat figured Nate wasn't going to return to the subject unless he was directed. "Do you think she knew he owned the building?"

"Of course. She had to list the owner on her application to open the bakery. She had to know who she was writing her checks out to every month, right?" Nate looked back and forth from Seth to me. "Why all the questions? I told you, the restaurant isn't going to be built now."

"Exactly." Cat pulled out her cell and dialed her uncle. When the call went straight to voice mail, she hung up without leaving a message. He'd show up for dinner sooner than later and she could tell him then. Besides, what did she really know except the victim's plans?

"Know your victim, know the killer," was one of Uncle Pete's favorite sayings. When he was talking about his job, that is.

Nate watched her closely as she put her phone on the table. "No way. You think Dee Dee could do something like this? She's a pain in the butt, I'll give you that, but she's local. She's not some outsider with homicidal tendencies."

"You're telling me she can't be a killer because she was born here?" Cat couldn't believe what she was hearing. "You can't believe that."

"People who grew up here are different. We care about each other. Well, I know that doesn't describe Dee Dee either, but it's the truth. We look out for each other." He frowned, apparently realizing he wasn't helping paint the bakery owner in a good light. Finally, he repeated his first point. "She grew up in Aspen Hills."

"Look, I'm not saying she's a killer. Just that it appears she had motive. Who killed Finn will be decided by people in law enforcement. Like Uncle Pete." Cat glanced at the clock. "I need to get ready for my seminar."

Seth stood and walked to the kitchen door with her. Lowering his voice, he put a hand on her shoulder as he talked. "I'll hang with Nate until he's done with his inspection. You kind of shook him up with the whole Dee Dee thing."

"I can't believe he didn't think of it before and tell someone." Cat glanced around Seth to watch as Nate used his phone to access his e-mails. "He's kind of naive."

Seth pushed a stray lock of hair out of her eyes. "He's a good guy. But yeah, he tends to see the best in people. Even when they cause him work."

Cat kissed Seth, letting her lips linger on his. "He's a lot like you in that matter. I guess that's why you two are friends."

Seth grinned and went back to the table. Cat heard the slap of his hand on Nate's back before the kitchen door closed. She didn't have time to worry about Nate right now. She had to be ready for the seminar on being a working author for the group. Although she knew a few of them were already at that place, maybe she could still impart some wisdom from her experience.

She ran upstairs to grab her file folder and go through the notes she made after every session. The questions she was asked were different each time, but the focus of the meeting was always about knowing when it was time to become a full-time writer. Unfortunately, that was one question she couldn't answer. Because it depended on a whole lot of factors in an author's life. But she could point out a lot of the things they needed to consider before they jumped into what might be an empty pool.

When she went downstairs again and entered the living room, all the writers were already there with pen and paper ready. She glanced at the clock. "The good thing about this being such an informal retreat is we can start things early if we want. Just let me grab a bottle of water and we'll begin."

"Oh, no hurry. We were just talking about the local murder. It's so interesting hearing what the local community says in real life. I mean, it's all anyone's talking about." Anne waved Cat out of the room. "Go take care of things. We'll be here when you get back."

Cat hurried to the dining room, hoping she wouldn't miss any of the gossip about Greyson's murder. This group was using the unusual circumstance to increase their knowledge about their chosen subject matter, murder mysteries. Maybe she should ask Uncle Pete to come and give a talk about police procedures. Except he always seemed busy during the retreats. Like with a murder.

She hurried back into the room and heard Colleen's response to Anne's comment.

"I bet the reason everyone is talking is because the guy was a famous chef. It just sounds like the perfect subject for a murder mystery." Colleen sipped on her coffee. "Cooking Can Kill. Or maybe Dying for Dinner Service."

Bren shushed her. "We're here to listen to Cat's story and grill her for all the juicy insider secrets, not brainstorm a plot for a new mystery. Go ahead, Cat, let's get started. I know I have a list of questions I want to throw at you."

"Yeah, I'm ready too." Rick grinned at Colleen. "Besides, I call dibs on the chef murder idea. I'm so writing that as soon as I get home. Maybe it will be a series—the Gourmet Food Writer Mystery series."

"And the guy has the bad luck of all his subjects for his interviews winding up dead?" Cat grinned. "I can play the 'what-if' game too. But Bren's right, we do have a lot to cover before you head off to lunch, so let's get started."

They'd only been talking for about ten minutes when Shauna hurried into the living room. "Sorry, Cat, I don't mean to disturb you, but there's an urgent call."

Cat didn't know what it could be about unless something had happened to her folks. She rose from the wide-armed reading chair where she'd been sitting. "I'll be right back."

Shauna shook her head. "Sorry if I wasn't clear. The call is for Bren."

Chapter Thirteen

Cat waited for Bren to return to the group. When ten minutes passed and she hadn't, Rick stood. Cat shook her head and put a hand on his arm. "Let me go check on her."

When she got into the foyer, Bren wasn't on the phone; she was sitting on the bench, looking out onto the yard. She smiled when she realized Cat was there, but the emotion didn't hit her eyes.

"Are you okay? Seth can drive you to the airport if you need to get home." Cat sat next to her on the bench.

"Wouldn't he love that?" Bren muttered, then shook her head. "Sorry, I am just realizing I've been a complete and utter fool."

"So there's nothing wrong at home?" Cat was confused.

Bren shook her head. "I guess I should tell you the whole story because I don't think that's his last call. My boyfriend is anxious. That's the good name for it. It's feeling now like I've excused his bad behavior for a while. The other name for it is controlling. He likes to know where I am. At all times."

"So you being here must be hard on him."

Bren laughed. "You could say that. He just gave me an ultimatum to come home today or move out when I finally come back."

"Because you came to a writers' retreat?" Cat didn't understand the man's logic, but she saw the pain on Bren's face.

"He says I'm being selfish and not considering him. He accused me of being somewhere shacked up with some guy." Bren took a deep breath. "I knew making the decision to turn off my cell would be an issue, but I guess I was ready for the fight. My writing is important to me. And if he can't see that, well, it's his loss. I just hope I still have clothes to pack when I get home."

"He wouldn't mess with your stuff, would he?"

Bren nodded, and this time a real smile curved her lips. "Darn right he would. The guy's crazy. I should have seen it before, but I thought his attention was cute. It made me feel wanted."

"Well, at least you have a few days left here before you have to deal with all of that. Put it all away and I'll tell Seth and Shauna not to let any calls go through to you from the guy." Cat hated to see the woman in such pain.

"I'm sure he won't be nice when you tell him I won't take my calls. So I'll apologize in advance for the blowback they'll get." Bren frowned, glancing out the window. "I hope he doesn't decide to get on a plane and bring the fight here."

Cat patted her hand. "If he does, we'll deal with

it. I happen to have an in with the law here in Aspen Hills. You just let us know if you see him or feel uncomfortable."

Bren took a deep breath and let it out. "Thank you for being so nice. I haven't been my best since I've been here. But it's given me a lot of time to think about what I want in my life and what I don't."

"Well, that's not what we advertise, but I'm glad the separation has given you some clarity." Cat wondered if once Bren was home in Chicago, she'd forget about her decision and go back. It happened more often than not, but Cat hoped Bren would beat the odds. "So, shall we go back and talk about the writing business? Or do you need some time alone?"

"Heck, no." Bren wiped her cheeks with both hands, then stood up. "I want to reclaim my life, and the retreat is apparently the first step in doing this. Let's talk books."

Cat followed her into the living room and saw the concern on the other writers' faces, but no one said anything when Bren rejoined the group.

"Now that we're all back, what were we talking about?" Cat curled back up in the chair and picked up her notebook. "We were just starting to talk about the changes in the business, traditional, self-published, or hybrid, right?"

Anne nodded. "I know you're firmly in the traditional camp, but can we discuss the pros and cons of all of those?"

Cat met Bren's gaze and saw that the woman had her notebook and pen in hand. She was ready to move on. At least for right now. Cat turned back to Anne. "Just because I published the traditional way doesn't mean I don't understand the changes in the industry. Let's not make this a one or the other discussion. Let's talk about the path for each."

They talked right up to when the clock struck noon. Cat glanced at her watch. "I didn't mean to keep you so long. I feel like we've got some threads to still discuss. Do you want to meet tomorrow at ten and we can continue this? It's up to you. Thursday's are usually a free write day."

"I'll be here." Rick closed his notebook. "I've got some questions about what you talked about today that I'd like to get some input on."

"It's not often that I get to be a part of a group discussion about the book business." Anne stood and stretched. "Let's do writing sprints when we get back from lunch and then I'll be ahead of my word-count goal for tomorrow."

The group murmured their approval of the schedule change and moved toward the foyer to go to lunch. Bren sat her notebook and pen by her laptop on a side table. "I'm leaving this here. I'd rather not go back to my room where I left my cell. I think I'm going to turn it off for the rest of the week."

"Sometimes having some distance with the issue gives you clarity." Cat gathered her notes and put a stickie on where they'd start back tomorrow. "Your stuff will be fine here. The house is yours for the week."

Bren paused at the door to the foyer. "You may regret saying that. I'm a pretty messy roommate."

With that she disappeared and Cat could hear the voices as the group decided where to go to lunch. By the time she'd straightened her folder and gathered up the cups and plates, the writers had left for lunch.

She took the dirty dishes into the kitchen and started unloading the tray into the sink. Shauna came in as she was just finishing.

Shauna set a basket of towels down on the floor. "You didn't have to do that. I would have cleaned up the living room."

Cat put the tray away on top of a cabinet and then refilled her coffee cup. "I wanted to be helpful. Sit down, we need to talk. We have a situation."

Shauna grabbed a bottle of water and sat. She folded the clean towels as she listened to Cat's retelling of her discussion with Bren. When Cat was done, Shauna folded the last towel and ran her hand over the top of it. "I figured something like that was going on with her. She was way too tied to that phone. I had a boyfriend like that for about two minutes. Then I told him to take a walk."

"We just have to screen any calls to Bren on the house line. From what she told me, he's pretty determined." Cat wondered if the guy would really hop a plane just because Bren wouldn't answer his calls. Just to be safe, she added, "And if anyone shows up in the next day or so, we need to be on alert. Seth needs to be part of this discussion too."

As if she'd called him, Seth walked in the kitchen door. He walked over to the sink and washed his hands. "Shauna, I got the garlic planted for you in a bed right next to the barn. I think there's room for a little herb garden too, if you want me to set it up for next spring."

When he turned around, both women were watching him.

"What? Did I walk in on something again? Seriously, if you guys are going to have private conversations, you need to go into the study or somewhere I won't bust in on you." He set the towel down. "I'll go check out my e-mails. I have a bid in on a project at the college that should be coming through anytime."

Cat shook her head. "You came in right on time. We need to talk about something."

Shauna made deli sandwiches for lunch while Cat filled Seth in on Bren's predicament. When she finished, he stood and went to the fridge to grab a soda.

He took the plate Shauna handed him and sat next to Cat. "If I'd have ever thought about treating you that way when we were dating in high school, my mother would have called me on the carpet."

"And we wouldn't have been dating anymore." Cat took her own plate from Shauna. The sandwich was stacked high with sliced pastrami and then she'd added pickled onions and a horseradish dressing. Cat could smell the tang of the dressing and her mouth watered. "Thanks, Shauna. This looks great."

"The slaw has cabbage and apples so I hope you like it." Shauna sat with her own plate. "I'm through two boxes of apples already and I'm doing a second batch of apple butter. It's on my to-do list for this afternoon. What are you all doing?"

"I'll prep that herb garden if you want. Maybe you can come out to the barn with me before you start cooking and I'll show you what I'm thinking."

Seth picked up half of his sandwich and groaned. "I love me some pastrami."

"I can do that." Shauna looked pointedly at Cat. "Are you coming out with us or do you have other plans?"

Cat squirmed a bit in her chair. She'd been meaning to stop by Dee Dee's bakery to see if she could find out if the baker had known she was about to lose her building. "I'm going into town for a bit."

"Cat . . ." Shauna started, but Cat held up a hand.

"Before you go off on me, I'm going to the bakery to see if Nate's information was true. I'll be careful. I don't need Dee Dee mad at me. We'll never get Nate out of here if she keeps filing complaints." Cat took a bite of the slaw. Tangy and sweet, the side seemed like a perfect match to the heaviness of the beef in the sandwich. "This is good."

When Shauna didn't respond, Cat added, "And I'm going into the station to see if I can catch Uncle Pete. If he doesn't have this information, it might take the spotlight off Jessica."

"That woman deserves to be worried if she was having an affair with her brother-in-law. Who does that?" Seth said in between bites.

"Judge much?" Cat asked, but really, she agreed with Seth's comment. If Jessica had been having an affair with Greyson, it meant one thing: Cat hadn't known the woman who she used to call a friend at all. "Sorry, I didn't mean that. She says she wasn't and it's hard for me to see Jessica doing that. She and Tyler were the perfect couple. Michael and I used to laugh about how our marriage was a poor comparison."

The other two at the table were silent as Cat processed what she'd just said.

Then she picked up her sandwich. "I guess, seeing how we wound up divorced in the end, we were right. But I can't believe I was such a bad judge of Jessica's character."

Seth put his hand on her arm. "People change, Cat. No one knows what goes on in a marriage or a relationship for that matter, besides the two people who are involved. It happens all the time."

"Yeah, think of all the neighbors of serial killers who comment on what a nice guy he was."

"Except for that little problem we had with our animals disappearing, one after another . . ." Seth added.

"And the backyard gardening he liked to do late at night," Cat finished. "You're both right. I shouldn't be kicking myself. But there weren't any signs. Truly, I believed they were in love. Maybe I was wrong."

"Or they were in love when you knew them." Shauna sipped on her lemonade. "Besides, even if she was having an affair with the guy, it doesn't mean she'd kill him. Her husband maybe, but why would she give up a piece on the side? That doesn't make sense, especially when you look at Greyson. That guy was a Greek god. He must have been amazing in the sack."

"And with that, I'm out of here." Seth finished the last of his slaw and picked up the half of the sandwich he hadn't eaten yet. "I'll be upstairs checking my e-mails. I'll stop and get you when I go back out to work on the new garden. I think you'll like what I have planned."

Cat and Shauna watched him leave the kitchen, then burst out laughing.

"That man of yours is a little bit conservative in talking about sex." Shauna finished her own slaw, then picked off a slice of the pastrami and popped it into her mouth.

"What can I say? His mom did raise him right. He's definitely not one to kiss and tell. The group we hung out with didn't even know we were dating until we showed up at homecoming together." Cat smiled at the memory.

Shauna studied her. "All joking aside, you be careful when you go talk to Dee Dee. I don't want to hear that you slipped and fell into one of her ovens."

"You're referencing the wicked witch in Hansel and Gretel. I don't think Dee Dee's that bad."

Shauna set her sandwich down and stared at Cat. "Seriously? Have you met the woman? That's exactly who she reminds me of."

Cat curled her fingers into claws and held them up toward Shauna. "I'll get you, my pretty. . . ."

"Wrong story, but right idea." Shauna nodded to Cat's plate. "Do you want more of the slaw?"

"Actually, I'm stuffed. I'm going upstairs to grab my tote and my notebook." She took her plate to the sink. "Honestly, I'll be careful. I just want to help Jessica if I can. Even if she isn't a friend anymore, she was at one time."

Shauna opened her tablet. "I get it. But if you aren't back by two, I'm calling Pete and having him send out a search party."

"That's what friends do. They call in the troops when need be." She paused before leaving the kitchen. "Thank you for being a true friend. I really appreciate you."

"Here to serve." Shauna grabbed a basket of apples and put them on the table. "Now get out of here so I can get busy."

During her walk into town, Cat practiced the questions she wanted to ask Dee Dee. She was risking the cease fire they'd agreed to on Sunday. Cat was going to have to be careful how she phrased her questions so it didn't seem like she was accusing the woman of murder.

When she got to the bakery, a crowd was gathered around the entrance. Cat moved in to stand by the bookstore owner, Tammy. "What is going on?"

"Dee Dee's going off on some guy from the city. From what I can hear, he's trying to serve her eviction papers."

A police car pulled up to the curb and her uncle got out of the passenger seat. He paused and looked at Cat. "Is there a reason you're here?"

"Yes. I was coming to talk to Dee Dee about who owns the building, but I think I got my answer." A crash came from inside the bakery.

"Paul, get in there and restrain Ms. Meyer before she hurts that guy." He motioned his deputy inside the building, then turned back to Cat. "You go home. I'll come by this evening for dinner if that's all right with Shauna."

"Of course, we'd be glad to have you." Cat heard a cheer from the spectators near the front. "Uh oh, Dee Dee must have gotten a good swing in."

"I better get in there before Paul shoots someone." He pointed a finger and repeated, "You go home."

"Yes, sir." Cat grinned at Tammy, who moved to the sidewalk and away from the bakery.

"I guess he told you." Tammy smiled as she watched Cat's uncle move his way through the crowd, telling people to leave the premises.

"He worries." Cat glanced back at the bakery and wondered who had come to evict Dee Dee if Greyson had been her landlord. Maybe Nate was wrong about that. She decided to head to the library and see if she could access the town's ownership records online. "I've got an errand to run at the college. So we'll see you Friday?"

"Looking forward to it. I'm bringing a ton of craft books that are related to mystery writing as well as a slew of the recent releases. At worse, we'll have a great discussion." Tammy paused at her store's entrance. "Thanks for including me in your retreat. It's nice to get out and talk to writers once a month. It keeps me working on my own manuscript."

"I didn't know you were a writer."

Tammy beamed. "I haven't told a lot of people, but I started writing a novel a few months ago. I guess you gave me the bug."

"Well, good luck, and if you ever want to grab some coffee and talk, just let me know. I'd love to sit down with you anytime besides retreat week." Cat turned to head to the college library.

"That would be awesome. I'll call you next week. It will have to be evenings after the store closes. Is that okay?" Tammy was almost vibrating with energy.

"Sure. Just call and we'll set something up." Cat waved and took a few steps away.

"You're the best," Tammy called after her.

As she walked away, Cat wondered if she would regret making the offer. Sometimes new writers were more interested in someone telling them how good their work was rather than listening to ways it could improve. But she'd give Tammy a few meetings to talk. Besides, it might be like talking to retreat guests. Now it was time to find out more about Dee Dee's building.

Chapter Fourteen

When she got to the library, Cat headed straight to the reference section. Miss Applebome was at the desk. Not who she wanted to see. The woman still hated her for borrowing a book without checking it out a few months ago. It wasn't like Cat was stealing it. It just wasn't available for regular checkout and she needed it to get Linda to talk. She took a deep breath and stepped forward. "Miss Applebome?"

The woman didn't look up.

Cat spoke a little louder. "Miss Applebome?"

"I'm not deaf, Ms. Latimer. I'm just waiting for the question." This time she did look up. "Or were you just checking to see if I was awake before stealing another book?"

Cat felt her face turn beet red. "I told you why I took the book. It's not like I was going to keep it or anything."

"I was pulling your leg. I'm busy. What do you want?" Miss Applebome went back to looking at her computer.

"I was wondering if the library has access to the city or county records where they store the building deeds. Like who owns a particular property?" Cat rattled off her question, not sure if she was making sense.

"Are you looking at doing a title search on your house? The town keeps building ownership records back to the founding. But I thought you did that research years ago when you bought the house?"

The woman never forgot anything. "I did. Actually, it's not my house I'm wondering about. It's one of the buildings downtown. I was wondering who the owners were."

"For what purpose?"

Now, the librarian watched her carefully. Cat figured the woman could spot a lie before it even left someone's mouth, so she decided to be totally honest. "I want to know who owns the bakery."

"And you didn't answer my question. For what purpose do you want this information?" Miss Applebome looked at her watch. There was no way it was time for her to leave. But maybe Cat should just come back in the evening when a less experienced librarian was on the desk.

"I think it might have something to do with Greyson Finn's death." Cat decided to put all her cards on the table.

"I thought you might be investigating again. You really need to learn to keep out of things that aren't your business." Miss Applebome wrote something on a sheet of recycled scratch paper and handed it to Cat.

"What's this?" She glanced at the neatly scripted words.

"It's the user name and password you'll need for the town archives. Try not to get yourself killed." Miss Applebome gazed at her with such concentration, Cat took a step back. "I'd hate to be the one to tell your uncle what you were doing."

Cat swallowed hard. "He knows. I tell him everything."

And that was almost the truth, but the ancient librarian seemed to sense the hesitancy in the statement. She turned back to her computer. "I certainly hope so, Ms. Latimer."

Cat stepped away from the desk, hoping she wouldn't be asked more questions. It was almost impossible to lie to the woman. Especially to her face. She just had that look. Cat's mother had the same look, and Cat had never gotten away with a lie when she was growing up or even now that she was an adult.

She hurried over to the computers and keyed in her password. The college had allowed her to keep her teaching access, probably in hopes that they could talk her into some adjunct classes sooner or later. Cat hoped her financial situation wouldn't cause her to need to take them up on the offer, but you never knew in the book business. One year you could be up, the next down. Royalties were hard to plan for. The retreat was holding its own, but Cat knew it had to pay off the remodeling costs before she could really count the income as profit.

She got into the town's website and then found the records link. Carefully, she keyed in the user name and password that Miss Applebome had given her. When she looked up the address, she saw the building had been through several owners in its over 150 years of existence. The last sale was to a holding company, the FFF. They'd bought it ten years ago.

Cat dug deeper into the scanned paperwork and found that the initials stood for the Finn Family Foundation. And Greyson and Tyler were full partners along with their mother.

Cat wondered if Greyson had always thought he'd expand his restaurant chain into Aspen Hills. But ten years ago, the town was just a college town. The families who came in for parents week didn't stay around or have vacation cabins.

Now the town was growing with a lot of the new residents working remotely from home or commuting into Denver. It wasn't a drive Cat would want to make, but the housing prices outside the Denver city limits made the drive less worrisome. Had Greyson decided the town had grown enough to support a high-end eatery? The Mexican place they went to for the close of the retreat on Saturday nights was high end and usually packed. Rumors said that the restaurant was owned by a famous chef out of the Southwest, but he'd never put his name on the place.

She wrote down all the information she had about the property, including the realtor who did the deal ten years ago. A bank or financial house wasn't listed at all, which was strange. She keyed in her own address and checked the records when she, Michael, and the bank had bought her Victorian. The realtor was listed as well as the closing title company and the bank that held the lien. The bakery property only had realtors and a closing company. Had the family come in with cash to buy the building?

Then she went back to the main page for the town's website and looked for the business license page. Hoping the same password would work, she breathed a sigh of relief when it did. Thank God for Miss Applebome's thorough nature. She looked up the Happy Cupcake. The name of the bakery didn't reflect the owner's personality. At all.

Dee Dee had just renewed her business license and had paid the extra money to get the five-year license instead of the annual one. Cat remembered the exact moment when she and Shauna had filled out those papers. The five-year license was the one Shauna had talked Cat into purchasing when they'd opened the Warm Springs Writers' Resort. Cat had argued that if the resort failed, it would have been a sunk cost.

Shauna had just smiled as she finished filling out the paperwork. "Then we better not fail."

Cat smiled at the memory. Shauna had more faith in the success of the resort than Cat had ever had. But then again, Cat overthought everything.

Like how upset Dee Dee would have been with Greyson when he told her he was ending her lease. Mad enough to kill him?

But then why was she so upset about this new lawyer coming in and telling her they were ending her lease? Especially if she'd already known? Cat hated to do it, but she mentally scratched a thin line through Dee Dee's name as a suspect. She didn't think the woman was that good of an actress.

She reached to close out the session, then thought about something else. She went back to the property ownership page and keyed in Tyler and Jessica's house. Was it purchased in their name?

When the owner loaded onto the screen, Cat wasn't surprised. The couple didn't own their house, the Finn Family Foundation did. Cat wondered who was in charge of the foundation's funds. Was it Tyler's mother? Or had it been Greyson? Or was it mild-mannered Tyler? He didn't have a job, or at least he hadn't when she'd known the couple. He'd called himself the house husband.

So many questions, but no answers. And even if she had the answers, was any of it tied to Greyson's death? Or was she just snooping into the details of a former friend's life. She wasn't sure, but Jessica had asked Cat for her help. And there was no way she would go into this blind. She wrote down the rest of the information and closed up her notebook.

It was time to have a heart-to-heart with Jessica.

By the time she'd gone to the English Department and talked to Lori, Jessica had left for the day. "They are doing a memorial tomorrow at the Lutheran church here in town. I'm sure Jessica and Tyler would love to see you. It's at one. Then they have to go into Denver where they're having an even larger memorial service. You know you're someone when they have two funerals for you."

"He had a lot of people in his life."

Lori shook her head. "I don't want to go out that way. Alone, with only family and customers to mourn me? He should have been married, not mooning over his brother's wife."

Cat was shocked at Lori's statement. "Did you know they were having an affair?"

"Actually, no. I suspected it because the guy met her here at her office a few too many times. When I asked her about her brother-in-law's visits, they stopped meeting here. But I'm sure they didn't just stop meeting." Lori winked. "They definitely had eyes for each other."

Cat thought about Jessica and Tyler all the way home. She could have sworn the couple was deeply in love. Of course, she thought she and Michael were the perfect couple too. And they might have been had he not felt the need to hold so much secret. Was that what had broken Jessica away from Tyler? Holding secrets?

She hadn't come to any conclusions by the time she got to the house. Uncle Pete's car was in the driveway, and as she glanced at her watch, she realized she was late for dinner.

Maybe her uncle could shed some light on his thoughts on who had killed Greyson. Maybe the investigation was over and the killer already behind bars. But she knew that was too much to ask. These things took time, no matter how fast they seemed to go in the television shows.

She bustled into the kitchen and set her tote down on the far cabinet where Shauna stored her larger appliances. She ran to the sink to wash her hands, then sat at her place and started filling her plate with the meat loaf, mushroom gravy, and mashed potatoes on the table. When her plate was filled, she picked up her fork to take a bite and realized everyone was watching her. Setting the fork down, she met their gaze. "What?"

"I don't know, I guess I expected to find you here since I sent you home after I ran into you at the bakery." Her uncle pointed his fork at her. "I think you even said you were going home."

Cat shook her head and filled her fork with a large bite of the meat loaf. Her stomach was growling. "No way. I needed to go to the library for some research. You can ask Miss Applebome—she saw me there. We even talked."

Uncle Pete's eyes narrowed as he watched her eat. "I'm sure you said you were going home."

"No, you said I was going home. I just didn't interrupt you." She pointed her fork at him in just the same way. "You were busy and didn't have time to listen."

Seth watched the interaction between the two. "And round one goes to Cat. But let's not call the match yet."

"Shut up, Seth." Cat glared at him. Then she addressed her uncle. "While I was at the library, I found out something interesting. Do you want to know or not?"

He stared at her a long time before he answered. "Might as well. I'm down to investigating Greyson's gambling habit to see if that's what got him killed."

"The Happy Cupcake's building is owned by the FFF, which stands for the Finn Family Foundation. Greyson was planning on evicting Dee Dee and opening a restaurant in the place where the bakery is now."

Her uncle finished his meat loaf and then nudged Seth. "Can you pass the meat loaf and the gravy this way? Shauna, this is outstanding."

"Thank you. I'm glad you like it. It was one of my mother's recipes." Shauna beamed at the praise.

Cat couldn't believe it. "Did anyone hear what I said? Greyson was evicting Dee Dee."

"No, actually the law firm he hired was doing it this afternoon. According to the guy who I saved from getting a cake in the face, the eviction has been in progress for about a month. This service was the first she'd known about it."

Of course, that matched with the fact that Dee Dee had just paid for a new five-year license the day that Greyson was killed. Maybe she hadn't done it. Which put all the light back on Jessica. "So you don't think she's the killer."

"She has an alibi. She was in Denver with a friend the night Greyson was killed."

Cat frowned. "No she wasn't. I talked to her at the bakery that night."

"After you left, she closed the shop and went to visit a boyfriend in Denver. The guy said she stayed there all night." Uncle Pete poured gravy over his meat loaf and what was left of his potatoes and his green beans.

"But he might have lied," Cat declared, but even she didn't believe it anymore.

Uncle Pete shrugged. "Maybe, but the fact she was surprised by the eviction today doesn't bode well for that being the motive."

Cat focused on eating and trying to think. Every time she thought the trail led away from Jessica, it always just died or led straight back.

"Look, I know you're worried about your friend. But just let me do my job." Uncle Pete's voice was softer, calmer, than it had been earlier. "And stay out of trouble. I worry about you. It's not safe to go poking the bear when you don't know if he was the real killer or not."

Cat stayed thoughtful during dinner, trying to keep up with the general conversation going around the table. But her heart just wasn't into the small talk. When Shauna pulled out warm apple pie with cinnamon ice cream she shook her head.

"I'm going in to check on the guests. Then I'm heading to bed. It's been a long day and I'm worn to the bone." She kissed Seth and Uncle Pete on the cheek, then nodded at Shauna. "I'm doing a second seminar tomorrow at ten. Can you have the treat table refilled after breakfast?"

"Of course."

Cat could see the worry in her friend's eyes but she just shook her head. "I'm tired. I'll see you all tomorrow."

When she went into the living room, the guests were all huddled on the couch and chairs, watching a movie. Anne paused the television when she saw Cat. "Come in and join us. It's *Murder on the Orient Express.* Rick's never seen it."

Cat leaned against the door frame and took in the group. Everyone was there including Molly. The groups always seemed to absorb the Covington attendee into their tribe sooner than later. Sometimes the student fit in so well, the line was seamless. "That's okay, I'm beat. So if you don't need me, I'm heading upstairs."

"Are you all right?" Bren asked, sitting up straight from her spot on the couch next to Rick.

"I'm fine. It's just been a long week. I'll see you

all in the morning for the rest of the publishing story. Have fun with the movie."

Cat was glad she didn't need to join the group. She *was* tired. And mostly she thought it was because she still hadn't dealt with her feelings about Jessica lying about her book. With the whole Greyson murder, this issue seemed a little petty. And if she brought it up, Jessica would pull the grief card to avoid talking about it anyway.

The next morning, Cat awoke to a feeling that she'd missed something. She thought about yesterday but nothing rang a bell. When she got down to the kitchen, Shauna was on the laptop. She didn't look up until Cat had poured herself a coffee and sat across from her. "Working on the cookbook?"

"Actually, no, I was talking to my brother. We connected on Facebook last night. He wants me to come to New York for a week."

Cat sipped her coffee. "Sounds great. When are you going?"

"I'm thinking next week. Once the guests get out of here. I might even have Seth drop me off at the airport at the same time." Shauna stood and pulled cinnamon rolls out of the oven. "Would you take care of Snow and the dwarves?"

"Of course. But I'm not riding your horse. I haven't ridden since first grade when I fell off and the horse stepped on my foot." Cat shuddered at the memory. "Then Mom made me walk to school by myself."

"Didn't you live about two blocks away?"

"What's your point? My foot had been stepped

on by a horse. I was distraught." Cat put the back of her hand on her forehead.

"You're such a whiner." Shauna smiled. "Well, if you think you'll be okay by yourself, I'm going to tell Jake I'll be there on Sunday night. I don't know how long I'll stay but I'll plan on being there a week. Unless things go south and then I'll come home."

"He's your brother; what could go wrong?"

Shauna stood and refilled her coffee cup. "I have a bad feeling that Mom told him about the money I inherited. I'm pretty sure he's going to try to sell me on some investments."

Cat hoped not. Shauna didn't deserve to have a brother who only wanted to know her now that she had money. But it had happened before. She was trying to think of something encouraging to say when the back door burst open.

Uncle Pete stood in the doorway, his face red. Glancing around the kitchen, his gaze fell on Cat.

"What's wrong?" Cat could see the distress in his face.

"I need to talk to Seth—where is he?"

Chapter Fifteen

Seth came in from the hallway. "I'm right here. What's going on?"

Uncle Pete poured a cup of coffee and looked at Cat. "Okay if we use the study? I need to ask Seth a few questions."

"About what?" Cat stood and put a hand up between her uncle and Seth. "You're not taking him into a private room to talk. You can talk here."

"Cat, that's not possible. Seth, grab some coffee and meet me in the study." Uncle Pete walked around the table on the other side from where Cat stood, frozen in place. "Cat, just relax. It's not something for you to worry about."

"If it's not something for me to worry about . . ." Cat started to ask, but Uncle Pete had already left the kitchen. She turned to Seth as he was filling a travel mug with coffee. "What is going on with him? Why does he want to talk to you alone?"

"Actually, I think I know, but let me find out. Whatever he asks me, I promise, I'll tell you after he leaves." He leaned down and kissed her softly on the lips. "I love you, Cat."

And with that he strolled out of the kitchen and toward the study. Cat started to follow but Shauna grabbed her arm. "Let them talk. You sit here and eat something. I have a feeling it's going to be a long day."

Cat sank into a chair and sipped her coffee, ignoring the cinnamon roll Shauna set in front of her. "I'm going to Greyson's funeral today at one. Do you want to come along?"

"Do you want me there as a friend?"

Cat finally broke her gaze from the unmoving kitchen door. "Yes. I think I need you there with me. Jessica, well, she can be difficult and demanding."

"I take it she still thinks you can keep your uncle from charging her in Greyson's murder." Shauna pushed the roll closer to Cat and picked up her own fork. "Go on, eat. You're going to need your strength."

"Why? What do you know? There's no way Seth's involved in this. No freaking way." Cat narrowed her eyes.

"I didn't mean Seth. You have a seminar as well as this funeral. I know how much being around that many people drains you." Shauna held up her fork. "So eat. You're grumpy because you're hungry."

"I'm grumpy because my uncle is questioning my boyfriend about a murder that I know he didn't commit." Cat stared through the wall like she could see into the study. Then she broke off a piece of the roll and popped it into her mouth. "I thought Uncle Pete liked Seth. I know he never liked Michael, but I always thought it was because of Seth. He thought

I'd chosen the wrong guy. And I guess he was right, in a way."

"Cat, calm down. You don't even know that the murder is what they are talking about. It could be something totally unrelated."

Cat laughed but the sound held no humor. "You know that's not true. If it wasn't police business, they would have talked in here in front of us."

"Okay, you're right there, but there's no use stewing over it. Seth said he'd tell you what he could." Shauna glanced at the stove. "I should make you an omelet. The protein would be better for your nerves than all that sugar. I was just going to have the rolls for breakfast, but I could add some substance to the meal."

Cat dropped her gaze away from the wall and looked at her friend. She seemed as upset as Cat felt. But she knew she was the one causing her friend's distress. "Look, I'm sorry for going postal on you. I know it's not your fault. But this investigation has me twisted up. Probably because of Jessica and her unreasonable demands. I'm beginning to think she did kill the guy—I can't find anyone else who had motive."

"Add me to the list," Seth muttered as he came into the kitchen with Uncle Pete following him. "Apparently I owed the guy money."

"You owe money to Greyson Finn?" Cat felt broadsided. She hadn't seen that one coming.

"Well, his records show I owe him money. I borrowed a few thousand from him to buy tools when I first started up the handyman business. I paid him back, every cent, either in cash or work on his brother's house. I guess I should have gotten a paid-in-full receipt since the accountant is now saying I didn't pay it off." Seth went over and re-filled his cup. "I guess I better go through my records and find what I can to prove I don't still owe the debt. Do you mind if I spend some time at my apartment this afternoon?"

"Sure, anything you need." Cat glanced at her uncle. "So you thought Seth would have killed this guy over a few thousand dollars?"

"No, I didn't think Seth killed him, but I had to clear up the issue so we could cross his name off the list. I was just surprised when his name came up in the investigation." Uncle Pete nodded to the cinnamon rolls. "Any chance I could get one of those?"

"I should say no," Cat responded.

"You're not the chef." Shauna pointed to the table. "Go sit down and eat. You need to be back to your happy and sparkling self before your session later this morning."

Seth set his coffee near hers and then went back for a roll. "It's Thursday. Why do you have a session on Thursday?"

"Because they still wanted to talk." Cat took another bite of the roll. She had to admit, at least to herself, that eating was making her calm down a little. She looked at Seth. "Do you need help going through your records?"

"You're kidding, right?" He grinned at her. "Don't give me that look. I see the box you throw your receipts into until tax time. I have a system and I don't need you messing it up."

"She never could keep her room clean." Uncle Pete sat and Shauna handed him a roll. "Thank you. This is the best thing that's happened today."

"This isn't pick on Cat day." Cat took a deep breath and focused on eating. She needed to figure out what this new information meant, if anything. "Uncle Pete? You said you talked to the accountant? Is he the guy who handles the family foundation?"

"What family foundation?" Her uncle set the fork on the plate.

Cat sighed. "I told you last night. It's the holding company that they bought the bakery building with. I just wondered who was in charge of it."

"That's right, you did say something. Sorry, it slipped my mind." He pulled out his notebook. "And to answer your question, the accountant didn't mention the foundation at all. He said he handled Greyson's financial affairs."

"So he should have known about the family foundation. Why wouldn't he at least mention it?" Cat pressed the point.

"I don't know, but I'll be talking to him again." He finished his roll and stood, taking the plate to the sink. "Seth, let me know when you find that documentation and I'll take it with me to reinterview this guy. Seems like the guy is only telling me what he wants me to know."

After Seth and Uncle Pete had left, Cat felt drained. She glanced at the clock and groaned. "How is it already nine?"

"We've been chatting here in the kitchen for several hours. And then Pete stopped by. . . ."

Cat held up her hand. "Stop, I know what happened. I'm just so drained after all the excitement this morning."

"I don't think Pete's even close to figuring out who murdered Greyson." Shauna grabbed a jar of peanut butter and spread a thick smear on a slice of bread. Then she repeated the action with some strawberry preserves she'd put up earlier that summer. She handed the completed sandwich on a paper towel to Cat. "Here, you need the protein. You should have let me cook you an omelet earlier."

Cat sighed. "This will work perfectly. Tell me you're going with me to the memorial service."

Shauna sank into a chair. "I had hoped I wouldn't have to go to another one so soon after Kevin's, but if you need me, I'll pull out my little black dress."

"I'm sorry. If this is too hard, I can do it myself." Cat felt like a heel. She should have realized what she was asking. Especially since Shauna had evaded the question when she first brought it up.

"I told you I was going, and I will." Shauna opened her laptop. "I better get busy working on the cookbook. I'd like to have a first draft done before I head to New York next week to see Jake."

"I'd be glad to read through it if you want." Cat wasn't much of a cookbook expert, but she could edit or wordsmith if Shauna needed her.

"Actually, I have someone beta reading it and testing out the recipes. If it passes through that test, I'll let you read for typos and stuff."

"Who's your beta reader?"

Shauna glanced up at the clock. "Your seminar is about to start."

Cat jumped out of her seat and refilled her coffee. She was already in the living room and waiting for the writers to show up when she realized that Shauna hadn't answered her question.

Anne was the first to arrive, notebook in hand

and chatting with Molly. Then came Rick and Colleen. Finally, just a few seconds before ten o'clock, Bren hurried into the room and quickly took a seat.

Cat turned from the conversation she'd been having with Molly about her experience and looked at Bren. It was obvious she'd been crying. Cat caught her gaze but Bren shook her head. Whatever it was, she didn't want to talk about it. Cat looked around the room.

"Well, we're all back. Do we want to make a list of what we need to cover? I want to make sure I answer all your questions." She turned to the flip chart and started writing down the points she'd remembered from yesterday. When she was done, she turned around. "So what else?"

The group called out so many items and questions, Cat didn't know if they'd finish the ask-the-author session today either. But they had one more get-together planned on Friday night after dinner to talk about the retreat, so she could squeeze some of these answers into that time frame if she needed to.

Taking the first item and crossing it off the list along with one farther down, she started talking.

When noon came she'd crossed off all but five items on the list. She glanced at the clock on the living room wall. "We did better than I thought we would. Why don't you all go eat and we can finish this up Friday night. Remember the owner of the Written Word is going to be here tomorrow to talk about the author/bookseller relationship. You'll love listening to Tammy."

"We could delay lunch if you wanted to keep going." Colleen glanced up from her notebook. "I could bring in some cookies."

Cat shook her head at the suggestion. "I'm sorry. I'm attending Mr. Finn's memorial service later this afternoon so I need to start getting ready."

"Are you scoping out the mourners for suspects?" Rick closed his notebook. "You know, they say it's always the spouse or someone close. Was this guy married?"

"Nope. I guess he was one of Denver's most eligible bachelors." Cat ripped the page off the flip chart and folded it, then put it in her folder.

"That doesn't mean he wasn't seeing someone." Anne stood, her notebook tucked under her arm. "Sometimes famous people keep their relationships secret because they want to look available."

Or they're seeing someone who isn't available. Cat hated the thought, but it was logical. As they moved out of the room, she pulled Bren aside. "Are you okay?"

"I was stupid and answered my phone this morning. I thought maybe he'd calmed down and we could have a rational conversation. Instead, I got a verbal beat down. I finally just hung up on him. I had to turn off my cell because he kept calling back." Bren leaned back against the doorway looking drained. "I don't know what I ever saw in that guy."

"They can be charming at first." Anne spoke so softly, Cat wasn't sure she had heard her. She patted Bren's arm. "You're doing the right thing. No one should make you feel less of a person. Our relationships are supposed to bring us up, not tear us down."

Bren bit her lip. "I know, but . . ."

"There are no buts in this situation, dear. You need to make a clean break of the man." Anne took her by the shoulder. "Let's go grab some food and we can make a plan for when we get back to Chicago. We'll come over with a bunch of movers and we'll get you out of there."

"You'd do that?" Bren seemed to brighten at the thought, then deflated again. "But I have nowhere to go."

"That's not true. You can stay with me until you get your own place. I have a lovely two-bedroom condo just off the lake. You'll love it."

Cat watched the two women walk toward the rest of the group, who enveloped them and their conversation like a family. She was still standing in the foyer when Shauna came out of the kitchen.

"There you are. I made us some sandwiches to eat before we go to this thing. I know I'll need something in my stomach." Shauna glanced around the empty foyer. "Are you waiting on someone?"

"No, I was just thinking." Cat moved toward her friend. "Let's eat so we can get ready. The church is only a few blocks away. Do you want to walk?"

When they got to the church, they joined the group of mourners flowing up the stone steps to the entrance. News crews were stationed behind barriers the town usually used for lining the streets for a parade route. This was probably the first time they'd been pulled out for a funeral.

Shauna stepped closer to Cat. "You don't think they're filming this, do you?"

"Actually, I know they are filming it. But don't worry. I don't think we're high end enough to get on the evening news." Cat glanced around at the others entering with them. "I just saw the mayor and his wife going into the church. And the president of the college wasn't far behind. It's kind of a who's who in Aspen Hills."

Professor Turner hurried up the stairs to walk with them. "I'm so glad I saw you. All of the department is supposed to be here, but I guess I'm late. I haven't seen one professor . . . well, besides you."

"I'm not really a professor." Cat brushed a leaf off his coat.

"Nonsense, once a member of our family, always a member. Besides, you're part of the college as your late husband's widow as well. So I guess you have two seats at the table. Or one really close to the dean." He took his fedora off as they walked inside and handed it and his coat to a college student who was manning the coatroom. Then he helped Cat off with her jacket. Shauna had chosen to go without a coat since her dress had long sleeves. "Shall we enter the chapel?"

Professor Turner held the door open and Cat wondered how many more people could fit inside the huge cathedral. There didn't seem to be room for two more people, let alone three. As she made her way closer to the front, she noticed a striking blonde sitting with the family, dressed in black, a black veil pushed back so she could wipe away the tears on her cheeks. Cat was just about to ask Shauna if she knew who the woman was, when Professor Turner grabbed her arm and pushed her into a row.

"You too, Miss Shauna," he said. Cat heard his words but before she could react, she was sitting in the pew with Shauna beside her and Professor Turner squeezing onto the edge. She could feel him pushing for more room.

Cat pressed against the man sitting next to her. She lost her balance when he moved over and she almost fell into him. Grabbing his arm to keep herself upright, she finally looked into his face. Dante Cornelio smiled back at her.

"Catherine, I should have known you'd be here." He leaned over her. "Miss Clodagh, so nice to see you again, even under such sad circumstances."

Shauna mumbled something that sounded like an acknowledgment to Dante's welcome, but Cat wasn't sure.

"Dante, I didn't realize you were in town," Cat stammered, not sure what to say. Dante Cornelio was one of the heads of a mob family that Michael had gotten messed up with. And it had gotten Michael killed. Of course, that hadn't been Dante's fault. The men had been friends, but Cat had been trying to stay away from the mob-connected, too handsome guy who sometimes lived down the street. She'd promised as much to both Seth and Uncle Pete. Now, Professor Turner had squeezed her into a too small seat right next to the man.

As if he'd read her mind, he leaned over and

whispered something to the man sitting next to him. The man nodded, then pointed to the side of the church. He spoke directly to Dante before he left his seat. "I'll be right over there when you're ready."

As soon as he'd stood, Dante moved over in the pew giving Cat room to breathe. "There, that's much better. I hate being packed in like sardines, don't you?"

"Your friend didn't need to leave. I was okay." Cat moved half over into where Dante had been sitting to give Shauna some room. She turned back to look at her friend, who was glaring at her. She leaned closer and hissed, "What?"

"Don't talk him into having the guy come back and sit. I've finally got blood flow back in my legs." Shauna rubbed her leg through the black dress.

A chuckle on the other side of Cat made her realize that Dante had heard their conversation. If she was going to be in trouble anyway, she should find out how Dante knew Greyson. But first she wanted to know who the woman at the front of the church was.

She leaned in close and discreetly pointed at the woman. "Do you know her?"

"Of course, that's Greyson's girlfriend or significant other or current shack-up. It depends on what side of the argument you're on." He lowered his voice. "Sandra Collins is a very well-known decorator in Denver. I hear they met when she was redoing his latest restaurant and he had her redo the house to her specifications, then asked her to move in with him. It was quite the classy touch."

"So who's arguing?"

Dante adjusted his coat. "The family. Now that his share of the family money is up for grabs, they'd like her to go away quietly and not make a claim on what they see as their money."

"That's horrible." Cat wondered if people talked about her that way. After all, she inherited Michael's insurance as well as bank accounts and the house that became paid off at the time of his death. Michael liked his insurance. It was like he'd known he'd be the first to leave this mortal plane. Wow, sitting here in the funeral had her revisiting a lot of things in her head. Instead of wallowing in her thoughts, she needed to get Dante talking about Greyson again.

"So were you close to him?"

Dante's eyebrow went up just a tad. If Cat hadn't been watching for any reaction, she would have missed it. "You mean Greyson? Are you asking if he was family?"

"No," Cat answered too quickly. "Oh, no, was he?"

Dante chuckled. "Not everyone I know is part of the family."

"I know. That was silly of me to assume." Cat tried to backpedal. There was no way she wanted to get Dante mad.

"You have a right. And, Catherine, I would never lie to you."

Cat felt Shauna's knee bump and knew what her friend was saying. "Anyway, enough about me. How did you know Greyson?"

"I visited his restaurant several times. The man was a genius with food. I'd talked to him about investing in an expansion, but he said he had enough investors."

"Really? When was this?" The music was coming to an end and Cat knew she wouldn't have much more time to ask Dante anything.

"Just last week when I was here." Dante glanced at the flower-draped coffin at the front of the chapel. "Maybe he should have taken my offer."

Chapter Sixteen

"Are you going to tell Seth?" Shauna hurried to catch up with Cat, who had bolted out of the cathedral as soon as the service was over. She moved her into the line of people that was going away from the parking lot where most of the mourners were heading. The family had to drive to Denver for the second service that would be held at an even bigger church in the city. Cat hadn't even seen Jessica, the crowd had been so large.

Shauna pulled her over to the side and off the sidewalk under an oak, and when she looked around to see that they were alone, she asked again. "Are you going to tell Seth?"

"What are you talking about?" Cat wasn't sure what Dante had said that had gotten Shauna so worked up about Seth. Cat had been more concerned about Dante's implication at the end of their conversation. "You don't think he'd kill someone because he didn't go into business with him, do you?"

Shauna glanced around for a second time. "You don't?"

Cat took her friend's arm and they started walking toward home again. "I don't know what to think with him. I mean, he seems so reasonable. But he's like petting a sleeping tiger. You never know when he's going to wake up and bite your arm off."

"That's about as good of a description as I've heard. The guy is crazy hot, but there's just something dangerous underneath. You can smell it."

Cat laughed. "I think that's his cologne. Anyway, to answer your question, yes, I'm going to tell Seth. And Uncle Pete. If they want to blame anyone for sitting me down next to Dante, they can talk to Professor Turner. That guy has strong hands for such a little wimp."

"That's for sure. I saw you almost fly into Dante. Good thing the man is built." Shauna looked at Cat, who had stopped walking and was staring at her. "What, I have eyes. I'm not dead, you know. And yes, I remember he's trouble. But wow, just wow."

"I'll tell him you admire him the next time we bump into each other." Cat worried that there would be a next time, sooner than she wanted. "So did you get any vibes from any of the mourners? I couldn't really see a lot of people because of the stupid hat the woman in front of me was wearing."

"Mrs. Rice."

Cat jerked her head around and scanned the street. "Where? I've been successful in avoiding her since last month."

"No, silly. Mrs. Rice was the one with the hat. I thought you would have recognized her. She gave me such a dirty look when we first sat down because we giggled. Then she saw Professor Turner and it was all sunshine and light. You don't think our neighbor has a crush on the good professor, do you?"

"Weirder things have happened." They were walking past Mrs. Rice's house now but the woman was still at the church. "I wonder why she was at the memorial though."

"Oh, all the old-timers were there. I heard at the grocery store that her bridge club members were all going out to The Diner for lunch afterward." Shauna was peering around the barn to the back pasture. "I haven't seen Snow out grazing today. I hope she's not sick."

"Horse flu?" Cat didn't know how a horse could get sick.

Shauna shook her head. "Maybe I should rethink this trip to New York."

"Don't be like that. I can call a vet if I think she's not doing well." Cat wondered if she would know or not. "Besides, I'll have Seth check on her daily while you're gone. He's more the horse type."

"And you have an excuse for Seth to be over here when you have the house to yourself," Shauna teased.

"Actually, we probably need some couple time. I don't think we've been out on a real date for over a month." Cat wondered if this new issue with the money Seth borrowed from Greyson would make it even harder to get together. "But yeah, I'm on the same wavelength."

They walked up the driveway and entered through the back door. When they came into the kitchen,

Anne burst in from the hallway on the other side. "You need to come. I can't get her to stop crying."

Cat and Shauna rushed to follow Anne into the living room. "What happened?"

"We were at Reno's and someone brought her the house phone," Anne explained when Cat put a hand on her arm. "Anyway, he was on the line. He said he'd found her and he could always find her, so she might as well just come home."

Rick stood at the living room door looking furious. "If I could reach that guy, I'd beat him to a pulp."

"Don't say that. You have to be strong for Bren. Show her there are good people out there who don't use violence or harsh words with others." Anne put a hand on his forearm and even Cat saw the instant relaxation.

"You're right. How come you always know the right thing to say?" He took in Cat's and Shauna's appearance. "I'd forgotten you'd gone to the funeral. Did you figure out any new suspects?"

Cat pushed the mental image of Dante out of her head. There was no way he was involved in Greyson's murder. Maybe she should see if he had even been in town that weekend. Of course, that wouldn't mean anything. The guy had his own private plane.

"We better go talk to Bren. Maybe we can talk murder suspects later." Shauna pushed Cat past Rick and into the living room.

"Oh, I am so sorry. I knew why you were here. Please, go ahead." He swung an arm like he was Cat's new bellboy, inviting them to step into the parlor. "I hope you can get her to calm down."

A sobbing Bren sat on the sofa. Colleen sat on Bren's left and Anne moved around Cat and Shauna to join the women on the sofa.

Cat moved in front of her and sat on the coffee table to bring her face aligned with Bren's. "Hey, are you all right?"

Bren nodded, then shook her head. Then she nodded again. "I don't know. I know I shouldn't let him get to me. I just thought since I'd turned off my phone, the next time I talked to him I could be in control. In charge."

"And he ambushed you." Shauna took Bren's hand. "You're shivering. Did you get to eat anything?"

"Not much. Our food had just arrived when the waitress brought Bren the phone. I guess she didn't think it odd for a customer to get a call," Colleen explained.

"They wouldn't think it odd at all. We all know where our favorite eats are and when we like to go to lunch. I've tracked Cat down several times when I needed to ask her something."

"Usually it's to have me bring home sugar or some type of spice you'd forgotten." Cat smiled at her friend.

"She's pretty predictable," Shauna added. "I can usually track her down with less than two calls."

"I think he went into my bank account and saw where we were going to lunch." Bren grabbed a tissue. "I have to get this relationship over and done with so he won't be following me around in Chicago. I like living there. I don't want to have to move."

"You'll be fine." Anne patted her back. "If he

starts this, you'll just file a restraining order. He'll get the hint."

Cat didn't want to point out that sometimes a restraining order didn't stop a determined stalker. They'd had experience with that before here at the retreat. "Well, let us know if you need anything. You're safe here. Do you want me to call Uncle Pete and ask him to reach out to the Chicago Police Department to go tell him to knock it off?"

Bren snorted. "I think Chicago's force is a little too busy to deal with a little phone harassment."

"We do have a pretty high murder rate, especially if you add in the suburbs." Colleen nodded, agreeing with her friend. "I have a link on my computer where I can go see all the reports."

"Why on earth would you do that?" Anne looked at her friend in horror.

Colleen shrugged. "It's research. I hate writing about the same type of murder over and over. How many times can you shoot a guy without your readers getting bored?"

"But these are real life murders." Anne wasn't giving up on expressing her distaste for Colleen's habit.

"I think it's brilliant." Rick moved farther into the room. "Besides, you can watch who gets caught and who doesn't. That's why I like looking at cold cases. It's a great way to get new ideas for your books."

Cat smiled at Shauna and they moved their way out of the room. By the time they got into the foyer, the writers' discussion had taken off. Cat glanced back at the group. "Bren will be okay. She has the support of a lot of people who care about her."

"It's nice to see them bond together. I worry about her going back to move out of her house, though." Shauna picked up a water bottle that had been left on the desk.

"Me too. I'm going to give Uncle Pete a heads-up on this. Bren might be surprised at how helpful the law enforcement in her town can be, especially with a heads-up that there might be a problem." Cat glanced down at her dress. "I'm going upstairs and getting out of this. What about you?"

"I'm going to check tomorrow's treats and breakfast items, but I'm heading upstairs too."

They left each other at the bottom of the stairs. Cat decided to do a little Google investigating on the grieving girlfriend she'd seen at the service. She quickly changed into jeans and a T-shirt, then headed into her office to boot up her computer. Maybe the grief was staged and she'd been the one to kill Greyson in the bakery. Especially if she thought he was cheating on her with his sister-in-law.

When she keyed Sandra's name into the web search she was surprised at the number of hits the woman had. She'd been active in the Denver real estate and design world. She'd penned several articles that looked well researched and well written. The woman wasn't a showpiece. She knew her business. Had Greyson threatened that in some way?

Cat skimmed through the available articles, then happened on a picture of the home she'd shared with Greyson. The white columns made the front of the house look more like a southern plantation than a Denver house. The house was restored and located in one of Denver's more upscale neighborhoods, Cherry Creek.

Cat wrote down the address and then grabbed her notebook. She had just enough time before dinner to make a quick trip to the library. Hopefully the password Miss Applebome had given her earlier would also work on the state or Denver property records site.

When she got downstairs, Shauna wasn't in the kitchen, so she wrote a quick note on the white-board and headed to the college.

The first password she'd tried hadn't worked, so she'd had to track down Miss Applebome. She caught her with her large tote and purse heading out the door. She touched her arm to get her to stop.

"What, Ms. Latimer? What can you possibly want now?" Miss Applebome looked at her watch. "You have three minutes before I'm officially off the clock."

"What's the password for the Denver property records? I tried the one you gave me and it wouldn't work." Cat rushed the words out, hoping she was asking the right question because it looked like she'd only get one. "I need to look up who owns a house in the Cherry Creek neighborhood."

Miss Applebome stared at her. Finally, she pulled a notepad out of her purse and scribbled something on a page. "You're determined, that's for sure."

Cat took the page and stared at it. When she looked up, Miss Applebome was already out the first set of foyer doors. She held up the paper and called after her, "Thank you."

"Your uncle is going to kill me," the librarian said, and then she walked out the second set of doors and disappeared down the library's wide stone steps.

Cat watched her for a minute, considering her words. "No, you won't be the one in trouble, I will."

She turned and headed back to the computers where she'd left her tote and notebook. She got into the Denver city records on the first try and keyed the address into the search engine. It took so long for something to load, she wondered if she'd been kicked out for looking at a dead celebrity's home address.

But it came up, and to Cat's surprise, the house wasn't in Greyson's name.

Chapter Seventeen

Cat tucked the printouts into her tote and looked up a phone number. When she made the call, the receptionist assured her that Sandra herself would be positively thrilled to meet with her at eight a.m. the next morning.

Cat figured "thrilled" wasn't the actual emotion the woman would have, especially if she figured out that Cat wasn't there to schedule a remodel of the house. But at least she had a good excuse to meet with her since she had transformed her Victorian into the retreat. She'd have to get up early and she might miss out on the first part of Tammy's seminar, but it was worth it. She needed to know if Sandra had a motive to want her boyfriend dead, which would put Jessica in the clear.

Cat wasn't sure why she was trying so hard to clear her ex-friend, especially since they still hadn't talked about her telling her students that she'd helped Cat write her books. That was unforgivable.

And if Jessica had killed Greyson, well, that would be something for Uncle Pete to deal with.

Now she was heading home for dinner and a meeting with the writers. The group had fallen into a practice of running writing sprints for at least an hour before they went to dinner. Then after dinner, they gathered around the television and dissected movies. This group was fun to watch.

When Cat came through the back door, Shauna looked up from her laptop. "I'm working on the cookbook tonight, so it's pizza for dinner. Seth's picking up our usual order and it will be here in about twenty minutes."

"I'll check in with the writers and be right back." Cat moved through the room and thought she'd made it out without talking about where she'd been, until she heard Shauna's question.

"Tell me, what did you find?"

Cat turned around. "I'll tell you at dinner. I need to update Seth anyway due to the Dante sighting. We can brainstorm who killed Greyson over pizza."

"It's not funny. You're putting yourself out there and Pete doesn't have a clue who killed the guy or why. The killer might get wind of what you're doing." Shauna had turned around in her chair and was watching Cat now.

Cat came back to the table. "Look, I'm not doing anything that would put me in danger. And I'm being smart about it. Tomorrow I'm taking Seth to Denver. I'd bring you but you need to be here for the guests and breakfast."

"Why are you going to Denver?" Shauna didn't look convinced that Cat was doing anything smart.

"Because Greyson's girlfriend owns a decorating business and I wanted to get some ideas about the house/retreat."

Shauna turned back to her notebook and her laptop. "You want to see if she has an alibi for the night Greyson was murdered. You know your uncle can just ask her these questions."

"I know. But I feel like I owe this to Jessica. We were friends once. Good friends. Besides, the woman might just have some innovative ideas about the retreat." Cat paused at the door. "If we can afford her."

"Money's not the issue, but if she thinks you are trying to pin Greyson's murder on her, she may be unwilling to work with us." Shauna waved her out of the room. "Go play with our guests. I'm busy here."

Cat smiled as she left. Shauna may not have had the writing bug when they first met, but now that she'd found her calling in cookbooks, she was hooked. Cat would find her working on the recipes for days when the retreat wasn't in session. It was hard to leave a project sitting for a week and now Shauna knew how Cat felt during retreat weeks. Although lately, she'd begun to work during the sprint sessions in the evenings. She didn't like missing the one today. But her time at the library had been fruitful.

She paused at the living room door. The room was quiet except for the clicking of laptop keys.

Anne glanced up then at the clock. "Five minutes until break. Get past that next stopping point."

Rick groaned and, glancing at his notes, started

writing again. Bren, Colleen, and Molly were all head down, furiously keying in their stories.

Cat left them and went to grab a water bottle out of the dining room. While she was there, she adjusted some cookies from one basket to another, cleaned off the table, and refilled the drink refrigerator. Shauna would just have to add the evening treats and bring out a new carafe of coffee and hot chocolate after dinner.

She heard the timer go off and grabbed her water bottle and headed into the living room. "How's it going?"

"We're just reporting words." Anne stood by the flip chart and wrote 897 under her name. "This is our second session. We'll have one more thirty-minute sprint before we head into town for dinner."

"I'm at 732 words. But I feel like I'm going to have to trash all of them," Rick called out. "This plot is killing me."

"That's the problem, you're supposed to be killing the victim," Bren teased. "I'm at 550 but they were all really good words."

"No filler words like 'so's' in the bunch?" Colleen elbowed her friend. "I'm at 623. But I'm in the middle so I'm totally lost on if the words will stay or not."

Finally, Molly raised her hand.

Anne pointed at her. "You don't have to do that; I'm not a teacher. What's your count?"

"I think I must be doing something wrong." Molly looked down at the figure she'd written on her notebook.

"Why, honey?" Now Anne's voice was softer, less teasing.

"Because I'm kicking everyone's butt." Molly grinned and held up her notebook. "I've written 1,020 words. I win the round."

Laughter filled the room and the unease Cat had felt after going to the library lifted. Writers could do that for her. They made the load just a little lighter. "Well, there's still cookies in the dining room if you need some fuel for the last run."

"Sounds like a plan." Rick stood but looked over at Bren. "Can I bring you something?"

Bren pushed herself out of the couch. "I can get my own. Besides, you'll probably take the last chocolate chip and bring me a peanut butter one if I let you choose."

Unwrapping her legs from the chair where she'd curled up, Molly jumped up. "I'm getting a cookie too."

When Anne and Colleen were the last ones in the room, Cat sat on one of the chairs. "You guys need me for anything? Any questions?"

"We're good. Thanks for setting this retreat up. I know we probably take over the house more than you're used to, but we're having a blast." Colleen opened the water bottle next to her laptop and took a sip.

"And making some amazing strides on our projects. Even Bren with all the upheaval is finding comfort in focusing on the words and the story instead of things in her life she can't control." Anne spoke in a low voice, hoping her friend wouldn't hear her words.

"Writing does that. It takes you away for at least a little while. And your group has been amazing. All I offer is a place to stay and write, some food, and a few seminars to talk about writing. The magic is what you make it." Cat sipped her water considering what she'd just said.

"It is magic." Anne nodded. "But it's also work. And we have five minutes before the last sprint starts so I better grab some fuel and take a comfort break before they get back in here to write. Or else we'll just talk away our time."

"Wait for me." Colleen followed Anne out of the room.

Cat walked around and picked up plates and empty bottles and took them into the kitchen. She dropped the plates into the sink and the bottles into the recycling. Shauna was still writing. "I'm going to work in the study. Let me know when pizza is here."

A grunt from Shauna was all she got in reply, but that was enough. Cat left the kitchen and moved into the study where she opened her notebook and reviewed what she'd learned. She wrote out the questions she wanted to ask Sandra the next morning and thought she'd be able to just act like the nosy Aspen Hills resident who wanted the gossip.

She glanced out the window and saw Mrs. Rice's house ablaze with light. Maybe she should ask the town's authority on all things gossip what she knew. She had been at the funeral. Maybe she'd picked up something that Cat had missed.

Cat wrote down on tomorrow's to-do list: "visit

Mrs. Rice." Her stomach turned just thinking about it. The woman was a master at the art of guilt. Even though Cat had nothing to feel guilty about, the woman would make her feel like she should be visiting more often. Or maybe calling her mother more.

She sighed and looked at her notebook. Too many unanswered questions to leave any possible rock unturned. She'd have to go talk to Mrs. Rice.

She was still dealing with her unease when a knock came at the door. Seth stepped halfway into the opening and smiled at her.

"Pizza's here. Are you coming to the kitchen?"

Cat shut her notebook and, bringing it with her, left the large antique desk and met him at the doorway. She kissed him and then moved under his arm into the hallway. "I'm starving."

Friday morning, Cat turned her alarm off and squinted bleary-eyed at the clock. Why on earth had she set an alarm for five a.m.? She dragged herself upright, then remembered, the Denver trip. She hurried into the shower and quickly dressed in what she considered her "author costume," jeans and a cute tank. Then she threw on a corduroy jacket over the top. Checking her look in the mirror, she decided she looked upscale casual.

She headed out to the hall and moved down to Seth's room. She knocked, but there was no answer. Assuming he was in the shower, she decided to go downstairs for coffee. She'd call him in ten minutes to wake him up if he didn't surface by then.

The house was quiet and still as she made her way down the stairs. She'd always loved the way the house felt first thing in the morning. When she was a professor, she'd left early to hit the gym before anyone else was even awake. Then she'd come home and write until she had to leave for her first class. It had been a good life. One she sometimes missed. She sniffed the air as she came down the last few stairs. Coffee was brewing in the kitchen. Shauna must already be up and getting breakfast ready for the retreat guests.

Instead of finding Shauna at the stove, Cat saw Seth sitting at the country table, reading the paper and drinking coffee. He'd already showered and dressed in good jeans and a T-shirt that didn't have either a sports team or a smart aleck saying on the front. He looked surprisingly presentable. He glanced up as she walked into the room and his smile almost melted her on the spot.

"Good morning, Cat. Ready for our little adventure?" His eyes twinkled as he watched her move to the coffeepot.

"I'm surprisingly nervous. I know I've played a part before, but the more I think about it, I'm not sure this Sandra *wasn't* responsible for Greyson's death." She poured coffee, then grabbed a couple of cookies from the bowl Shauna kept on the cupboard.

"I'm starting to agree with you. I'm apparently friends on Facebook with this woman, probably because I was trying to get her to shoot some work my way if she ever did a decorating job in Aspen Hills. I have a lot of designers on my friends list, just in case." He winked at her. "Anyway, I went back on her feed, and from what I could decipher from her posts, she had a big fallout with her SO a few weeks before his death. She even said she wished he'd just disappear out of her life."

"That's the same time as he transferred the house to her name only. Maybe they were on their way to breaking up?" Cat bit into the peanut butter cookie and groaned. Shauna had the magic touch with desserts.

"But last week she was back to praising the guy and his attention to her." Seth grinned. "I guess giving her a mansion free and clear is one way to prove your love."

"You could try it with me someday," Cat teased. "I'm pretty sure it would increase your position on the boyfriend scale by at least a few points."

Seth glanced around the kitchen. "From where I sit, you already have your mansion. I'm going to have to be more creative."

Cat bit into the second cookie and sighed. "It is a good house. Even when Michael and I were house hunting, this was the only one I seriously had on my list."

"Yeah, there's that issue, but the house can't be blamed for it." Seth stood and filled a travel cup with coffee.

"It doesn't bother you when I talk about Michael, does it?" Cat studied his face to see if she could see a lie if it came. But she shouldn't have worried. Seth was as up-front as he'd always been with her.

"The only part of it that bothers me is that I let you go in the first place. If I'd been smart, Michael wouldn't have had a chance to sweep you off your feet because you would have had the Mrs. Howard title long before you met him." He held out the bowl of cookies. "Do you want one more for the road? We better get on the road if you want to be back for Tammy's seminar."

Cat didn't know if Seth had cut the conversation short because of the topic or the actual time, but she was glad he had. She wanted to be sensitive of his feelings, but sometimes, the story she was telling included Michael. It was a part of her history now and Seth needed to understand that. She stood and moved toward the bathroom off the laundry room. "Pour me a travel mug and fill a bag with those cookies. I'll be ready in a few minutes."

When they'd gotten in the SUV, Seth was quiet for a few minutes as he moved quickly through town and out to the highway. As they drove by Jessica's house, the boys were getting into Tyler's Land Rover. Jessica stared at Cat as if she could read her mind.

They were on the highway before Seth spoke. "Do you really think she has it in her to kill someone?"

Cat sighed and turned in the seat to meet his eyes. "The problem is, I just don't know. She's a different person than who I thought she was when we were friends."

"Can someone really change that much?"

Seth's question echoed in her head as Cat watched the scenery pass by as they drove through the edge of the national forest between Aspen Hills and Denver. Could Jessica have really changed—from the fun-loving peer who she used to sneak off campus with and grab an ice cream cone between classes—to a stone-cold killer?

Cat finally turned back to look at Seth. "Maybe some people hide their dark side from everyone for years."

Chapter Eighteen

Cat and Seth listened to music he'd downloaded for the trip. Some of the music brought back memories from their high school dating years. When one of her favorites from senior year came on, she grinned at him. "You made a good mix tape for the drive."

"I don't think they call it mix tapes anymore. It's a playlist." He tapped his fingers on the steering wheel. "But more important, it's the playlist of our relationship. There's a song in there from every year we dated. Including the last two, after you finally came to your senses and came running back to me."

"I'm not sure that's exactly how it happened, but you can live in your fantasy world." Cat sipped her coffee. "I didn't ask: did you find the receipts for Uncle Pete?"

"All neatly accounted for. There is no reason for me to be on the naughty list." He grimaced. "Although I think clearing my name put Nate on the suspect list."

"Wait, how is that possible?" Cat set her cup down and wiped off the lid where she'd spilled after Seth went over a pothole. "Nate seems like a nice guy."

"He's a great guy who tends to lose too much during the poker game. I swear if that guy lived in Vegas he'd be homeless by now. I paid Nate's rent for several months. That's how I paid back Greyson."

"So then Nate owed Greyson instead of you." Cat tried to put the scenario in her words so she could understand. "I'm not sure why he mixed up money like that. How would he remember who owed him what?"

"Greyson was crazy smart about money. He was always giving us investing tips when we played poker. I guess he kept a log or something to keep track of who owed him money." Seth tapped his fingers on the steering wheel as he drove. "I hated telling Pete that Nate owed Greyson money, not me. Nate couldn't hurt a fly, much less murder someone. Especially over money. He's not that type of guy."

Cat didn't want to point out that a lot of murderers were people whose friends and neighbors had no clue of their darker hobbies.

Seth laughed. "Although I think the only one less excited to hear about Nate's motive was your uncle. He flat-out told me that his suspects in this case were more like the cast of that summer TV show. You know the one that he talks to Shauna about all the time."

Cat couldn't think of what the name of the show was, but she knew what her uncle was saying. He was addicted to reality television, even the really, really bad shows. "He thinks that everyone who could have wanted Greyson dead is too nice or soft to have really killed the guy."

"That about sums it up. I hope we find the grieving girlfriend to be a hard-eyed chick who'd rather cut you than talk to you." He turned off the highway and onto a section of freeway that would take them downtown.

"I wouldn't describe a decorator as hard." Cat pulled out her notebook. "From what I learned about her on the Internet, she chaired her sorority charity event all four years in college. And she still donates a week's worth of her business's profit to the humane shelter every December."

"Maybe . . ." Seth stopped and shrugged. "Sorry, I've got nothing."

Cat put the notebook back in her tote. "Yeah, this is probably a total waste of time."

Seth turned off the freeway and drove down a surprisingly quiet downtown street. It even had available parking in front of the building that held Sandra's offices. "Well, didn't we just win a lottery. Maybe our visit will be as lucky."

"From your mouth to God's ears." Cat stared at the art deco building as she climbed out of the SUV. She grabbed some quarters out of her purse and fed the meter for two hours. "I don't think we'll need all that time, but just in case."

"Stop being such a worrier. I swear sometimes you're just looking for the sky to fall." Seth met her on the sidewalk and put his arm around her waist.

She paused at the doorway. "Maybe this is a bad idea."

Seth pulled her to the side to let another woman

pass through the doorway. "Why are you so hesitant? This isn't like you at all."

Cat stared inside the expansive lobby. It looked pricy and she felt totally out of her element. She was being silly. She had driven all this way and she was going to get the information she came for. She put her hands on her hips, spread her legs a little, and looked up into the sky. Then she started counting in her head.

"What on earth . . ." Seth paused, watching her. "Wait, I know what you're doing. The Superman pose that's supposed to make you more confident. Do you do this a lot?"

She saw him glance around to make sure no one was watching. She took a deep breath and kept counting in her head. "Before every signing, especially if I have to present in front of an audience. Now give me a minute so I can keep track of how long I've stood this way."

He stepped in front of her, blocking her from the people walking into the building. Cat saw him nod to a couple who appeared to be watching her closely. "Good morning. It's going to be an amazing day."

The man responded with a nod as he held open the door for his companion, but the woman gave Seth a cheery response. "Good morning."

Seth glanced at her over his shoulder. "Are you almost done? There's a ton of people walking down the sidewalk."

Cat took one last deep breath, then stepped beside Seth. "What? Was I embarrassing you?"

He held the door open and hurried her into the foyer. "I was just hoping they wouldn't ask if you were having a seizure or something. You have to admit, it looks a little odd."

"Odd is fine as long as I feel better about my next steps. And I do." She punched the up button on the elevator. The car must have been waiting at the bottom as the up light blinked, and after Cat and Seth entered the elevator a mechanical voice announced that they were going up. Cat pressed the top button and the car rushed upward to the fifth floor. When the doors opened, they stepped out directly into a waiting room where a woman sat behind a large reception desk.

As they walked up, the woman smiled so brightly Cat imagined that her teeth must have been bleached to gleam that way.

"I'm here to see Sandra Collins," Cat announced, making her voice as perky as she knew the receptionist's answering tone would be.

Instead, the woman's voice was deep like dark chocolate. "You must be Catherine Latimer. Sandra's expecting you. I'll just buzz Chi Chi, her assistant, to escort you back. Can I get you some coffee while you wait?"

"Water would be lovely. I'm about coffee'd out." Cat downgraded the perky tone in her voice as she turned to Seth. "Do you want something?"

"Thanks, Kathi," he said, looking at the receptionist's nameplate. "A Coke if you have one. Otherwise, black coffee will do just fine."

"Perfect. I'll buzz Chi Chi and then go get your refreshments. I'll bring them to the meeting room so you don't have to carry them." Kathi pushed a button on her switchboard.

Cat and Seth went over to one of the white

couches to sit. She looked at the white rugs under all of the furniture and over the walnut flooring. "I wouldn't want to carry a cup of coffee over all this white."

"I'm not touching that one at all. Why you set me up for all these zingers, I don't understand." Seth picked up a copy of *Modern Western Living* and started flipping through the pages.

"It doesn't hurt anyone to be a little self-deprecating at times." Cat leaned in and looked at the magazine too. She dropped her hand and stopped his flipping. She pointed to a flower garden. "Wouldn't that look great outside the barn?"

Seth studied the layout. "Actually, that's almost what I was planning to do with Shauna's herb garden I'm making her on the left side of the barn door. I'm making a small water pond on the other side of the door and I'm using an old water faucet I found at an antique shop. That way the cats will have a place to go wash up before dinner."

"I don't think they actually use water to wash. . . ." Cat saw the way Seth wasn't looking at her and realized he was teasing. She slapped his arm. "You are in so much trouble."

A tall woman wearing heels that made her look even taller approached and paused in front of them. She appeared to be of Asian descent. Seth set the magazine down and they stood.

"Chi Chi Newby; if you would both follow me, I'll take you back to Ms. Collins. She's set up in the meeting room. I guess your call must have tweaked her interest because she already has some ideas sketched out for you to see."

They wove through hallways and finally stopped

at a glassed-in meeting room. Inside was the woman Cat had seen at the funeral. When they entered the room, Sandra stood and glided toward them, holding out her hand to welcome them.

"Catherine Latimer, I'm so glad to meet you. Dante told me you were at the funeral but we had to rush off to Denver for the second event. Such a sad day." She shook Cat's hand, then turned to Seth. "I'm sorry. I don't know your name."

"Seth Howard. I'm the local handyman in Aspen Hills. Cat has hired me as the main contractor for any work done on the retreat." Seth took her hand in his and gently shook it. "I have to say even though I wasn't able to be at the funeral, I'm so sorry for your loss."

"You are too kind. Would you both have a seat. Your drinks have already arrived." Sandra stepped back to her spot in front of a large coffee cup and a silver carafe. "Catherine, if you change your mind about coffee, I had them bring an extra cup."

"It's Cat, please. And I'm fine with water." Cat sat in the chair where the water had been set, which was across the table from Sandra. She wondered why Dante had felt a need to mention her attendance at the funeral but thought it best to get off that subject sooner than later. "So you and Greyson were a couple? I don't think I knew that."

"We were keeping it on the down-low. Greyson was a very private man." She turned and studied Seth. "I know where I've heard your name."

Seth nodded, a wide smile settling on his face. "Great. I sent you a letter when I opened my business hoping we could work together."

Sandra waved the idea away. "No, it wasn't that.

You played cards with Greyson. The man did love to play poker."

Seth smiled, but Cat could see the flash of hurt in his eyes. All the work he'd done to reach out had been treated like junk mail. "Guilty as charged."

Cat wanted to reach out but she thought better of the action. The less this woman knew about them, the better. "It was horrible, what happened to Greyson. Were you in town with him? I can't even imagine how you felt."

"No, I was coming back from a weekend in Cabo with a few friends. You can imagine my shock when I got to the house and found a message from the police. I mean, I'm not sure I even said good-bye to him when I left Friday morning. He was still asleep. He and I had such different sleep schedules, I didn't want to bother him." She smiled but the sadness showed through the memory. "He always called me a lark because I'd be up at six and he had just gotten into bed a few hours before."

"I am so sorry. That must have been horrible." Cat didn't even dare to breathe. The woman was telling her everything she wanted to know, without her even throwing out a question. Alibi, check—but did she have motive to hire out the deed? "It sounds like you had a perfect life together."

Now Sandra did laugh, but the sound was harsh. "Perfect? Not by a long shot. Let's just say Greyson hadn't gotten used to the whole monogamy thing. Anyway, I'm sure you don't want to hear my sad story about my boyfriend's trysts. You're here to talk about the retreat."

Cat nodded, but this time she did look at Seth as Sandra pulled out a sketchbook and turned it toward Cat and Seth. There, on the first page, was a pencil drawing of Cat's house.

"I got so excited when I got your call. I've seen your home. Greyson and I drove through Aspen Hills on our way to his brother's a few months ago. I made him stop and let me snap some pictures. I was planning to reach out to you about doing some work. It's really a lovely building and you've kept it historically accurate, at least on the outside." She pointed to the gingerbread at the top of the gables.

"That's been mostly recreated by Seth." Cat beamed at him, glad to have a chance to brag on his work. "He spent a lot of time at the Aspen Hills Historical Society section in the library looking for old pictures so he could recreate the look as the building was originally. When I bought it, someone had torn the original front eaves down and put up gutters."

"Oh, no." The look of shock on Sandra's face was real. She cared about her buildings, that was for sure. "Anyway, you've done a lovely job with the outside. I had some ideas to make it more welcoming for guests and even drew up a small commercial sign. Does the house have a name?"

When both Cat and Seth shrugged, Sandra went on. "I'm sure it does, especially with its history of being part of the college for so many years. I'll keep digging for that."

As she made a note, Cat leaned back. "I'm friends with Tyler and Jessica. Or I was before my divorce. You know how those things go; you tend to lose track of the other couples who were your marriage friends. How are they doing? I attended the funeral but didn't want to intrude on their grief."

"Grief? Maybe for the ongoing income Greyson brought in. I think Tyler was just happy that the thing between Greyson and Jessica was finally over. Even though one of them had to die to get there."

"You think Greyson and Jessica were having an affair?" Cat leaned forward, watching her.

"I know they were. At least they were before me. I can't be sure he stopped it when he said he did, but you have to trust the person you're with, right? Although he did go to Aspen Hills for those stupid poker games once a month." Sandra shook her head. "Sorry, I'm running my mouth without thinking. Let's get back to my plans for your house."

Sandra walked them through the changes she thought she could make and then, at the end of the presentation, handed Cat copies of the drawings in a folder. "It's all in there. What we discussed, very general estimates of costs and time frames. I know you host a monthly retreat, but I think we could get it done in between sessions. Especially if you have some pieces now we could use in the new design. Think it over and call me when you want me to tour the house. Then I could give you a more complete bid, including a final budget and time frames."

"Thank you so much for your time." Cat stood and held out a hand. "And again, I'm so sorry for your loss."

"Thank you." Sandra turned toward Seth. "Do you have a card I could have? I have another project coming up in the Aspen Hills area and would love to have you bid some work for me."

"Of course." Seth smoothly took a business card out of the top pocket of his shirt. Cat realized he must have come prepared, hoping the fact-finding meeting might give him a chance to leave his contact information.

They didn't talk until they were back out in the car. Seth started the car and pulled out onto the still empty street. "Well, what did you think? She has an alibi for Greyson's death."

"Yeah, but she really hated Jessica. Flames almost shot out of her eyes when I mentioned her name. And she doesn't like Tyler much either."

"Sometimes the girlfriend is more of an outsider to the family and can see the family drama clearer than those involved." Seth glanced at the clock. "Do you want something for breakfast besides the cookies you ate earlier? We have time to hit a drive-thru on our way back."

"Sure." Cat opened the folder and stared at the drawings of her house. Sandra had even put up a small yard sign with a blank spot for the name. Did the house have a name? She'd never even considered looking for that when she did the research. It would be nice if it was called something like Covington House or maybe Alexander House, that sounded really cool. Who had been the first dean who'd lived there? She'd have to do some research. Even if she didn't have the money to hire Sandra for the redesign, she thought she might just do the sign thing.

"Earth to Cat. What do you want to eat?"

Cat turned to Seth and realized they were already in line at the drive-thru. She glanced over the menu board and ordered. When they'd gotten their food, Seth pulled into a parking spot and shut off the engine. She sipped her orange juice and watched him. "I figured you'd just keep driving."

"We have some time." He unwrapped a breakfast burrito. "Besides, we haven't had a date for a while. I thought I'd take advantage of the opportunity for us to spend some time alone. So just to be clear, date night this week has been checked off."

"I'll give you this one. We don't get much alone time, especially when the retreat's in house." Cat watched him eat as she picked at her finger-sized hash browns. "We're okay, right? I mean, if you were having an affair with my sister, I'd know, right?"

"Do you have a sister?" He sipped on his coffee and turned her way. "How hot is she?"

"She's not hot at all. Besides, I don't have a sister." She slapped his arm. "Why can't you be serious for a minute?"

"You're the one tempting me with some unknown sister." He set his coffee down and turned the music down on the stereo. "But yeah, I think you'd know. You're talking about Sandra, right? She said she thought Greyson had ended it when they started dating."

Cat picked up her sandwich and arranged the English muffin so it was straight. Before taking a bite, she looked at Seth and shook her head. "I'm talking about Tyler."

Chapter Nineteen

Shauna was in the kitchen working on her laptop when Cat and Seth got back to the house. "I was beginning to wonder if you two took the day off for a little impromptu Denver date." She studied their faces. "Uh oh, what's wrong?"

Cat started to pour herself another coffee, then thought better of it. She went to the fridge and instead, poured a glass of the fruit-infused water Shauna had begun to keep on hand. Today, apple slices and mint floated in the pitcher. "We were just talking about the case."

"You think the girlfriend did it? You know that's an easy assumption and not always true." Shauna had been the victim of a similar assumption just a few months ago.

Seth grabbed a soda and shut the refrigerator door after Cat put the water pitcher back. "Actually, no. We went to talk to her. She might not be surprised that Greyson's dead, but she is visibly upset about it. She said that he had been having an affair with Jessica before they got together."

"Which Jessica denies, right?" Shauna closed the laptop. "I'm sure glad I'm not Pete. This investigation is a lot about he said, she said, and not a lot of facts."

"Well, I was thinking, maybe Tyler knew about the affair too." Cat watched Shauna's face. "Do you think he could have killed his brother over this?"

"I think it's a theory. Brothers have been known to kill each other. It's even a biblical story." Shauna glanced at her watch. "Pete's coming over for dinner. He called earlier to talk to you but I didn't mention where you two had gotten off to."

Seth grinned. "Just taking my girl to see the big city. And she even said it counted as date night. Besides, I might have gotten a job out of the trip."

Cat pushed the folder over to Shauna. "Check out her ideas. If you think we need to upgrade the decor, she might be the one we should look into hiring. She seemed to get the idea of the house-slash-retreat nature of the place."

Shauna patted the folder. "I'll look at this later. Tammy should be here any minute. Do you want me to help her get set up?"

"No, I'll do that. You probably still have to refresh the dining room after breakfast. This group likes their treats." Cat started toward the kitchen door to make sure the living room was ready.

"Hey, I almost forgot. Nate stopped by this morning. He was upset but he didn't say why." Shauna watched as Seth and Cat made eye contact. "Okay, you two, tell me what's going on?"

"It's my fault. When I took my receipts to Pete showing him I didn't owe Greyson a dime, there was one payment I made to Nate for Greyson." Seth cracked open his soda and took a gulp. "Now, it looks like Nate had motive and not me."

"Way to pass the buck, dude." Shauna shook her head. "I guess that could have been what had him troubled. He didn't say."

"I probably better call him and see what he wanted." Seth followed Cat out of the kitchen. "I'm going to use the study if that's okay. Then I want to get working on those flower beds we talked about."

"Let me know what he says." Cat put her hand on Seth's arm, stopping his movement. Then she kissed him. "Thank you for the lovely date."

"I do know how to woo a lady. Business meeting and a drive-in breakfast." He ran a finger down her cheek. "I'm serious about us getting out of here for a week. Have you thought about timing?"

"It can't be next week. Shauna's heading to New York to meet up with her brother. What about when she gets back? I'm still not committed to any new books, so it's a good time for the writing, and we'd still be two weeks away from the next retreat." Cat thought about her upcoming calendar as she talked. "Do you want me to make reservations? And where?"

"Let me handle it. I've got some money put aside for these types of situations." He grinned. "I'm thinking warm and sandy though. So don't forget to pack that yellow bikini."

"Sounds great." Cat left him and walked into the living room where she set up the table that Tammy liked to display and sell books from, as well as the podium and a flip chart, just in case. By the time she heard someone call out from the foyer, the room was clean and ready for the session.

"Cat, are you around?" Tammy was standing in the middle of the foyer, a book cart by her side filled with boxes. When she saw Cat come into the foyer, she dropped her shoulders and a sigh of relief escaped from her lips. "Oh, good. I was afraid I'd written down the wrong date."

"Nope, we're expecting you. I have you set up in the living room, as usual. Do you want some coffee or some water? Maybe a cookie or brownie? I'm not sure what decadent treats Shauna put out for today. Since the retreat's ending soon, she tends to go all out the last few days." Cat approached the woman slowly. For some reason, the bookseller seemed as timid as a field mouse. At times, in her store, she seemed normal, but whenever Cat saw her out and about, she tended to withdraw into the brown dresses she liked to wear that seemed to match her long loose hair and even her eye color. The woman would disappear in front of a brown wall. "Let me help you with your boxes."

"Oh, you don't have to do that." Tammy grabbed the handle of the cart possessively. "It's really heavy, you know, with books."

"Well, if you won't let me help you, I'll get you some coffee and some treats." Cat smiled. "Any favorites you want me to nab before the writers get down here?"

"I do love Shauna's brownies. They are so much better than the ones at the bakery." Tammy's eyes widened. "But don't tell Dee Dee I said that. She's a little touchy about Shauna's mad baking skills. I think she's afraid Shauna's going to open a competing bakery. I told her that was silly. Shauna has her hands full with the retreat. But you can't tell some people anything they don't already know."

"You and Dee Dee are friends?" Cat guessed she shouldn't have been surprised. The women had shops on the same block. But the two were like night and day in personality.

Tammy smiled. "I'd like to think so. I mean, she talks to me about her boyfriend and I listen. I guess I listen a lot. She really has issues with that guy."

"Oh, who is she seeing?" Cat tried to keep the question conversational, but this was the first time she'd ever heard of Dee Dee being nice to anyone, let alone being in a relationship.

"I probably shouldn't say, but you know him. It's Nate from the health department?" Tammy adjusted her tote on her shoulder, her face staining red. "I told Dee Dee that it was a total conflict of interest, but she said they never talked about work when they were together. You know what she means, right?"

"I get it." Cat tried to put Tammy at ease. She guessed that talking about sex wasn't something the woman did all the time. "I work with my boyfriend so I know sometimes the lines can be a little wavy. I don't know how Dee Dee kept the professional out of their lives."

"They were always breaking up. He'd say something that made her mad and next thing I knew, he was a 'turd.' But then the next time we'd talk, they'd be back together again." Tammy shook her head. "I'm waiting for someone who really loves me. Someone who will see me for the treasure I am."

"That's good."

Tammy glanced at the clock. "I need to get set up."

Cat watched as Tammy hauled the heavy cart into the living room. She was going to have to have Seth watch for the woman and offer to bring the boxes inside. No one would turn down help from good-looking Seth.

After getting Tammy settled, Cat went into the study. Seth must have already called Nate and left, because it was empty. She pulled out her notebook and, looking at the mess she'd made over the last few days, went to a clean sheet and wrote Greyson's name in the middle. Then she wrote all the names that she'd known about that had been in his universe. When she got to the poker game, she wrote down Seth and Nate and a question mark. Maybe there was someone else that owed the man money. She wrote down her question, then went to Jessica. Here she wrote a ton of questions. Why was she calling Greyson daily? Why would Sandra think she was having an affair? And if she was, did Tyler know?

She wrote Tyler's name on the sheet too, but she didn't feel it. The guy had been devastated when Cat had dropped off the basket of muffins.

Then she wrote Sandra's name. She sat back in her chair and thought about the meeting that morning. The woman had seemed genuinely affected by Greyson's death. Yet, she took on a new project the day after the memorial? *How would I react if something happened to Seth?* Could she pour herself into work or would she be staring into a television screen not watching the movies that played and thinking about their time together?

"People respond to grief differently," she said aloud.

"Yes, they do." Seth stood in the doorway. "I didn't mean to startle you but Shauna wanted me to come get you for lunch. Are you thinking about Greyson and Sandra?"

"Her, and everyone else who touched the guy's life. I didn't think it was that late. Tammy must have already left." She glanced down at the page and quickly scribbled Dee Dee before closing the notebook. "I guess there's a reason Uncle Pete's the professional in these matters and not me. All I keep doing is running in circles."

"I helped Tammy out to her van about thirty minutes ago. You've been in here for a while. And don't sell yourself short. You have good instincts. That's why Pete lets you play with these things. I think he appreciates having someone else he can bounce things off." He held a hand out and wiggled his fingers. "Come on, Nancy Drew, let's eat and talk about something else."

Cat stood from the desk and crossed the room, taking his hand. "Like your conversation with Nate? Did you know he was seeing Dee Dee?"

Seth laughed. "I think 'seeing' is a pretty broad term. He and Dee Dee had a few nights together after too many beers at Bernie's, but I doubt Nate thinks of it as a relationship. I suppose Tammy told you this?"

"Yeah, I guess she's Dee Dee's sounding board. And the woman is worried that Shauna is opening a competing bakery," Cat said as they entered the kitchen.

Shauna looked back at them from her position at the stove. "There is no way in the world I'd open a bakery. Do you know what time I'd have to get up? Not just one week a month, but every freaking day? Who's spreading such a vicious lie?"

"Dee Dee." Cat took in the smell of clam chowder and fresh baked bread bowls. "Yum. I didn't think I was even hungry until I walked in the room."

"That's why I love making soups in the fall. They fill the kitchen with warm, lovely smells." Shauna finished the last bowl and set it on the table. "Dee Dee has some trust issues. I think she's always waiting for the other shoe to drop. And if there's not drama going on, the girl will make some happen."

"Shauna and I made plans for the herb garden in front of the barn this morning while you were locked in the study." Seth grabbed a notebook and handed it to Cat. "Check this out."

"I drew the barn, so don't make fun of my artistic skills." Shauna sat and started eating. "But I think it will be lovely come spring. And if we get it set up now, I play with what I want to plant all winter."

They talked about the new garden and the upcoming change in weather. "I'm hoping next month stays warm, because if not, your writers are going to freeze on our hike." Seth glanced at the calendar. "We should still have good weather that week, but any later and we'd be pushing it."

"Let's sit down sometime soon and plan out next year's extra day's events and get the retreats on the calendar. That way we know what we're looking at so we can plan some vacations if we want." Cat looked pointedly at Shauna. "You did make your airline reservations, right?"

"I did, and I'll be riding with Seth when he takes the guests to the airport on Sunday. You'll just need to remember to come get me next Sunday." Shauna nodded to the house calendar on the counter. "I've put all my travel arrangements in there, in case you need to get a hold of me."

They finished lunch and Cat went out to the living room to clean up after Tammy's seminar. Rick sat in a wingback chair, a notebook on his lap. He was staring out the window that looked out onto the backyard.

"Sorry, I didn't realize you all were back from lunch." Cat hurried around the room, picking up cups and dishes.

"I didn't go with the group. I had some things on my mind." He closed the notebook. "Why do women always fall for the wrong guy?"

Uh oh. Cat set the tray down and sat on the chair next to him. "Trouble in paradise?"

"No. Just me being silly. I should have known I wasn't her type." He smiled but his eyes didn't match the emotion.

"Don't tell me that Bren's talking to her old boyfriend."

"He sent her roses this morning," Rick spat out. "Like a few flowers would make up for how controlling and possessive he's been this week."

"Bren's a smart woman. She can see through the smoke screen, I'm sure." Cat patted Rick's arm. "Have you told her how you feel?"

He sank back into the chair. "No. I thought it

might be better to wait until we get back and she's clear of the guy. I don't want her to think I'm poaching."

"If you like her, you need to tell her," Cat pressed. "She needs to know there's other fish in the sea."

"But what if she doesn't feel the same way about me?"

Cat could hear the fear in his voice. "Then you'll know and you can go on and just be her friend. She needs friends now more than ever."

"You're right. I can't believe I'm being such a jerk about this." He stood. "I'm running into town and grabbing a burger. Thanks for talking that out with me. I needed to hear another side."

Cat watched as he walked out of the room. She wouldn't say he had a spring in his step, but she thought he might actually talk to Bren now about his feelings. She sank back into her chair. "People are exhausting."

She finished cleaning up and took the dishes into the kitchen. No one was there so she checked the dishwasher to see if it had been run. Only lunch dishes were inside, so she spent a few minutes rinsing off the new additions. Doing dishes had always given her time to think, especially back in the day when she was teaching full time.

After she finished, she hurried upstairs and opened her word-processing program. She wanted to get more of this idea for a new book down before it totally disappeared.

A knock on the door brought her back to reality and Cat realized she'd written over five thousand words in one setting. She saved the document and made a note to read it tomorrow if she had time before the final dinner. Tonight, after dinner, they'd talk through what worked and what hadn't at this week's retreat. She might not be able to solve Greyson's murder, but she did a great job managing the retreat.

"Come in," she called out. Expecting Shauna, she was surprised when Uncle Pete came into the office and sat on her couch. "What are you doing?"

"Hiding from life. I know you don't want to hear this, but chucking it all and moving to Alaska is looking better and better." He picked up Cat's latest book and held it up. "This one was really good."

"You're reading young adult?" Cat couldn't hide her surprise.

He sat the book down. "You're my niece; of course I'm reading your books. I just hope you don't start writing that sexy stuff. I'll have to hide it from the guys at the station if you write that."

"I don't have plans to publish erotica, so I think you're safe." She crossed the room and sat next to him. "What's going on?"

"Everyone wants to know who killed this guy and I'm about to change my standard answer to 'who wouldn't have wanted to kill him?' Man, the guy was a tool. He loved having people under his thumb." Her uncle ran a hand through his hair.

"Power corrupts. Seth told me about Nate."

Uncle Pete sighed. "Unfortunately, Nate and Seth were small potatoes in this guy's game. He seemed to have his fingers in a lot of pies." He looked at her. "Including some he didn't own. Have you talked to your friend lately?"

"Jessica?" Cat shook her head. "Not since she came and tried to get me to have you back off. Are you serious about her being a suspect?"

Uncle Pete didn't answer for a long minute. "Can you talk to her? I want to give her the benefit of the doubt, but someone who would sleep with her husband's brother might not be concerned about a little murder to cover up the indiscretion."

"I'll talk to her. Sandra Collins seems to think the affair was already over."

Uncle Pete patted her leg and stood. "We better get downstairs or Shauna will come looking for us. I'm not surprised you talked to Sandra, but I'm not sure I buy what the woman is selling."

Chapter Twenty

After dinner, Cat glanced at the clock. She had thirty minutes before she was expected in the living room. Uncle Pete had already left and she and Seth were cleaning off the table. "Hey, do you want to go for a walk with me?"

"A walk?" He looked at the clock. "Don't you have a thing?"

"A meeting, a gathering, a seminar . . . you can call it a lot of different names. But I have thirty minutes."

He narrowed his eyes. "This is an investigation kind of walk, isn't it?"

"I want to see if I can talk to Jessica, so yeah, I might need you to wait for me for a few minutes." She put the last plate in the dishwasher and, after adding soap, closed the door and started the machine. "But don't go too far; I'm not saying I trust her completely."

"I'd love to come to your rescue. I haven't played knight in shining armor for a long time." He put the salt and pepper away and then opened the back door. "After you."

Cat wrote a note for Shauna and followed Seth out the door. As they walked by Mrs. Rice's house, her neighbor was down on her knees weeding the front flower garden in the evening cool.

Cat pulled on Seth's arm and walked faster, hoping the woman wouldn't see them. When they turned the corner, she slowed down, let go, and took a deep breath. "That was close."

"You don't have to run from her, you know." Seth looked down on her in amusement. "There is a phrase you can use. It's new, so I don't expect you've heard it much. It goes something like this: 'Sorry, but we don't have time to talk.'"

"Believe me, I've tried cutting her short. If she has something to tell you, nothing's going to stop her." Cat glanced up the street where Jessica was sitting on the front porch, watching her boys ride their bikes in the driveway. "She's out front. Can you walk around the block and I'll see if she'll talk to me?"

"She's probably already seen me."

Cat nodded. "I know, but it might feel awkward to have you standing out by the mailbox while we talk. I'll be fine. The fact she has seen you protects me."

"What, you think she'd kill you on her front porch? That's not very discreet." Seth squeezed her hand and laughed at the look Cat gave him. "Okay, I'm walking. Just don't forget about your meeting in a few minutes."

"You make one lap around the block and I should be ready. I'm not wasting time on this. Either she wants to talk to me or she can just talk to Uncle Pete and I'm out of it."

Seth walked past the house when Cat turned to cross the street. She thought she heard him murmuring, "promises, promises . . ." but she couldn't tell. She looked up at Jessica and took a deep breath.

When she got to the porch steps, Jessica patted the swing next to her. "Go ahead and sit down. I figured you'd be here sooner or later."

"We have some things to talk about." Cat sorted through all the things she wanted to tell her old friend but pushed away the ones that were just hurtful. They could be dealt with later. Once this murder thing was cleared up. She shook her head. Now Seth had her calling everything a "thing."

"Between us or this whole ugly Greyson problem?"

Cat was surprised that Jessica realized there were issues between them. "Let's start with Greyson's murder. I'm going to ask you again, were you sleeping with him?"

Jessica's face showed shock and her first glance was toward the boys to make sure they were out of earshot. "Lower your voice. I don't want my kids to hear that ugly rumor."

Cat leaned back on the swing and watched her. "Well?"

"No, I wasn't having an affair. Not with Greyson, not with anyone. I love Tyler. I have since the day we met." Jessica smiled a little as she obviously was remembering a better time. "But Greyson and I were friends. That's all."

"So why were you calling him daily before he

died?" Cat might as well get all the cards on the table.

Jessica shook her head, sadly. "We were planning Tyler's surprise birthday party. The guy turns forty next month. Can you believe it? We're all getting older, but forty? Greyson wanted it to be a huge bash. He had rented the Covington Common Hall for the party and there just seemed to be detail after detail."

"A birthday party?"

Jessica rubbed her neck. "That's why Greyson was here that night. He and I met at the hall to make sure it was big enough. Do you know how many people he had on the guest list? Not just Aspen Hills's mayor, but Denver's mayor and the freaking governor were invited. Greyson wanted Tyler to know how much he was appreciated and loved. I just wanted an intimate, fun party."

"Sandra said she thought you and Greyson had something going before she came on the scene," Cat prodded, not willing to give up the idea.

This time Jessica did laugh. "Sandra hated Greyson's family, and that included me. Anyone who took the limelight away from her was suspect in her mind. I hear she accused him of sleeping with his sous-chef last month."

"Was he?" Cat didn't know if Greyson had been a player, but if he had, then there might be more people on the suspect list than she thought.

"No. The guy was as faithful as the day was long. He told me once when we were planning the party that he thought Sandra was finally the one. I wasn't so sure. She can be a bit of a handful." Jessica glanced at her watch. "I've got to get the boys in and get baths started. Are we done? Are you convinced I didn't kill Greyson in a fit of jealous rage? You know me."

"Do I?" Cat stared her down. "The woman I knew wouldn't have told people she wrote my book for me."

"And the true issue finally comes out." Jessica put up her hands. "Yes, I said something catty like that. Why? I don't know. Maybe I was jealous. Maybe I was hurt. You didn't just leave Michael when you moved away. You left me. You didn't even tell me you were moving until the day you turned in your resignation."

Cat could see the pain in Jessica's face. "I didn't think . . ."

"Exactly. I know you were in a bad spot and I figured you'd reach out sooner or later, but, Cat, you never did." Jessica stood and wiped the tears off her cheeks. "I've got to take care of my family."

Cat watched as she stood on the top step and called for the boys. Then Jessica stepped down and met her kids on the way to the garage. Their gazes met, and for a second, Cat could see the devastation in Jessica's eyes.

She walked to the sidewalk where Seth waited for her.

"Did you get what you needed?" He put his arm around her shoulders as they walked home.

Cat didn't respond for a few steps. Then she nodded. "More than what I needed. And probably less than I deserved."

The confused look on Seth's face didn't go unnoticed, but Cat didn't want to explain. Seth must have felt her need for quiet because instead of responding, he gave her a squeeze, then let her go.

They walked together like that in silence, crossing the road. The house was in sight when Cat heard the sound of the cat meowing in the fenced yard next to her.

Mrs. Rice stood, watching her. "Are you okay? You look like you've had a bit of a scare."

"I'm fine, Mrs. Rice." Cat pasted on a smile. No need for the town gossip to get the news about her fighting with Jessica any faster than the phone tree would bring it. "Are you planting more bulbs?"

The woman laughed and took off her gardening gloves. "Guilty as charged. I do love a good row of tulips in the spring. The flowers feel like God's way of welcoming the change of seasons. I only hope I'm alive to see them blossom."

"Mrs. Rice, you're probably going to outlive all of us." Seth responded with the answer Mrs. Rice had been fishing for.

"Well, thank you, Seth, but even all that money didn't keep Greyson Finn alive now, did it?" She narrowed her eyes. "I don't want to say he deserved to be killed, but the way he went through women, I wouldn't be surprised to find out it was a tossed away lover. The man was a cad."

In for a penny, Cat thought. "Oh, really? I thought he was dating a decorator out of Denver. Don't tell me he had something on the side."

Mrs. Rice's eyes gleamed. "Not just one. I've heard he had several women on the string. One in each town between here and Denver. I can't believe how women will let themselves be used that way."

"No. That's horrible. Sandra's a nice person. I just met her today." Cat let outrage show on her face, even if it was really focused on the gossip going around about a man who couldn't defend himself.

"And what he saw in Dee Dee, I have no idea. It's not like the woman is even pretty." Mrs. Rice leaned down to pet her cat. Then she straightened and stepped out of the grass onto the walkway, the cat following her. "Yes, Mr. Peeps, it is time for your dinner. It was nice to talk to you youngsters."

"Wait, Mrs. Rice," Cat called out as the woman moved toward her walkway. "Why do you think Dee Dee was involved with Greyson?"

She turned and stared at Cat like the question was ludicrous. "Because she told me they were dating one day when I went into the bakery for some cookies for my bridge game."

Cat and Seth started walking toward the house. "Dee Dee was dating both Nate and Greyson?"

"I'm beginning to wonder if it's all a fairy tale." Seth shrugged. "Although looking at Sandra, I'm not sure the baker was Greyson's type."

"Sometimes men like variety, but yeah, I'm beginning to wonder if the gossip was just for show. From what I read about him, the guy did like the bachelor chef image." Cat opened the kitchen door and was surprised that Shauna wasn't hanging around. "I wonder if she went out to talk to Snow and the kittens."

"I can check if you're worried." Seth put a hand on the doorknob.

"Don't you have a game to watch tonight?" Cat shook her head. "Let her be. Just because I'm a mother hen about her lately doesn't mean you have to be."

"Okay then, you don't have to tell me twice." He grabbed a package of microwave popcorn out of the cupboard. "If you want to join me after you meet with the writers, I'll leave the door unlocked."

"I'm thinking I'll draw a hot bath and get some reading done." She smiled. "Go, team."

He called after her, "You don't even know what team I'm rooting for."

And that was the way she liked it, she thought as she made her way to the living room. She heard talking in the dining room, so she turned right and found the group filling plates with after dinner treats.

"You know I'm going to have to go on a diet as soon as I go home." Anne smiled at her. "I bet I've gained ten pounds this week."

"I'm going to have to give up sugar, again. Detox, here I come." Colleen took a bite of a brownie. "But it's been worth it."

"The college food service isn't even half this good." Molly held a cookie under her nose. "I might just have to come begging for treats during finals week."

"At least you're within walking distance." Colleen shook her head. "Maybe I have some extra miles I can use to come to the retreat and sneak food home every month."

"Okay, so you all like the food. Grab your plates and something to drink and let's go talk about the rest of the retreat. I'd like to know how you all did with word counts and other projects." Cat put two brownies on her plate and filled a cup with coffee. She promised herself it would be her last cup, but she knew she'd probably break that promise, especially if the session went long into the night. But it was worth it. Having these debriefing sessions gave her ideas on how to adjust the next session. What worked, what didn't.

Cat had left a notebook in the living room and she opened it up to an empty page when she got settled. Then she curled her feet up underneath herself and waited for the group to quiet down. "So let's start at the beginning. What did you want to get out of the retreat?"

Three hours later, and two more cups of coffee and a couple of cookies, Cat felt drained. Her notebook was filled with comments and good ideas, but even better, she could see the satisfaction on the faces of her guests. Molly had been quiet this retreat, but when Cat pressed her, the Covington student listed off a ton of things she'd learned and completed.

Cat was cleaning up the living room, setting the cups and plates on a tray, when she heard someone at the door. She turned to find Bren standing, watching her work.

"You scared me. I thought I was alone here." Cat glanced around the empty room. "Did you leave something?"

"Actually, no. I was just wondering if I could ask you something." Bren came in the room, and as she walked toward Cat, she picked up an abandoned plate and cup. She sat it on the tray, then sat down on the couch.

Cat sat too, wondering what the woman wanted

to talk about but knowing it wouldn't be a quick, yes or no question. "Sure. Is this about writing?"

Bren shook her head. "I guess what's on my mind is a more general life question. You were married before."

"I was married for five years. Michael was a professor at Covington, and when I graduated, they offered me a position too. Probably because they didn't want to lose Michael." Cat leaned into the chair and the memories. They had been happy, once upon a time.

"Do you think people ever change? I mean really change?" Bren pushed on without letting Cat answer. "Can you ever look at someone the same way again once you've seen their dark side?"

The question hung in the air as Cat considered the feeling of betrayal she'd felt after she and Michael divorced. Even now, with knowing the rest of the story, the betrayal still covered over the love. Could she have gone back after the reason for the divorce had been revealed? Probably not. And that was what Bren needed to hear.

"When my husband and I divorced, I was furious. I was hurt. And if he'd called me and apologized and explained, I couldn't go back. I think that kind of a relationship has a sacred bond. The two of you are building a life together. Each person needs to protect that bond because it's fragile and it can break." She picked up her cup and took a sip of the now cold coffee. Watching Bren, she noticed the woman wasn't wearing the rock she'd had on her left hand when she'd arrived in Aspen Hills.

"I think he's just saying the right things now

because he knows I'm leaving. He thinks he can make what he did disappear." Bren shook her head. "I'm surprised I got any writing done at all this week with all the drama going on in my life. I'm really not this way normally."

"Don't apologize for emotions. We all have them, and sometimes getting some distance gives you the clarity to remember who you are. Just keep that idea in your head. Who are you, and more importantly, who do you want to be? I don't know you or your boyfriend well enough to make judgments, but you do. Trust your instincts. I think you know what you need to do."

Bren glanced at her watch. "Thanks. I do know, but sometimes change is hard."

"And a little scary." Cat finished off the cold coffee. "I moved from Aspen Hills to California and then back home. I gave up two professor positions and became a full-time author with this side hustle. And I've never been happier."

Now Bren did smile. "So there's life on the other side of pain?"

"There's always life." Cat stood and picked up the tray. "If we're talking longer, I have to grab more coffee."

"Nah, I'm good. But I think I'm going to sit down here and journal for a while, if you don't mind. I feel the need for some dreaming." Bren held up a leather-bound journal she'd had sitting next to her. "My new adventure awaits and I need to get planning for it."

As Cat put the dishes in the dishwasher, she thought about the hopes and dreams that the house

had given a lot of the writers who had made their
way through the retreat. The week here changed
people's lives. Maybe not to the extent it had
Bren's, but the writers got stronger. More focused.
Maybe she could use that in the marketing somehow. Warm Springs Writers' Retreat, where dreams
become reality?

Chapter Twenty-One

Saturday morning was always filled with activity and a bit of melancholy for Cat as she knew the house would feel empty as soon as Seth left tomorrow to take the writers to the airport. Worse, tomorrow it would be empty as Shauna was taking off as well. As Cat dressed for her day, she realized this was the first time she would be alone in the house since she'd moved back from California. Even when she'd been married to Michael, she hadn't spent more than a few nights alone when he'd gone off to economics conferences. She'd been invited, but she'd spent enough time with his professor friends to know that she'd be bored out of her skull. Even the thought of having time to read hadn't drawn her out of the house.

She glanced around her bedroom. This had been their bedroom when she'd been married too, but now she had her own queen-size bed in the room, which was decorated the way she wanted. And she had the closet all to herself. Which would change if Seth asked her to marry him. Or they decided to move in together. She brushed a wrinkle out of the comforter. No use worrying about what hadn't happened yet.

When she came into the kitchen, Shauna was already up and baking. The cinnamon smell filled the room and made Cat's mouth water. "Good morning. I didn't think you'd be baking this morning. Don't you have enough food to get through the last couple of days?"

"Maybe, but then you won't have food for the week I'm gone. Make sure you put anything you need on the shopping list this morning because I'm going to the store right after lunch." Shauna sat a plate with two slices of French toast and bacon in front of Cat.

"You do realize I know how to cook. And I even know where the store is." Cat poured maple syrup over the toast. "And if I don't, we have these things called restaurants where I can go eat and just pay them for the meal."

"Funny girl." Shauna sat her own plate down and grabbed the syrup. "I just want to make sure you have food. Is that a crime?"

"Sorry, you're a good friend. And I appreciate your concern. I just don't want you to run yourself ragged taking care of me when we still have a retreat in session." Cat glanced around. "Have you seen Seth this morning?"

"He's already out and working at the barn. I love the design we made for the herb garden. I should be able to do some puttering next week when I get back. That and I'm taking Snow out for a long trail ride before the snow falls." Shauna pointed a slice of bacon at her. "We probably only have one more month of autumn. You want to make good use of it."

"Maybe Seth and I will go hiking one day next week." Cat bit into the bacon and almost choked when the back door flew open.

Nate Hearst stood in the kitchen and looked around, wildly. When his gaze fell on Cat, he moved toward her. "Cat, I really need to talk to your uncle. Where is he?"

Cat stared at the man. He looked crazed. "At the police station?"

"They said he was coming here. Are you sure he's not here?" Nate looked around the kitchen like his attention would find Uncle Pete playing hide and seek from him. "Maybe he's in the other part of the house."

Shauna held up a hand, stopping Nate from barreling into the hallway. "Look, we said Pete's not here. This is our home, not an open community hall. Calm down and have a cup of coffee and tell us what's going on."

At that, Nate shook his head and sank into a chair. "Sorry, I'm a little upset. I've gotten three calls this morning from the guys I play pool with down at Bernie's. Dee Dee's been saying we're a couple and I probably killed Greyson because I was jealous of the attention he paid her."

"Were you a couple?" Cat set a cup of coffee in front of Nate.

He shook his head violently. "No. I mean, yeah, there were a couple nights where we went to her place after closing down the bar, but that's not a re-lationship, right?"

Shauna shrugged. "I guess it depends on your definition."

The kitchen door opened. Seth and Uncle Pete came into the room. Nate stood up so fast he spilled his coffee. He grabbed a couple of napkins off the table and sopped up the liquid. "Chief, I really need to talk to you."

"I guess so since you tracked me down." Uncle Pete gave Cat a kiss on the head. "Do you mind if we use your study? Nate and I have some things to clarify since his last interview."

"There's nothing to clarify . . ." Nate started, but stopped when Uncle Pete held up a hand.

He poured a cup of coffee. "Bring your cup and follow me. We need to talk and there's nothing to be gained in airing dirty laundry with an audience."

Nate picked up his cup and followed Uncle Pete out of the kitchen.

Cat turned and looked at Seth, who was pouring his own coffee. "Uncle Pete doesn't think Nate has anything to do with Greyson's death, does he?"

Seth didn't answer until he sat at the table. "I don't think so, but he's kind of ticked that Nate didn't mention this when he interviewed him a few days ago."

Cat and Shauna stared at him.

"What? Katie called Pete when he was in the barn talking to me about the new garden spot. I think he wants a section next year to raise some tomatoes." Seth sipped his coffee. "Pete says gardening decreases his stress level. I guess he used to garden with your aunt."

"They had a huge garden, but he hasn't done

anything like that for years." Cat stared at the door, wondering what was going on with her uncle.

"I think he's worried if he does his own, he'll be too busy to water at times. This way, he has all of us to make sure the plants don't die." Seth glanced at his watch. "So today's schedule, all you need me for is Driving Miss Latimer to dinner and back, right?"

"We need to leave about five. We have five thirty reservations." Cat finished her French toast. "Shauna, you're coming with us, right?"

"Of course. I wouldn't miss Saturday closing dinner for anything." She stood and took her plate to the sink. "But I do need to get packing. I'll strip the beds when I get back next week so just pull out the trash in the guest rooms and close the doors. I'll take care of the rest."

Seth sipped his coffee as Shauna disappeared out of the kitchen. "I get the feeling she thinks we can't survive without her for a week. She offered to pick up groceries for my apartment this afternoon."

"I think I'll have enough food over here for the two of us plus an army. You might as well plan on eating dinner with me. If we don't eat what she makes up, she might think I starved myself." Cat stared at the door where Shauna had disappeared. "I guess she really needs this trip."

"Well, I'll be upstairs. I've got some work to do to get ready for next week. I'm doing a bid for our friend Sandra. She wasn't kidding when she said she wanted to throw some work my way. I guess networking is the way to get business." Seth walked around the table and, after filling up a carafe, kissed her. "I'm looking forward to next week. I might just take a day to play hooky with you."

Cat refilled her cup, then went over to where she'd left her tote bag and pulled out her notebook. She wrote down the notes from her talk with Jessica. The comment from Mrs. Rice. And now the connection between Nate and Dee Dee.

As she looked at the wheel she'd made with Greyson in the middle, one name kept coming up. Dee Dee. Except the baker had an alibi for the time of Greyson's death. And really, every time she looked at motive, Dee Dee being the killer just didn't make sense. There had to be another answer. She just wasn't seeing it.

By the time Nate and Uncle Pete came back into the kitchen, Cat had read through her entire clues notebook and rewrote the unanswered questions. Maybe she'd just go over to the bakery later today and see if she could get some answers.

Nate stormed out of the house without even glancing Cat's way.

"I guess the talk didn't go like he'd planned?" Cat nodded to his cup. "Do you need a refill?"

"I don't have a lot of time, but I'm going to take a break anyway." He refilled his cup before he sat down. "I have to admit, I'm not feeling like I'm making any headway on the Finn case. Nate's been keeping it interesting, but I know that kid couldn't kill someone, especially over a woman. He's a player. He likes his freedom way too much to be tied down."

"Dee Dee seems to think they're a couple. I've heard that from several people." Cat sipped her own coffee and watched her uncle's response.

"You need to keep your nose out of my investigation. I do have to say I'm happy to not run into your writers every time I turn around. What, does this group write romance or something?"

"No, they're mystery authors, but they are more interested in the community rather than the details of the crime. The murder came up several times, but mostly in a discussion on different ways to kill someone. I'm surprised no one has stopped by the station to talk to you."

"I've been out most of the week, but I would have heard if they had. You should send them to Shirley if they have procedure questions. She loves talking about all that writer stuff."

Cat thought about the notes she'd made about the case just before her uncle arrived. "Is there any way that Dee Dee could have done this? I can't see Jessica killing anyone and Sandra doesn't seem the type."

"Actually, I'm going into Denver to reinterview the girlfriend this afternoon. Some of her original statements about where she was haven't panned out." Uncle Pete looked at his watch.

"You can't think it's Sandra, she's . . ." Cat tried to figure out why she was so convinced that Sandra was innocent, but unless her alibi held up, she didn't have much to go on. "She just doesn't seem like the type."

"But Dee Dee does? Are you sure your conflict with the woman over the health department calls isn't clouding your judgment?" He stared at her, challenging her statement with his gaze. He used to do the same thing when she had complained about a teacher being unfair. Or a bad day at school.

"It's not that I don't like her. I admit, I don't, but she's so temperamental. I hear stories about her anger issues all the time. It feels like something she could do." Cat smiled as she grabbed a cookie. "It's a good thing I'm not in your shoes. I'd have a lot of innocent people in my jail because of a feeling."

"Going with your gut isn't a bad thing, but you have to have more evidence than just a feeling. And right now, the best lead I have is taking me to Denver to talk to Sandra." He finished off his coffee and stood. "Are you going to the Mexican place down the highway for dinner tonight?"

Cat thought her life might just be too routine. But darn it, she liked the place and so had the guests she'd taken there. "Guilty as charged. It has great food."

"And strong margaritas." He kissed her on the top of the head. "I'd worry about you but I know Seth is playing designated driver this evening."

"He's being paid to do the driving—don't let him make you feel sorry for him." Cat followed him to the doorway. "Hey, Mrs. Rice said something funny yesterday. She said that Greyson and Dee Dee were seeing each other. Do you think that's true?"

"Your neighbor needs to check her sources on her gossip. I haven't heard one peep about that and I've been knee deep in Greyson's life. I know his routine as well as he did when he was alive, and Dee Dee wasn't a part of the guy's life."

After Uncle Pete left, Cat wandered through the empty downstairs. The writers must all have been at the library for the morning, getting in those last few hours of research time. Seth was working on his bid. And Shauna must be packing. She could go outside and play with the kittens for a while or maybe go talk to Dee Dee at the bakery so she could mark off some of those questions she hadn't found the answers for.

She hesitated as she grabbed her tote bag, but then she shook off the unease she felt about going to talk to the woman. Even her uncle had said Dee Dee wasn't involved in Greyson's death. She'd be safe.

She wrote "TOWN" on the bulletin board but figured she'd probably be home before Shauna even saw the message. She slipped a cookie into a plastic bag and threw a bottle of water into her tote. There was nothing wrong with being a little prepared for everything.

Mrs. Rice waved at her through the large plate glass window in her living room. Mr. Peeps was in her arms, and even at the distance Cat was from the house, she could see the hiss that came over the cat as he watched her walk by. What in the world had she ever done to the stupid cat? As if he'd been able to hear her, Mr. Peeps fought against Mrs. Rice's hold and batted at the window. Cat walked faster to try to get out of his vicinity.

As she walked into town, she ran the cast of characters who might be involved in Greyson's death through her mind. If Dee Dee was truly off the list like she believed, then she'd have to go through her notebook and the list again and comb out the one person whose alibi seemed less than solid.

When Cat reached the bakery, the café chairs in the front were all upside down on the table. She frowned and glanced at her watch. It was eleven on a Saturday. The bakery should have been bursting with people right now. Instead, the windows were dark. Cat tried the door. It was locked.

Tammy called out from the front of the bookstore where she was washing windows. "She's not open. I don't know if she's sick or not. I haven't had the time to give her a call."

"Did she say anything last night?" Cat walked over to the bookstore and watched as Tammy finished washing off the window in the door.

"No, and that was weird. I always poke my head in when I'm closing up, just to make sure she's doing okay. But she was normal. Kind of quiet, but it would be expected, giving the circumstances."

"You mean Greyson's death." It appeared Tammy was convinced that Dee Dee and the murdered chef were an item, even if Uncle Pete thought the idea ludicrous.

"She's such a sensitive soul. I bet when he moved in with that decorator it probably broke her heart. And now, she's just a nobody and that woman gets all the sympathy." Tammy held the door open for a couple who were coming up the walk to the store. "Welcome folks. Feel free to look around. I'll be right in."

Cat waited for the older couple to disappear into the store before answering. "Hey, did Dee Dee mention being in a relationship with Nate?"

"The health inspector? That Nate?" Tammy started laughing. "I thought we talked about this earlier. He was in love with her. Dee Dee told me he begged her to go out with him. She let him take her to dinner a few times, but I think they were just friends. Dee Dee liked to exaggerate sometimes."

Cat wondered what other stories Dee Dee had told and how many of them contradicted themselves. She said her good-byes and headed home for lunch.

The kitchen was empty and the stove cold when Cat returned from her wasted walk into town. Her note was still on the board. Maybe Shauna had just lost track of time. Cat went through the kitchen and up the stairs to the third floor.

She knocked on Shauna's door. "Hey, do you want me to order pizza or have Seth run into town for some burgers?"

There was no answer. Cat opened the door and glanced inside. Shauna's suitcase was out on her bed, packed with clothes. It was still open but it looked like Shauna had finished most of her packing already. Cat crossed the room and glanced into the bathroom. No Shauna. Now she was beginning to worry. She went to the window and glanced out to the backyard. Shauna could see the pasture from the window and Cat saw Snow out grazing. So Shauna wasn't riding.

Cat left the room and headed to the stairs. Seth was just coming down from the attic where he had set up a desk for his office on retreat weeks.

He grabbed her arm before she could go downstairs. "Hey, what's got you in such a hurry? I take it Shauna has lunch ready?"

"No." Cat pulled away and started down the stairs. Seth followed her. "What do you mean, no?"

"I mean, lunch isn't ready. Shauna doesn't appear to be in the house." Cat paused at the second-floor landing, then walked over to where the guests' rooms were. She knocked on the first door. No answer. Using her pass key, she opened the door and walked through the room, making sure Shauna wasn't hurt or passed out. Entering one room after the other, she cleared all the rooms, even the one without a guest this week. No Shauna. Seth stood in the hallway, watching her, concern in his eyes. She could barely meet his gaze after she checked the last room.

"Don't get worried, yet. She could be doing laundry. Or out in the barn with Snow." Seth put his hands on Cat's forearms to steady her. He met her gaze. "Right now, she's just not where she is supposed to be. It doesn't mean anything."

Cat hoped he was right. Because if anything had happened to Shauna . . . She shook her head. She wasn't going to think the worst.

"You go check the barn. I'll clear the rest of the house." Cat took a deep breath, trying to keep the fear at bay. "We just saw her at breakfast."

Chapter Twenty-Two

Cat had gone through all the rooms in the house, including the basement. When she came back upstairs, she dialed Shauna's phone. She heard the ringing in the foyer. She ran from the kitchen. A woman stood at the desk.

"Thank God, I thought something had happened to you." Cat rushed toward the hotel desk but as she got closer, she realized the red hair was really blond. It wasn't Shauna at the desk, but Bren.

She held out the phone. "I had just come in from lunch in town when I heard this go off. Isn't that Shauna's phone?"

"Yeah." Cat cut the connection and slipped her phone into her pants pocket. She took Shauna's phone from Bren. "Hey, you haven't seen her, have you?"

"No, not since yesterday. I came back early from lunch because I wanted to get this scene down before I lost it." Bren moved toward the living room. "Your car is parked across from the post office downtown. Maybe she went shopping or something?"

The car. Cat's shoulders dropped. Of course, Shauna had mentioned she was going shopping. She must have just forgotten about the time. Hoping the concern she felt didn't show on her face, Cat smiled at Bren. "That's right. I'd forgotten she was going to get some supplies. Thanks and good luck with your scene."

"No probs." Bren waved as she disappeared into the living room. Cat glanced out the front. The SUV with the Warm Springs Resort logo on the front wasn't sitting out front like she'd left it the last time she'd driven anywhere.

Seth came in through the front doorway. "She's not in the barn and I've walked the entire property."

"She's at the store. Bren told me she saw the car in town. I'm going to walk in and see what's keeping her. Why don't you come in with me and you can run and get us burgers for lunch from The Diner?" The fear Cat had felt had disappeared. Shauna used the grocery story as her source of gossip. With the murder happening this week, she'd probably just lost track of time.

When they got to Main Street, Cat saw the car in the grocery store parking lot. "So we'll meet at the car?"

Seth patted his pockets. "Sure, I have my keys if I get done first. I shouldn't be more than fifteen minutes. Call me if you need help with the groceries."

"I think she was just getting a few things to tide me over until she got back." Cat shook her head.

"I told her not to worry about it, but she said she needed some travel-sized products too."

"She's really excited about this trip. Even though she doesn't talk a lot about her brother, she must miss him." Seth kissed her and then pulled his phone out of his pocket. "I'll call in the order while I'm walking. Hopefully that will save some time. I'm starving."

"Well, I won't leave you waiting in the car long then." Cat waved and crossed the street to the grocery store. She glanced at the checkout counters first—no Shauna. Then she slowly made her way down the edges of the store. Not in produce, not at the butcher counter, not at the bakery. When she went by each aisle, she paused, scanning the row for Shauna. Finally, she was back up front at the checkout stations. A man in a yellow vest smiled at her.

"Can I help you find something?" The man's name tag read Roger.

"Hi, Roger. My friend Shauna Clodagh came in this morning and I'm just looking for her." Cat didn't know where she might be but maybe she was in some cubby drinking coffee and chatting in the back.

"Shauna didn't come in this morning. She has the retreat this week. I probably won't see her until Sunday afternoon." Roger turned toward an elderly woman and pointed to an empty checkout line. "Mrs. Anders, Sally on number five can help you."

"But she said she was coming to the store. Her car's out front." Cat put a hand on Roger's arm as the man started to step away, clearly done with the conversation.

He frowned and turned toward the large windows in the front of the store. "You're right. It is out there. Hold on a minute."

He went to the checkers, one by one, and they each shook their heads after looking at Cat. Then he stopped by the service desk and picked up the phone. Finally, he came back to where Cat was standing. Her gut was twisted in a knot and she knew what he was going to say before he opened his mouth.

"Sorry, no one has seen her." He pointed toward the service desk. "Why don't we go over there where you can sit and I'll call Pete."

"Call Uncle Pete? Why?" This couldn't be happening. Shauna was going to walk through that door laughing about her adventure and be shocked that Cat came to track her down.

"It appears she's gone missing. I'm sure you'll want your uncle's help in finding her." He put a hand on her back and tried to move her out of the main aisle.

"You call Uncle Pete. I'm going to go looking in the other stores." Cat shook off his hand and his concern. Shauna wasn't missing. She couldn't be.

Cat pulled out her phone and dialed Seth as she walked out of the store. When he picked up, the tears started to fall. "Seth, she's not here. I'm going to check the stores around and see if I can find her. She has to be somewhere."

"Check the car. I'm on my way."

She heard him talking to the restaurant staff but she hung up the phone and hurried over to the car. It was empty and unlocked. Which wasn't unusual. Cat didn't lock the car when she took it for errands either. Aspen Hills just wasn't that type of town where you worried about such things.

She was about to close the door when she saw the slip of paper on the passenger seat. She grabbed it and read Shauna's grocery list as well as her other stops. She had listed "book for flight" on the top. Was she in Tammy's store, lost in the stacks and trying to find a story to keep her busy during the flight?

Cat put the note into her pocket and took off to the bookstore that was only a block away. Shauna had probably been inside when Cat stopped to talk to Tammy. Speed walking down the street, she crossed against the light since there were no cars on either road. At the bookstore, she pulled open the door and the bell rang out.

Tammy looked up and smiled. "It must be my lucky day. It's not often I get to see you twice. Do you need something for the retreat? Or is this research?"

"Is Shauna here?" Cat glanced around the small bookstore.

Tammy shook her head, worry creasing her brow as she picked up on Cat's concern. "I haven't seen her for a week at least. I mean, in the store. I saw her yesterday at the retreat and she said she was coming by to pick up some reading material. I pulled a stack of recommendations for her to look at but she hasn't come in yet. Why? Is something wrong?"

Cat moved through the bookstore much like she had at the grocery store even though it was smaller and, besides her and Tammy, completely empty.

She paused at the counter. "You're sure she didn't come in? Maybe she's in the back?"

"I can check. I'll check the bathroom too, but, Cat, I don't think she's here." Tammy held up a finger. "Hold on."

Cat took a deep breath and pulled out the list again to study it. A book and the groceries. Nothing else. Where had Shauna stopped in between the grocery store and the bookstore? Cat turned and looked out the window at the closed-up bakery.

Cat moved toward the door.

"Cat?" Tammy's voice stopped her. "She's not back there."

"Tammy, do me a favor and call 911. Ask them to call Uncle Pete and tell him that I'm going to check out the bakery for Shauna. He'll know what I'm talking about."

"Cat, no one's at the bakery. I told you earlier, I called Dee Dee when I saw she was still closed this morning." Tammy started to follow her.

"Just call 911 for me. And if you wouldn't mind, stand outside and watch for Seth? He should be coming by soon." Cat didn't wait for a response. She hurried over to the bakery's front door and tried the handle. Locked. Then she peered into the dark dining area. No sign of life. If Dee Dee had Shauna, they were in the back.

She made her way down the narrow walkway between the bookstore and the bakery. In the back alley, there were two parking spots for the bakery. One had a white van with the bakery name and logo on the front. The other was empty. The door to the van was open as was the back door to the bakery.

Cat snuck around the van and peeked in the front and back windows. It was empty. But the keys were in the ignition. Cat made her way up the stairs to the back porch staying close to the wall of the building. She could hear someone talking as she got closer to the doorway.

She peeked inside and saw Dee Dee standing over Shauna, who had been tied to a chair. A gag was in her mouth, but Cat met her gaze.

Shauna blinked twice, letting Cat know that she had seen her.

Cat leaned back against the wall and out of view of either Dee Dee or Shauna. What on earth was she going to do? And why would Dee Dee do this?

You don't ask residents of crazy town why. For some reason, the thought made her calm down just a bit. As she stood there, she heard Dee Dee talking to Shauna. She picked up her phone, dialed 911, and adjusted the volume, holding the phone toward the doorway. Hopefully Katie would be listening and hear what was going on so she could send someone to help.

"You just had to stick your nose into my business. First, you steal my recipes to put into that book of yours, then you try to steal Nate. Yeah, I've heard about how he was all over you at Bernie's. Men are pigs, all of them. But it's women like you who tempt them. He was hitting on someone new a few nights ago. I bet you didn't know that, did you? You and that Sandra who thought she could take Greyson away from me."

Cat listened as the woman raged about the unfairness of life. If she'd been able to respond, she would have pointed out the fact that Dee Dee had been after two men at the same time and the duplicity of that, but she didn't think telling the woman that would help Shauna's chances. She tuned back in to the rants.

"So, you're just going to have to disappear into the woods. That's the nice thing about living so close to a forest. There are lots of little creatures who will think of you as a tasty treat after I leave your body there. And as long as I keep you tied up well, I won't even have to kill you myself. Bear, wolf, or mountain lion—I'm pretty sure one of those will find you long before your friends even know you're missing."

Cat glanced around for something, anything to use as a weapon. She had to keep Dee Dee from putting Shauna in the van at all costs. She sat the phone down on the porch floor, up against the wall, and hoped that someone was still listening. Then she picked up a board that had come loose from a pallet. Hopefully Dee Dee didn't have a real weapon or she'd be coming into a knife fight with a toothpick. But she had to do something.

She hefted the board and stepped into the doorway. Dee Dee was poised above Shauna, a wooden paddle she must have used for her ovens held upright and ready to swing. Shauna ducked as Cat cried out, "Stop it, Dee Dee!"

Dee Dee checked herself midswing, missing

Shauna and hitting the chair. Shauna fell over to the floor and Cat could see her trying to free herself. "The police are on their way; put down the paddle."

"It's called a pizza peel, not a paddle. Seriously, don't either of you know anything about cooking?" Dee Dee's eyes were bright with madness. "And it works really well to knock someone out. I guess in Greyson's case, it broke something in his head because by the time I came back to check on him to see if he'd come to his senses yet, the guy was stone cold."

"You can't kill someone because he doesn't love you." Cat stepped closer, her fingers gripping the wood, but she could feel the sweat forming on her palm. Where were the police? It couldn't be more than two blocks to the station from here.

Dee Dee cackled in glee. "Oh, but I can. You know that. Greyson needed to control his family and stay out of my bakery. He wanted to close me down. After all I did for the guy, he was going to let his family take over my building? That wasn't going to happen."

"And yet, it's still happening, even with Greyson gone. You got served eviction papers, right? Who are you going to kill to stop that? The lawyer, Greyson's family, the judge who approved the order?"

"I might not be able to stop it, but I don't have to let her steal my recipes or my chance at happiness with Nate." Dee Dee smiled. "And maybe you can come along with her. I hear bears need a lot of food in the fall to allow them to hibernate."

She stepped toward Cat. Shauna's foot had come

loose from the ropes after the chair had fallen over. Cat saw Shauna kick her foot out to trip her and then Dee Dee was flat on the floor. Cat ran over and pulled her arms behind her back, then she sat on her butt. Dee Dee squirmed under her.

Shauna inched closer but Cat couldn't use a hand to take off the gag since she had a death grip on Dee Dee's arms. It was all she could do to hold on. The woman bucked like a bronco in the rodeo.

"Well, isn't this a site?" Seth's voice came from the open doorway.

Two police officers burst into the doorway and stood over Cat and Dee Dee, guns drawn.

She looked up at one of them and nodded to Dee Dee. "Do you want to help me with her? Or are you going to shoot her?"

They looked at each other and one officer holstered his weapon. "If you weren't the chief's niece, you'd be in cuffs too."

"If I wasn't the chief's niece, I'd probably be home reading a book and this murderer would have gotten away with her crime and a few more before you guys caught her." When the officer put cuffs on Dee Dee, Cat pushed herself up and off the woman.

"You witch. No one is going to believe you anyway. It's all circumstantial," Dee Dee screamed at Cat as the officer dragged her to her feet.

Cat ignored her and pulled the gag off Shauna's mouth. "Are you okay?"

Seth helped her get Shauna and the chair upright, then using his pocket knife, he cut off the ropes that had bound her. Shauna stood and rubbed her wrists.

"I'm fine, just furious. And to think, I came to the shop to apologize for taking one of her recipes and making it better." Shauna stared at Dee Dee, who was being led out of the back room of the bakery and toward the police car. "I told her I was going to credit her and the bakery for the idea and that might get her more customers. Then she went off on me about losing the store and Nate and the next thing I knew, I was sitting here, tied up."

The other police officer came and handed Cat her phone. "Smart idea. Katie has the confession all recorded back at the station. This trial might be a slam dunk because of you."

"I'm just glad you got here in time. What took you so long?" Cat took the phone and slipped it into her back pocket.

"We were on a lunch break and it took Katie a few minutes to reach us." He looked out toward the squad car. "Your uncle is on his way back from Denver. I guess he didn't need to reinterview Ms. Collins after all."

He tipped his hat and headed out the door. He paused at the doorway. "Henry will be coming back after we get her into one of the cells. We'll need to secure the scene, so if you wouldn't mind leaving soon, we'd appreciate it. Your uncle says he'll interview you all later."

Seth put his arm around Cat and another around Shauna. "Let's go get lunch. I'm pretty sure our order's ready by now."

Chapter Twenty-Three

The second pitcher of margaritas had just arrived and Cat refilled her glass. She was still shaky about the events earlier in the day, but Shauna and Seth seemed to have put it all behind them. Shauna was talking to Colleen about all the sightseeing she wanted to complete while she was in New York the next week.

"Jake says he's going to get me on the floor of the stock exchange." Shauna grinned at Cat. "You want me to buy you a stock or two while I'm there?"

"It might be shortsighted, but I'd rather have a snow globe of Central Park." Cat grinned at her friend. Warning bells were going off about her brother, but Shauna had promised not to make any financial decisions about the money that Kevin had left her during the week. Cat hoped that Jake's newfound interest in his sister wasn't based on the size of her bank account. She thought it might just break Shauna's heart if it was. "Just remember what we talked about."

Shauna held her glass up for Seth to refill. "Tell

your girlfriend that she doesn't have to worry about me like some mother hen."

Cat wanted to remind Shauna that if she hadn't gone looking for her today because she was worried, she might be spending the week dodging wild animals in the woods rather than avoiding the wolves of Wall Street. But a glance passed between them and Cat knew that Shauna was thinking the same thing.

"Cat, stop mothering Shauna. Shauna, be careful out in the big city. They like to eat country bumpkins like us." Seth poured the icy golden liquid into her glass. "We like having you around."

"I survived in LA for five years before I even met Cat, so I'm not such a country bumpkin." Shauna elbowed Seth. "Not like you, who was born here in little Aspen Hills."

"I did my traveling during the army years. I'm proud to be a native Coloradoan. There aren't many of us left." He held up his glass of Coke. "To the Warm Springs Writers' Retreat. You're never boring."

"You sound like you're surprised." Anne held her glass up. "To those who write, and those who teach, and those who read. We all love stories."

They all sipped their drinks. Then Rick stood up. He looked at Cat and nodded. "I'm going to do this in public so I can't back out, so I'm asking all of you to keep me accountable."

"You're giving up drinking?" Molly asked.

"No, it's donuts. He's going sugar free," Colleen supplied.

Anne shook her head. "We know it's not coffee. He wouldn't be able to survive."

"Let the man talk." Bren, who sat next to Rick, looked up at him and smiled. "Go ahead, Rick. How can we help you?"

He took a deep breath. "Bren, I know you're still involved and you have some things to clear up when we get back to Chicago. But I want you to know I've been in love with you since the day you joined our critique group. I didn't tell you then when you were single, and I should have. If you think you might feel something for me, I'd love to take you out on a date as soon as you feel ready."

Bren stared at him and his cheeks reddened.

Rick slipped back into his chair. He didn't look at her. "Or not. Either way, I want us to continue to be friends. You can forget all the things I just said and we can go back to being friends."

Bren took his face in her hands. "Why would I do that?"

She smiled as she searched his face. Then she kissed him. Slow and sweet. When she finished, she picked up her glass and took a drink. "You better be expecting my call. Because as soon as I have my life back in order, I'm taking you up on that offer."

The table cheered as a clearly shocked Rick stared at Bren. As the food was delivered, she nudged him with her elbow. "Stop staring or I'm going to change my mind."

Rick picked up his fork. "I've had the best time here in Colorado. And I finished a first draft of a book this week. What more could a guy ask for?"

Molly sighed. "I'm going to miss all of you. I can't believe I have to go back to class next week and just be a graduate student again."

"You're never *just* a graduate student. No matter

what you do during the day to expand your education or work to put food on the table, you're a writer. And you need to carve out the time to make sure you stay an author." Cat dipped a chip into the salsa. "Face it, Molly, you're one of us now."

As the evening came to a close and they were back at the house, Cat found herself alone in the kitchen with Shauna. Feeling the courage that comes from a few drinks, she sat down at the table after making coffee. "Can we talk?"

Shauna sat a plate of cookies in front of Cat and filled her own cup. "I know what you're going to say. You think maybe Jake is looking at me with new eyes because of my money. And believe me, the thought has crossed my mind too. But I'm not taking any account information and if he brings up the subject, I'm going to shut it down. I want to know my brother, not the broker he is during the day."

"What if they are the same person?" Cat knew people who lived their job 24/7. She just hoped Shauna's brother wasn't one of them.

"Then I get a hotel and have a nice week visiting New York City. I'm not going in thinking that this will be a fix for our family dysfunction, but I'm willing to give him the chance." Shauna smiled. "And I appreciate the fact that you're concerned. I don't think I ever thanked you for saving my life today."

"I don't think I saved your life."

"Okay, but I do. I saw the look in Dee Dee's eyes when she started to swing that paddle. She wanted me dead. Not because of Nate or the recipe. I think she found out she liked killing people. A lot."

Shauna shuddered. "It makes me cringe just talking about her."

"Well then, let's just not talk about it. Did Uncle Pete clear you for leaving tomorrow?" Cat yawned and sipped her coffee. Tomorrow morning was going to come faster than she wanted.

"He's coming by before breakfast to do my interview. I told him he could talk to you then too." Shauna's smile looked evil to Cat.

"What time is he going to be here?" Cat took a cookie and broke it in half, nibbling at the sweet treat.

"Five. But you don't have to be downstairs until six. After he interviews you and Seth, we'll have breakfast and the guests will have their brunch ready. You're going to have to put away the leftovers if they don't finish before I leave."

Cat stood and went to the sink to rinse her cup. "I better head to bed then. And I do know how to put away food."

"I'll call you before I get on the plane to remind you," Shauna called after her.

Cat waved as she left the room. "Go to bed."

She knew Shauna would set up the kitchen and the dining room before she went to bed. The girl only needed half the amount of sleep that Cat did. And she worked out every day. There was something seriously wrong with anyone who didn't sleep seven to eight hours a night. Seriously.

Sunday morning came faster than Cat had hoped. A knock on her door woke her up. She sat up, bleary eyed. "Yes?"

"Your uncle's here and you are supposed to be downstairs in twenty minutes." Seth stood at the doorway. He looked showered, dressed, and kind of hot in a too clean and awake way. "I was sent back upstairs to get you moving."

"You could just tell them I'm awake." Cat put a pillow over her head to block the overhead light that Seth had turned on when he entered the room.

"I could send your uncle up with a pail of ice water."

Cat threw the pillow off the bed and crawled out. She made her way into the bathroom. "Go away. I'm up now."

"Didn't you used to be a morning person?" Seth asked as she entered the bathroom.

She stuck her head out the doorway. "Not before my coffee."

Shutting the door, she still heard his laughter coming through the walls. She turned on the water to the shower and sank into its warmth.

When she got downstairs, Seth was the only one in the kitchen. He looked up and smiled. "There's my lark. How are you this morning?"

"Tired. I'm not used to going out on Saturday evenings and closing down the place." Cat crossed the kitchen and poured herself a cup of coffee.

"Those writers of yours know how to party. I didn't think we were going to get them into the car before one." Seth folded the paper back. "Maybe we should make a one pitcher rule at dinner."

"They were helping Rick and Bren celebrate. I guess their acknowledging their feelings for each other was a long time coming." Cat put a croissant on a plate and grabbed the jar of strawberry jam.

She held one out to Seth. When he nodded, she sat a second one on the plate and went to sit next to him. "True love overcomes all barriers."

Seth watched her smear jam on one of the croissants and then took it from her. "Do you truly believe in that?"

"True love? Of course. I'm a romantic at heart. You should know that by now." She licked the jam off her finger and then repeated the process for her own croissant. "Don't you? How could you look at those two last night and not believe in true love?"

"I wasn't talking about them."

The sentence hung in the air, but before Cat could respond, Uncle Pete and Shauna came into the kitchen.

"Good, I didn't want to use the ice water this morning." He refilled his coffee. "Come into the study and let's get this thing over with."

With a quick glance at Seth, Cat took her coffee but left her plate on the table. She moved it out of Seth's reach. "Don't touch that."

Listening to his laugh, Cat resigned herself to the fact she was going to have to make another one when she got back into the kitchen. Men were so predictable.

As she went into the study, she realized her uncle was sitting behind Michael's desk. So this was an official interview, she thought. Power play and all. She sat in her reading chair and curled her legs up underneath her. "What do you want to know?"

"Tell me everything from the time you realized Shauna was missing." He pulled out a pen and started writing in his notebook.

Cat recounted yesterday's activities, trying to keep the fear she'd felt throughout the ordeal under control. She wasn't reliving the experience, just telling her side of things. It was important to Dee Dee's trial to have all the facts. Still, she felt a little shaky when she finished. She went to take a sip of coffee and realized it was empty.

Her uncle saw the action and nodded to the carafe on the desk. "There's more in there."

Cat got up and poured herself more coffee. "I know it's crazy to be upset now. Especially since it's over, but all I want to do is hide under my covers until I forget it ever happened."

"You were lucky."

Cat nodded her head. "I know. If I'd been any later, Shauna would have already been dead."

"No, Cat, that's not what I meant." Uncle Pete's voice was warm and comforting. "You were lucky you didn't get yourself killed. You need to keep yourself out of these investigations. One day, your luck is going to run out."

"I didn't go to investigate. I went to find my friend. I called the police station when I realized she was missing." Cat returned to her chair, setting the coffee down on the end table.

"No, you had Roger from the grocery store and Tammy from the bookstore call. You didn't call until you wanted Katie to record the conversation. And how that even worked, I don't know. Again, I repeat, you were lucky."

"No one thought Dee Dee was the killer. She was just a royal pain in my butt. And when I realized that Shauna was probably trying to be the nice guy

and patch up their differences, that's when I knew
Dee Dee had her. I never thought she would con-
fess to Greyson's murder." Cat picked up the coffee
and drank, but instead of making her relax, the
coffee tasted bitter.

"You suspected her. You even asked me about
it. I guess I'm going to have to give your hunches
a little more weight. You have some natural talent
at this investigating stuff." He nodded to the
door. "That's all I need. Go get your boyfriend so
I can yell at him for not calling me too. Then I
think I'll stay for breakfast. Shauna says we're
having waffles."

Blueberry waffles to be specific. Cat sent Seth
into the study and made herself another croissant
because as she predicted, hers was gone.

"He said he didn't want it to dry out on you."
Shauna laughed. "I'll have waffles ready in about
five minutes."

"I want a croissant too." Cat finished spreading
the jam, then without sitting, took a big bite out of
the treat. After swallowing, she glanced at Shauna,
who was watching her. "You ready for your trip?"

"Yes. I had to go into the library in the study and
pull out a book to take with me since I never got to
the bookstore yesterday." Shauna slapped her forehead. "And I didn't get to the market."

"Like I told you, I know where the store is if we
need food. But books, we have plenty; so tell me,
what did you choose?" Cat finished her croissant and
refilled her coffee cup. Then she sat at the table,
folding Seth's newspaper.

"An Amish mystery. It looks like we have the

whole set, so I took the first two books. If I don't like it, I'll buy something in the airport. I have about an hour before my flight takes off." Shauna poured waffle batter into the baker, then sprinkled blueberries over the top, and closed the lid. "What are you doing next week?"

"As little as possible." Cat smiled. "So if you want to talk, call me."

Shauna poured two glasses of orange juice and set them on the table. "I will, I promise."

Cat knew there was more to that promise than just calling if she was lonely, but she let it be.

After breakfast, the writers gathered in the foyer. Everyone was there and packed, except Shauna. Cat had sent her upstairs when she tried to finish up the dishes. Now, she came down the steps, her suitcase in hand. Seth stood by Cat's side watching.

"She'll be just fine." His words were soft but she nodded so he would know she had heard him.

"Miss Baker, a word if you don't mind?" Uncle Pete called Bren over to the side of the foyer. Cat moved with her. He looked up and frowned at Cat but didn't tell her to leave.

"What can I do for you?" Bren looked confused at being singled out.

He handed her a card. "I've talked to a friend in the Chicago police force and he gave me this number. When you're ready to move your stuff out of the apartment, call him and he'll come with you."

Bren's eyes widened. "But I didn't think . . . I mean, they must be busy. I don't want to take up their time."

"And we don't want you getting hurt. From what I've seen, you need some backup when you go to move out. And while friends are nice, having a police officer by your side will keep your ex-boyfriend from acting on any bad behavior he might be considering."

Bren threw her arms around Uncle Pete and hugged him. Cat smiled as his eyes widened. She mimed patting her on the back and her uncle mimicked the action.

"Thank you so much. This means the world to me." Bren stood back and wiped tears from her face.

"Well, you just take care of yourself and don't move in with someone unless you're completely sure. And if you are, you might as well marry the guy." Uncle Pete took out a handkerchief and wiped at his eyes. "Maybe an old-fashioned idea, but you deserve a complete commitment."

Cat turned and smiled at Seth, wondering if he found the same humor in her uncle going all soft over a guest, but he wasn't watching her or the interaction. Shauna, on the other hand, was wiping tears from her own eyes.

"Denver express is leaving in a few minutes. If you have luggage that's not in the car, you better get it outside. We're going to be tight this trip," Seth called out.

Cat said good-bye to all the guests and then turned to Shauna. "Have fun but be careful."

Shauna smiled. "Same to you. See you next Sunday."

Cat and Uncle Pete stood and watched the group leave. He put his hat on and started out the door after Seth drove off. Then he turned back. "I swear,

Cat, your retreats are getting more interesting by the month."

And then he was gone. Cat cleaned up the dining room. Then she made a sweep of the living room. By the time she'd gone through all the guest rooms and pulled off all the linens and stuffed them in the laundry shoot to the basement, she was tired. But instead of taking a nap, she went out to the barn to check on Snow and the kittens.

She'd have to add this to her daily to-do list so she wouldn't forget to feed and water the zoo when Shauna was gone. Her friend did a lot around the retreat and around the house. Cat figured she'd know exactly how much this week when Shauna was gone.

She was still sitting outside the barn, playing with the kittens, when Seth came back. He sat on the straw bale next to her. "Everyone's off to parts unknown."

"I hope Shauna has a good time with her brother." Cat set down the kitten who'd been sleeping on her lap.

"She will. That woman is as tough as nails. If he doesn't want to be a good brother to her, she'll just change the trip into a spa week and leave it at that." Seth picked up the kitten that was trying to climb up his jeans. "I'm putting in that bid tomorrow for the Collins job, but then I'm clear for the week. Do you want to spend some time together?"

"Sounds like a plan. I know we haven't had a real date for a while. I'm sorry I'm keeping you so busy." She batted her finger at the all-white kitten.

"We're building a future. I know it's your business, but I hope I'm more than just a hired hand around here. I hope I'm part of the team." He put a hand on her knee but didn't look at her.

She turned toward him. "I think we're a good team. You, me, and Shauna. The retreat needs all of us to be successful."

Seth grinned. "I was hoping you'd say that. I've been doing some planning for the next session when we take the group out for a day hike. I think we could do this as part of all the retreats when we have good weather. You know exercise helps clear your brain so you guys can write more."

Cat shook her head. "Let's just get through this one and then we can see about adding a session."

He leaned over and kissed her. "I was thinking we should add it on Thursdays."

As the kittens played around their feet, Cat and Seth sat and talked about the future. Their future with the Warm Springs Writers' Retreat and their future as a couple.

Life was good, Cat thought as the kittens slept around their feet. Especially when there was family to surround you. She liked her life just fine. And there was no way she was giving up even one of the kittens. They were part of her life now, for better or worse.

Seth stood and pulled her to her feet. "Let's go grab something to eat at The Diner. I'm feeling lazy tonight."

"Me too. Although let's have dessert at home. Shauna left us an apple pie." Cat put an arm around his waist and they made their way back to the house where they locked up before walking into town for dinner.

Life was good.

Dear Readers,

One of the joys of writing the Cat Latimer mystery series is imagining the food that Shauna bakes for the retreats. Of all the kitchen arts, baking is my favorite. Mostly because of the lovely smells a loaf of bread or a batch of cookies fills the house with. I've had scones before, but this recipe makes me think of October's chilly mornings and sitting with a book and a cup of coffee. Don't be afraid of baking scones, it's just a sweet biscuit.

Lynn

Cranberry Scones

Preheat oven to 425 degrees F.

In a large bowl, mix:

> 2 cups flour
> 2 tsp baking powder
> ½ tsp salt

Add:

> 4 Tbsp cold butter cut into chunks

Mix the cold butter into the flour with a pastry knife until the mixture looks like small peas.

Add:

> 3 Tbsp sugar
> ½ cup dried cranberries

In a small bowl, beat together:

> ½ cup half and half
> 1 large egg

Add wet mixture to dry, but don't overmix. Then knead the dough no more than a dozen times. Roll out onto a floured surface and cut the circle into 8 wedges. Place the scones on a lightly greased cookie sheet and brush some half and half on the top.

Bake for 10–14 minutes. Serve warm with butter.

Enjoy.

Catering and Capers with
Isis Crawford!

Nail-Biting Romantic Suspense
from Your Favorite Authors

Grab These Cozy Mysteries
from
Kensington Books

Forget Me Knot
Mary Marks
978-0-7582-9205-6 $7.99US/$8.99CAN

Death of a Chocoholic
Lee Hollis
978-0-7582-9449-4 $7.99US/$8.99CAN

Green Living Can Be
Deadly
Staci McLaughlin
978-0-7582-7502-8 $7.99US/$8.99CAN

Death of an Irish Diva
Mollie Cox Bryan
978-0-7582-6633-0 $7.99US/$8.99CAN

Board Stiff
Annelise Ryan
978-0-7582-7276-8 $7.99US/$8.99CAN

A Biscuit, A Casket
Liz Mugavero
978-0-7582-8480-8 $7.99US/$8.99CAN

Boiled Over
Barbara Ross
978-0-7582-8687-1 $7.99US/$8.99CAN

Scene of the Climb
Kate Dyer-Seeley
978-0-7582-9531-6 $7.99US/$8.99CAN

Deadly Decor
Karen Rose Smith
978-0-7582-8486-0 $7.99US/$8.99CAN

To Kill a Matzo Ball
Delia Rosen
978-0-7582-8201-9 $7.99US/$8.99CAN

Available Wherever Books Are Sold!

All available as e-books, too!

Visit our website at **www.kensingtonbooks.com**

Follow P.I. Savannah Reid
with
G.A. McKevett